Praise for Hwee Hwee Tan's
FOREIGN BODIES

"A novel of distinction . . . alm‌[...]‌omplished for a twenty-three-year-old."

—*The Economist*

"If Flannery O'Connor had written the screenplay for *Midnight Express,* it might have turned out somewhat like this startling and remarkable debut novel—academic glam, international intrigue, and Christian redemption all stirred up in the same wok. . . ."

—*Kirkus Reviews*

"This lively combination of mystery, youth culture, and spiritual awakening is wonderfully unique. . . . Fast-paced and totally unpretentious. A completely absorbing first novel."

—*Library Journal*

"*FOREIGN BODIES* explores serious themes with an enviable lightness of touch. Hwee Hwee Tan has made a witty, confident, not to mention brave debut."

—*Literary Review*

"A smart and challenging book. . . . An exciting addition to trans-cultural literature."

—Edwidge Danticat, author of
Breath, Eyes, Memory and *Farming the Bones*

"Fast-paced, streetwise. . . . Tan's good ear for the spoken word is everywhere apparent. . . . What is impressive, especially in so young a writer, is Tan's assurance and her seriousness."

—*Independent*

foreign bodies

A Novel

Hwee Hwee Tan

WASHINGTON SQUARE PRESS
PUBLISHED BY POCKET BOOKS

New York   London   Toronto   Sydney   Singapore

To Paul Mullen

This book is a work of fiction. Names, characters, places and incidents are products of the author's imagination or are used fictitiously. Any resemblance to actual events or locales or persons, living or dead, is entirely coincidental.

WSP

A Washington Square Press Publication of
POCKET BOOKS, a division of Simon & Schuster Inc.
1230 Avenue of the Americas, New York, NY 10020

ISBN: 0-671-04170-3

First Washington Square Press trade paperback printing January 2000

10 9 8 7 6 5 4 3 2 1

WASHINGTON SQUARE PRESS and colophon are registered
trademarks of Simon & Schuster Inc.

Cover design by Brigid Pearson
Front cover photo credits: inset by Telegraph Colour Library/FPG
International; bottom © Wendy Chan/The Image Bank

Printed in the U.S.A.

foreign bodies

CHAPTER 1

DAY ONE: SUNDAY (VERY EARLY) MORNING

Mei

'Are you a Singaporean citizen, over twenty-one, and a lawyer?' he said.

I recognized that voice at once, the English accent, the voice roughened by too much tar and endless lager sagas. It could only be Andy. Now the above question might seem fairly innocuous to the casual eavesdropper, but in this instance it caused me a great deal of aggravation. Believe me, if Mother Teresa was in my place, if she was asked the same question under the same controlled circumstances, it would be enough to make her chuck her role as the saint of the century and send her screaming down the streets, going apeshit, looking for babies to kick. Why was Andy's question so provocative? I'll tell you why. Firstly, not only because it was one in the morning (and looking at my glow-in-the-dark Casio clock, I saw that it was 1:16 a.m. to be exact), but secondly, and more importantly, Andy knew, that I knew, that he knew, the answer to all three questions, because five hours earlier he was supposed to meet me outside Tung Lok Shark's Fin Restaurant to celebrate my getting the licence to practise law. Of course, Andy didn't turn up. I hate eating alone, so I went home early, and woe to me – I returned to the flat only to find my mother having a karaoke night with her mah-jong playmates. So instead of feasting on Abalone Delight and Peking Duck, I spent my evening trying to block out the sound of fifty-something housewives wailing songs from the Karaoke Hit List From Hell, songs like 'Sealed With A Kiss', 'Singapura, Oh Singapura (Sunny Island Set In The Sea)', 'Tie A Yellow Ribbon Round the Old Oak Tree', 'Que Será Será', and 'Ne Xin Li Ken Ben Mei Yao Wo' (or 'Your Heart Never Had Me'). Trust me, you haven't seen something truly Satanic until you've seen your mother belting out 'Chain Reaction' complete with Diana Ross hand actions and bum wiggles. So, as you can imagine, when Andy phoned, I was in less than a good mood. What would you do – after the pain in your ears has subsided, when you've finally managed to fall asleep – what would you do, if you were woken at one in the morning by someone who had stood you up five hours earlier, and asked three completely inane questions?

I pondered my options, rolled over the choices that came to mind, and finally decided upon the calmest, the most apposite, indeed, the most mature response. I slammed down the phone. It rang again, and I picked it up and said, 'I'm very pissed off now, and you have about five seconds to make me un-pissed-off, preferably using a technique which involves three words or less, or else this phone is going down again.'

Silence on the other end as Andy paused to think of those all-important three words. As our Andrew ponders upon those crucial phrases, perhaps now would be a good time to introduce him. This is a tricky process because of the Eugene Connection. Andy wasn't really a friend, he was more like a friend-in-law – I knew him through Eugene. Eugene was my neighbour-cum-childhood playmate. When we were kids, we had great adventures together, like investigating 'The Case of Mrs Lam's (Possibly) Murdered Maid', but that's another story. Now pay attention, here's where it gets complicated, because Eugene is one of those people with those intricate, exotic backgrounds that most normal people like me would kill for. During his teens, Eugene and his parents emigrated to Holland to open a Chinese restaurant. He returned to Singapore for a few years to complete his National Service, then he went to university in England, where he met Andy. They became best friends, and spent their undergraduate years cultivating their passion for soccer, kebabs, and Cocoa Bombs. Anyway, post-graduation, when Andy (unsurprisingly) couldn't get a job in England, he decided to go East to seek his fortune.

Andy finally thought of those three magic words – 'I'm in jail.'

Now it was my turn to be speechless.

So Andy said, 'Have I used up my words quota yet or can I say more?'

I graciously granted him permission to speak.

'They think I'm the head of a soccer gambling syndicate. I'm supposed to be like some octopus, with tentacles all over the place, in Asia, Europe, everywhere. Imagine that – little ol' me. Head of a multi-million betting empire. I don't know whether to be flattered or outraged.'

'Have you been charged?'

'I've been arrested under – what was that phrase again? – the Common Betting Act. They said it was a "bookable offence". What's that in normal English?'

'It's legalese for "You're in big trouble."'

'So, as you see, I need someone to bail me out. And the police said that that someone had to be Singaporean, and over twenty-one. And I thought, hey, I've got a friend – not just an acquaintance, but a *good* friend, who fits that description perfectly. Plus she's just got her law licence.'

'I'm impervious to flattery at one in the morning.' But once again, I knew I had to do it. I had to rescue Andy again.

Andy was always stumbling into trouble. I don't think he ever had a plan in life, but if he did, it was probably to live a life of complete cluelessness. He would do something outrageous, after which he would flash his trademark stricken-yet-ingenuous look: he would widen his doe-like eyes, scrunch his mouth and flap his hands as if trying to fend off any accusations of misconduct. 'It's not my fault,' he would invariably say, 'I don't know how that broke*/I don't know how the snot got sprayed all over your CDs*/I didn't know you weren't supposed to smoke that in this country* (*delete as applicable) — it just *happened*.' I was used to getting him out of trouble. In the past few months, he had depended on me to bail him out, in the metaphorical sense. I didn't mind that. It's just that I never expected to have to bail him out *literally*.

Ah well. Some were born to guardian angelhoods; others have guardian angelhoods thrust upon them. I fall into the latter category. Eugene came to Singapore for a few months, to help Andy settle in, but last week I had to take over from Eugene after he got a phone call from his parents, demanding that he return to Holland to help them run their Chinese restaurants.

'My father wants to open two new branches in Leiden and Utrecht', Eugene said, 'called Triple Pagoda, or Moon Dragon Flying Round Lotus Umbrella, or something stupid like that. I better go to Holland and stop him before he does any more *pei-say* things like that. Can you imagine, he even wants to put *bami* balls on the menu?' Eugene stuck a finger down his throat, and pretended to gag.

So Eugene entrusted Andy to my care. 'You got to take care of him for me. We're like brothers. Like Frank and Joe Hardy. Like Butch Cassidy and the Sundance Kid.'

'Butch Cassidy and the Sundance Kid weren't brothers,' I said.

'*Ai-ya*, you lawyer types are so pedantic,' Eugene said. 'But hey, seriously, Andy needs help. You know what he's like. I need someone to look after him for me.'

That someone had to be me. I didn't really have a choice. I remember when I first saw Andy. He stood out from all the other passengers at the arrival lounge, surveying his surroundings with innocent awe. His face looked so fragile – skin white as fine china, as if one touch would shatter it into a powder of dust. Pale like marble, with wisps of red hair, and fine, fragile features, he would have looked terribly pre-Raphaelite, but for the freckles and glasses. With those plump cheeks, curly red hair and brilliant blue eyes, he looked like a baby angel, empty of guile, filled with pure, naive joy. One look at him and I knew that I had to dedicate my life to protect that innocence, preserve that purity, shelter him from an evil and cunning world. Even though his red head towered a foot above me, I felt a deep need to go up and pat him on the head.

Andy had this helpless boy charm, the kind that brought out all the maternal instincts that I never knew I had. When I first saw him I suddenly had all these unnatural urges – I wanted to bring him home, sit him down on the sofa, place the remote control in his hand, and say, 'You just stay here watching the highlights from the Premier League while I go into the kitchen and happily spend three hours brewing a bowl of red date soup for you.' Once, while watching *Four Weddings and A Funeral*, I had a vision of myself smiling up at him, barefoot and pregnant, like some model out of a Ministry of Community Development poster. And I was like – Holy Jesus, what's happening to me? Why am I thinking these evil thoughts? Why have ten years of feminist education suddenly evaporated?

That's why I have spent the past few months cleaning up after Andy. Recently, there have been many of Andy's 'It Just Happened' incidents. Like the time we were at Newton Circus, when Andy ordered a cup of Ovaltine. He poured the Ovaltine into a saucer, blew on it to cool it, then added some vodka. 'It's called Cocoa Bomb,' he said.

Afterwards, we made our way to my new car. Now I know that Andy loves my car, because when he first saw it, he knew a lot more about it than I did – 'Unbelievable! You've got the best model in the range. As Jeremy Clarkson says – not only does this car combine the smooth ride and responsiveness of a gasoline engine with the fuel economy of a diesel, it also has three-channel anti-skid brakes, and a computer-controlled traction control system. Cool.' However, I didn't buy the car for any of those reasons. I bought the car because I fell in love with its one genuinely distinctive feature – its green-tinted glass roof, which Andy proceeded to make even more distinctive by being sick all over it. That night at Newton Circus, I learnt another dubiously useful lesson, which I shall pass on for your instruction and edification: if someone pukes on your car roof, it will set off the alarm.

'Sorry, I didn't mean to do that. It just happened. It must have been the curry.' Footnote: even if he's drunk three gallons of beer, it's never the alcohol that causes Andy's awesome feats of regurgitation – it's always something else – like the kebab, or the crisps, or the Wagon Wheels. When I point that out, he says, 'Don't *you* tell *me* what to eat Miss Slim-Fast, Miss Ryvita-With-Jam. You're just jealous because *I* don't have to worry about my thighs.' That's another thing that drives me nuts, the way Andy mainlines Mars bars and liquorice without gaining a pound. I think he's signed a pact with the Devil – how else can you explain how Andy manages to maintain the body of an Adonis while subsisting on the fantasy diet of a nine-year-old?

Another time when there was a lot of cleaning up to do was during Andy's first MRT trip. There were these big signs plastered all over the train station, these drawings of a cup and a plate of steaming food, with a huge red cross stamped across them. For those lacking the ability to interpret visual symbols, a caption underneath that warned us that the possessors of food and drink in an MRT station would be subjected to a five-hundred dollar fine. I told Andy to hide his bottle of Cocoa Bomb in his bag, but he said, 'I'm not going to let any foreign government dictate *my* eating habits.' So we were standing on the platform, waiting for the train, and Andy starts recounting Fallensham United's latest victory, jiggling his hands as he tried to reconstruct Varney's last-minute winning piledriver. Of course he spilled his drink all over the floor. He took off his T-shirt, got down on his knees, and went – 'Shit shit shit shit shit' as he tried to mop up the brown mess. Then this huge mother of a voice booms out from some hidden PA system. The cameras had been watching us all this time, that panoptic system that governs the public transport system. The voice said, 'Will the topless man please make his way to the Central Control Station.' As usual, it was down to me to deal with the grim grey-uniformed MRT wardens, grovelling on Andy's behalf, soothing things over in the Singlish lingo that only the natives could do – '*Ai-ya*, sorry about my friend *lah*. He's *ang mo*, you know what they're like. He just got off the plane, he came from this small *ulu ulu* town in England, very *sau-ku*, he doesn't know anything. You give him chance, okay or not?'

'Okay, this time we give him chance,' the station manager said, 'but next time he do this again, we *ou kong* him a lot of money.'

It was Andy's first encounter with Singlish, so after we left the control station, he asked me, 'What were you talking about?'

'I told them you were this stupid white foreign country bumpkin,' I said, 'and they said they would let you off this time, but if you litter again, they'll fine you five hundred dollars.' I explained to Andy that though people like me and Eugene could speak perfect English, we reserved our 'proper' English for foreigners, job interviews and English oral exams. With friends or family, we always used Singlish, that is, Singapore slang. Singlish is a type of pidgin English, where English words are arranged according to the rules of Chinese grammar, and sentences are sprinkled with the occasional Chinese, Malay and Indian words. Singlish sounds like 'broken' English – to foreign ears it can sound unintelligible, uneducated, even crude. However, we didn't speak 'broken' English because we lacked the ability to speak the Queen's English; we spoke Singlish, because with all its contortions of grammar and pronunciation, its new and localized vocabulary, Singlish expressed our thoughts in a way that the formal, perfectly enunciated, anal BBC World Service English never could. Besides, who wants to talk like some O level textbook, instead of using our own language, our home language, the language of our souls?

I don't speak either standard English or Singlish consistently. When I'm with friends like Eugene, I enjoy switching between the Queen's English and the *Ah Ma*'s English, randomly, arbitrarily and often in mid-sentence. It's just the Singaporean way, this totally jumbled, multi-lingual lingo – just part of our melting pot, *rojak* way of speech, thought and life.

I didn't know how Andy managed to get arrested, but based upon previous experiences, I could probably guess correctly. Every Saturday over the past few months, Andy would get together with Eugene and their other punter friends to bet on soccer results. I told Andy he would get arrested if the police caught him, but he wouldn't listen. He's obsessed with soccer. A month ago, I was yabbering away for about five minutes before I realized that I was talking *at* Andy, rather than *to* him. I hit the back of his head, and he jerked to attention.

'Sorry – just thinking about class tomorrow. I'm thinking of giving the kids Defoe. He can be, really, uh, deep.' Andy shook his head and blinked a couple of times to clear his head. 'Right,

I'm with you now. "Justice is always violent to the party offending, for every man is innocent in his own eyes." Marvellous quote from "The Shortest Way With The Dissenters".'

'You weren't thinking about Defoe or justice,' I said. 'Don't think you can smokescreen me with all that literary crap.'

'I was thinking about Defoe!'

'No you weren't. It's the same every Saturday night. You sit there, practically catatonic. When I jerk you to attention you always insist that you were thinking about Updike's latest novel, or the Bosnian peace process, or the Tory party conference at Blackpool, but I know you're lying. I've seen that glazed look before. You're replaying the winning volley by Mikhailichenko against Man United. You can disappear into your own little fantasy world for hours. Your mind's like a VCR on perpetual rewind.'

Andy raised his palms in surrender. 'You know me too well. I started off thinking about Defoe, about justice, then I thought about how unfair it is that Man U win all the time, and before I knew it I saw the ball dropping over Mik's left shoulder, his right foot pivoting, smashing the ball in mid-air.'

'Mentally, you've never developed beyond puberty. You're twenty-two going on twelve.'

Andy stuck an imaginary knife in his back, twisted and turned his body, his face contorting in mock agony. 'That was a completely unprovoked attack, but I know you love me anyway.'

'I never could resist little boys,' I said. 'I know I keep nagging you about this, but one day your obsession with soccer is going to get you into trouble.'

'I'm not obsessed.'

'Yes you are. What's the name of the wife of the coach of the goalkeeper of the England team?'

'Meg.'

'And you say you're not obsessed. Which brings me back to

9

what I was scolding you about before you went into your dream world. You know who Meg is but you can't remember the name of my niece.'

'*Zhen Chou, Zhen Cai* – it's not that big a difference. It was an easy enough mistake to make.'

'There *is* a big difference. *Zhen Cai* means "genuine fortune". *Zhen Chou* means "really smelly". I don't think my niece appreciated being called "stinko" at her birthday party.'

'Oops.'

'Oops indeed.'

'I can't help it if you've got such a big family,' Andy said. 'Fourteen aunts, twenty uncles and millions more nephews and nieces. It's difficult to keep track of names.'

'*I* can remember the names of *all* your relatives.'

'Considering that just includes my mother and father, that's hardly a serious mnemonic challenge.'

Only last week, Andy promised me that he would stop gambling, but tonight I knew that he must have lied. I guessed that despite his claims to be a reformed man, tonight, he must have backslid and run the betting house again, only to be raided by the police. I decided that it was probably good for him to rot in jail for at least a night.

'Where are you?' I asked.

'I'm in the lock-up at the Central Police Station. Come and bail me out now. Please.'

'Forget it,' I said, 'I'll bail you out tomorrow.'

'Why can't you come now?'

'It seems to have slipped your notice that it's half-past one in the morning. You might be surprised to learn this, but the courts aren't open at this ungodly hour, so I can't apply for bail now anyway. I'll see you in the morning.'

'I'm sorry I couldn't choose a more convenient time to ybe arrested. So you're just going to let me rot in jail then?'

'Don't worry, you won't rot. This is Singapore. Parliament outlawed bacteria in nineteen seventy-eight.'

'Oh go ahead, make fun of me. It's fine by me. Never mind, you can come tomorrow. I'll just have to sleep in this dark, small, stinking cell for an entire night, with only a chamber pot for companionship. I hope you enjoy your air-conditioned room. I don't mind. I hope you're not feeling *guilty*. I hope you'll be able to sleep *in peace*.'

'Don't worry, I will.' I put down the phone.

'*Ai-yoh*, so late already who call?' My mother came into the living room.

'Andy,' I said. 'He got arrested for running a soccer gambling syndicate.'

My mother slumped into the sofa. 'I *knew* this was going to happen. I keep telling you, it's the tree.'

'Oh Mummy, not the tree again.'

'It is!'

Andy lived in a flat above us, and my mother blamed everything bad that happened on the big Flame of the Forest outside our apartment block. 'Bad *feng shui*. It's true what Master Chou said. When he looked at our block, he said if got big tree planted outside your main door, very bad luck. If money wants to flow into your house, it cannot come in, because the tree is blocking the money. Also, this type of tree, so big, no good – demons like to come and live in it,' my mother said. 'I was talking to Mrs Lam tonight, and we both agreed that it's all the government's fault. You know the last few months we keep writing, write to everyone – the HDB board, the MP, keep asking them to cut down the tree but they don't want. You see, now this sort of thing happen. So bad luck. Your friend get arrested in our block, it'll be all over the newspapers. Like that, everyone will think our block got curse. Our property price sure to drop, next time we want to sell the flat, it's going to be *very* difficult. I tell you, next time election come, I won't vote for this government. Ask them to do a simple thing – cut down tree – they also don't want.'

'So you're saying that the demons in the tree made the police arrest Andy. I knew there was a logical explanation for all this.'

'Hah, you always think so funny to make fun of me. I never go university like you, but I'm not stupid. *Feng shui* is true. What did Master Chou tell us at the community centre?' She shut her eyes and frowned. 'Fortune . . . is not a random occurrence of chance, but has a vitality of its own, a . . . energy that moves, that can be attracted . . . enhanced . . . manipulated.' She smiled proudly at being able to remember Master Chou verbatim. 'You wait here, I show you something.'

She ran to her room and returned with a leaflet.

WIND & WATER CENTRE
Master Chou
Geomancer & Metaphysician
A.C.S. (American Chirological Society, National School of Palmistry, University of France)
Advised the USA Embassy (Singapore) on their ground-breaking ceremony (1994)
Consulted by the Government for the work site at Marina Bay MRT Station (1988)
Interviewed by SBC in the 'Tuesday Report'
Prediction of China Tiananmen Event & Gulf War (Features in Asia Magazine)
Specially been invited to provide Chinese Name for one ASEAN regional Airline
In life who can help you out of dark corners?
Call 234 7888 or Mobile-Phone 267 8897
or pager 889 7771 or Fax 678 9098

'You see, even the big businessmen in Singapore and Hong Kong, even the US embassy believes in *feng shui*. University people,' my mother said. 'This Master Chou, he's very famous. He can do *feng shui* for our flat, only one thousand and seven hundred dollars. Offer ends next Wednesday.'

'Forget it.' I didn't want anything to do with these so-called *feng shui* experts. I knew how they operated. Master Chou would come into the flat with his trigram, which looked suspiciously like a spider's web and walk around the room shaking his head. Then he would stroke his long white beard, jiggle his fingers as he calculated our fortune, tell us to move our hibiscus plant from the living room to the kitchen, and then charge us two thousand dollars for his advice.

'And I don't want you to do any *feng shui* arrangements yourself either,' I told my mother. Last month she bought a DIY *feng shui* book. I returned one night to find my room filled with purple cushions, and a lamp radiating red light. My mother insisted that the red light gave my bed a prosperous aura. I told her that it made my room look like a Turkish brothel.

'Are you going to be Andy's lawyer?' my mother said.

'Yes. Why do you ask?'

'Don't think about the case while you're in bed. If you want to think about your work, think about it at your desk. Master Chou say if you mix home and office, your energy will clash. I keep telling you not to read your files in bed, but you never listen to me, that's why you can't get married. I don't want to say things like what I'm going to say now – very bad luck – but I think you should know.' My mother took a deep breath. 'If you don't get married soon, afterwards you become an old maid, you'll be all alone. You're nearly thirty. Your expiry date coming up. You wait too long, you'll get left on the shelf.'

'Mother, getting married isn't like going to NTUC.'

'Getting married is *exactly* like going to NTUC. Shopping

for a husband is the same as shopping in the supermarket. I warn you, once you're over thirty, very difficult to get fresh men. You wait too long, you can only get divorcees. Recycled material. Second-hand goods. So if you see got good bargain, remember – grab first, worry later.'

'Was Daddy a good bargain then?'

That shut her up. For five seconds. Then she said, 'All I'm saying is that you're at the right age to get married. I got married when I was your age.'

'And we both know what a mistake *that* was.' In her desperation to get off the shelf, my mother married a businessman fifteen years her senior. My father died from a heart attack a few years ago. I do not miss him.

'Your generation different now,' my mother said. 'Last time, divorce very difficult. But now, after you're married, you don't like it, can always refund or exchange. That's what divorce is for.'

'The reason why I'm not married,' I said, 'is because I don't *want* to get married.'

'How can you say that? I tell you, Mummy's not going to live for ever. After I die, you all alone, how?'

'Life without you might actually be pretty pleasant,' and as soon as I said that, I regretted it immediately. I knew what her next words would be.

'Why do you hate me so much?' my mother said.

I could have told her why, but I figured that she probably knew the reasons already. So I just said, 'I don't hate you,' and went to my room.

The reasons had nothing to do with anything that was happening *now*. The seeds of trouble and deceit were sown ten, twenty years ago, and now, we reaped the results.

Nearly twenty years ago, my grandfather accidentally swallowed a fish bone. He was rushed to General Hospital, where they x-rayed and ECG-ed him, but they couldn't find anything wrong. The surgeon announced, 'We've examined his oesophagus, but when we introduced the scope into the gullet, he suffered an intense reflex spasm. We were unable to examine the oesophagus as far down as we would have liked.'

I nodded.

'We're going to give him some barium. Hopefully that will reveal any obstructions in the body when we take an x-ray.'

I nodded again. I didn't understand anything he said, but it sounded like a good idea.

They fed him the white liquid, but my grandfather caught a fever. Panadol relieved this, but two days later, a stroke struck him down. All I remember about my grandfather in his final days, is his fingers gripping the rails of the bed. At that age, I wasn't tall enough to see any further.

'What's wrong with *gong gong*'s fingers?' I asked.

'Gangrene,' my mother said.

The doctor came in and said, 'We've carried out some tests and detected an abscess behind his pharynx. We'll have to drain it to prevent infection.'

My grandfather was in a terrible condition, so the doctors performed the operation quickly, and didn't look for a foreign body. He died from septic poisoning a few days later. He suffered for an entire month, and nobody knew what caused it. We only discovered what killed him after the autopsy.

'There was a fish bone stuck in his oesophagus,' the coroner told us. 'Four cm long. It pierced his oesophagus, cut into his heart, the upper left chamber.' The coroner tapped his chest. 'The bone caused all the infection, formed small blood clots. The clots travelled in the blood to his fingers and toes, that was what caused the gangrene. The clots killed him.'

All the problems that came up on this present Sunday, they

all arose because of the foreign bodies within us – things that happened in our childhood, some big, some small, but all significant; things that happened ten years ago, but still control our lives today; things from our yesterdays that will decide what we drink, dream and doubt, till the day we die. But you can't see those things, because they're not on the outside.

The press got it all wrong, of course, surprise, surprise. You wouldn't *believe* the articles they printed about us. For them, it was all so simple: Andy was the foreigner, the evil outside influence, the *ang mo*; Eugene was the Singaporean kid led astray by corrupt Western expatriates; and me, I was the local, naive, *sauku* mountain tortoise of a girl who should have listened to her mother and not fallen for a criminal like Andy. All the experts in the world could never figure out what was wrong with us, because our wounds were lodged deep, hidden from the sharpest eyes, the most advanced machinery. But now, we're all going to have to have our turn – first me, then Andy and then finally, Eugene. We're each going to tell you tales from our youth, tales of how we got our wounds. So forget first impressions, ignore what you see on the outside: these are our real stories, the stories only we know, the stories of our foreign bodies.

Mei

When I die, I'm not going to have a funeral like my *gong gong*'s. My funeral will be a quick and simple affair. People would arrive at three, say nice things about me, then leave at five.

When my *gong gong* died, his funeral lasted forty-nine (7 × 7) days. An army of priests gathered outside my grandfather's house, ready to storm Hell with their rituals and rescue him from the demonic clutches of *Yuen Thou Wong*.

During the afternoon, I drank Fanta orange while the saffron-robed monks beat their gongs under a red canopy. The tock-tock-tock of their gongs mingled with the background music – the Bee Gees singing 'Staying Alive'. To this day, I don't know who chooses the music for funerals. The only thing I know is that the same inappropriate music plays at public functions in Singapore all the time – I've yet to attend a wedding where they *haven't* played 'Please Release Me'.

It's usually terribly humid in Singapore, but today it was so bad it was like breathing soup. I hid under the red canopy, because on a day like this, five minutes under the sun and my black hair would be hot enough to fry an egg on. We tried that at a Brownies' camp once but that's another story.

My grandfather's photo sat on the red altar, flanked by bronze urns and brown joss sticks. In that starched, wide-collared white shirt, he looked unusually mild. In real-life, blown-up size, with his crew-cut (dark on top, grey at the sides), rough tanned leathery skin and Marlborough breath, he looked like a sergeant. He often acted like one, for it was his birthright, as the patriarch, the head honcho of the family, to boss people around until he got what he wanted. Though my grandfather looked naturally stern, his pot belly, cultivated via the mass consumption of Guinness Stout and KFC, gave him a cheerful aura reminiscent of the Laughing Buddha. He didn't dress fancy – he went everywhere in his roach-bitten singlet and khaki bermudas, but there was one accessory he was genuinely proud of. He loved to play with his dentures, punctuating his sentences by lifting up his bottom front tooth. It was a gold tooth, and it was his only luxury.

I coughed. There was smoke everywhere – grey smoke from the joss sticks, black smoke from the cars and trucks that whined past, and puffs of cigarette smoke from the monks having their tea break in the corner. I finished my twelfth glass of Fanta. Orange is a lucky colour, so it's the only drink, apart from Chinese tea, that's served at our family functions. Though sick of Fanta, I asked for yet another glass of orange because there was nothing a kid of eleven could do at funerals apart from drink, choke on smoke, and wonder which level of Hell the deceased had descended to.

My grandfather was in Hell, and he was taking me with him. My grandfather always taught me that everyone goes straight to Hell – 'You are guilty until proven innocent.' Two bull-headed, long-tailed, trident-bearing, toe-tapping creatures waited constantly by your bedside, ready to drag you in chains once you've breathed your final breath. Our fate was sealed a few years ago when we went to Haw Par Villa. This was the garden of the gods, a real tourist-magnet, the home of the Golden Buddha, the Prosperity Buddha, the Health Buddha, the Longevity Buddha – well, you get the idea.

My grandfather couldn't care less for the statues. No, instead he made a beeline for the cave with the 'Ten Courts of Hell'. Boiling in oil, disembowelment, sawing in two, eye-gouging, tongue-plucking – all these tortures were recreated in wax, with a loving attention to detail – we're talking blood, pus, intestines, sliced breasts, stray eyeballs. Nothing was left to the imagination. One thing was clear: forget Dante's *Inferno*, there is no Hell like the Chinese *tei yuk*.

My grandfather pointed at the first exhibit, 'Rats Gnawing Off a Man's Tongue'.

'That is what happens to liars,' my grandfather said.

I knew then that we were going to Hell, for my grandfather lied about my age at the box office, shaving three years off my actual age to get me into Haw Par Villa for free.

My grandfather suddenly clamped his fingers on my wrist. 'There are things that even Haw Par Villa dares not show. Tortures like the Exploding Water Torture. The demons stick a hose into your mouth, then pump you full of water. When your body gets big big, they jump on you and – boom!'

I saw my heart, kidney and intestines sprayed across the walls of Hell.

'This is what happens to children who are not *xiao xun*,' my grandfather said. 'This is how they're punished if they have no respect and forget their elders.' He flipped his golden tooth out of his mouth and drew it back again.

Then he told me a tale that served as a guide, a sort of 'How to Reduce Your Time in Hell' story.

Once upon a time, there was a boy who lived with his widowed (of course) mother. He slogged all day planting rice, but his earnings only enabled him to buy a single bowl of rice. The conversation at the dinner table usually went like this:

'Mother, take this single and only and last bowl of rice that we might ever get for the next two months.'

'No, son, I'm not hungry,' she lied. 'You need the rice to give you strength to plant more rice.'

'Mother, I'm not hungry.' His stomach growls.

'But son, you're so thin.'

'But Mother . . .'

You get the idea. Of course the mother gets the rice in the end. That night, a thunderstorm wakes the mother. She screams. The boy rushes into the room and hugs her all night until the storm dies.

After a few weeks, the mother snuffs it (tuberculosis would be an appropriate agent of death). So, after his mother is in the grave, whenever there is a thunderstorm, the son runs to the graveyard and hugs the grave, crying, 'Don't be fearful, Mother, I'm here to protect you.'

After he finished his story, my grandfather dropped his Marlboro and stamped on it with his flip-flops. 'After *gong gong* die that time you know what to do right?'

I shook my head.

'You must visit my grave, talk to me, bring things for me to eat. Are you going to do that?'

I didn't say anything.

My grandfather nudged me. 'After I die, you going to feed me or not?'

'I can't.'

He glared at me. 'Why?'

'I'm a Christian.'

'Since when?'

'Last week.'

'Who did this to you?' he enquired in that shocked tone people reserved for victims of child abuse.

'Uncle Cheong.'

Children have heroes whom they idolize beyond sense or

reason. Possessing a transformative vision, they invest the object of their adulation with sublime qualities unseen by the common eye, a vision one often finds in poets, and second-hand car dealers. In my eyes, Uncle Cheong could do no wrong. Even his farts smelled like Aramis No. 7. With the heart of Mother Teresa and the body of Tom Cruise, Uncle Cheong was my hero, and whenever he came to visit, for a week I would be 'Uncle Cheong did this, and Uncle Cheong did that'. I loved the way his wavy black hair fell naturally over his broad shoulders, but Singapore Immigration didn't share my admiration for his coiffure – the airport officials always demanded that he cut his hair short or they wouldn't let him into the country. He just laughed them off. The skin around his eyes crinkled whenever he smiled, which was often, and whenever he flashed his dimples, I just melted.

Perhaps, now that I'm older, if I met him today, I would view him differently. Maybe I would see him through adult eyes, my aunts' eyes, see him as a rootless, idle, no good, useless bum. But I'll never know – he died in a boating accident when I was in my teens. Who was the real Uncle Cheong? Was he a tramp, beggar, vagabond, or an adventurer, crusader, pilgrim? Juxtaposing fragments of malicious gossip with shimmering projections of my fantasies, I constructed my image of Uncle Cheong – he was the collage of our Imaginations.

Uncle Cheong spent his life travelling around the world, doing missionary work for Operation Mobilisation, or TEFLing, teaching English in Third World cesspits. I always thought Uncle Cheong was like Michael Landon in *Highway to Heaven* (only less soft-focus), an angel roaming the universe, going where good needed to be done. I pictured him wandering around rugged ruins, all stubbled and bulging biceps, looking like the guy out of the Camel ad (only without the cigarettes). Uncle Cheong was a free spirit, a dreamer. When you listened to him you could hear fireworks, exploding constellations, sweet jazz music booping across the muddy banks of a wide emerald river. In Uncle Cheong I saw a life spent cruising exotic lanes in the East and hip alleys in the West, working in desert cities where the humidity frosted the windows, where men cycled through sandy streets, pulling carts of ice yellow with sawdust. There he would open his window, to let in the thick smell of spices, the reckless butterflies and the song from the women, the psalm that rose above the golden city. Sometimes I dreamt of him wandering streets innocent of asphalt and corners untainted with street lights, sleeping in houses that cracked loudly as the cold night air contracted the wood, waking to walk in fields of gold, chewing oaten stalks until the sharp sweetness filled his throat.

Uncle Cheong dazzled me with incredible stories, tales of men who through faith shut the mouths of lions, slew giants with a sling and a stone, turned armies of invaders to flight – stories that did what all stories should do: announce a history, while proclaiming a mystery. Stirring me with his smooth voice, his words came alive, hypnotized me and, all around, I could feel the flower buds buzz, the electricity crackling through the mud of the earth. Everything became sensitive to the touch.

'Jesus said that if we had faith as small as a mustard seed, we could toss mountains into the sea.' Uncle Cheong said that we could stop the sun in its tracks, turn rivers to blood, make locusts sweep through the nation – all these things have happened before and can happen again. There was more to life than meets the eye, more than I could possibly imagine. 'Faith is seeing what you can't feel, taste, hear or touch, seeing with your soul, not your eyes. There exists a parallel universe, an invisible world, where the unseen is more real than the seen – that's the ultimate reality. What do you see when you look at the sun? Do you see a golden disc, or thousands of angels singing "Holy, Holy, Holy"? That's what Blake tells us. We need to use our Imagination, see the world not with, but through the eye.'

Uncle Cheong told me the story of Elisha, how the army of Syria surrounded his house. His servant panicked, but Elisha prayed, 'Lord, open his eyes, that he may see, that those who are with us are more than those who are with them.' Suddenly his servant saw the mountain filled with angels in fiery chariots.

Uncle Cheong told me that only if I surrendered all – 'your fears, your goals, your life to God, don't care about friends or family or whatever' – only then would I be able to find something amazing, miraculous, bright, glistening, shining with joy and rapture, life above the earth, soaring in the heavenly realms, way beyond the blue.

I became a Christian because I wanted to be like Uncle Cheong. I wanted the jazz alleys, the burning sands, the road black with ice, a life raised to a visionary pitch, soaring above the earth to the heavenly kingdoms. On the God-awful streets of man, Uncle Cheong's excitement, mystical devotion and sheer hunger touched me, taught me how to deal with the pit and prunejuice of life. He could out-road Kerouac any day. I didn't see Uncle Cheong often, but whenever he visited me, I knew there would be cries and wild eyes, rocking and roaring, horns, snares, sticks, kicks. Whenever he arrived, I could hear a portal whine open, gushing holy white light on to the grey cement floor. All I had to do was lift my foot and step into a new, magical world, a world shimmering with tremendous possibilities. And then I knew – big-deep-bass-strumming-in-the-heart kind of knowing – that if I became a Christian, somewhere along the line there would be visions and everything. Somewhere along the line the pearl would be handed to me.

*

'If you become a Christian, after I die, who will take care of me?' my grandfather said.

'I don't know.'

He drilled his finger into the side of my forehead. 'You everything also don't know. You better don't listen to your Uncle Cheong. You want to end up like him? He's so useless. He doesn't care about anybody, only care about Jesus. After his wife died, you see him do anything for her?'

I shook my head.

My grandfather grunted. Then he said, 'You Chinese – how can you become a Christian?'

I was going to say 'I don't know' again, but I decided that silence was the best policy.

'Now you're a Christian, but you can always change your mind. You can un-Christian.' His voice grew soft. 'So after *gong gong* die, you can take care of me. So do you want?'

'Want what?'

'Do you want to un-Christian?'

I couldn't answer his question.

'You love me more or you love your Uncle Cheong more? You want to go Chinese Heaven or Christian Heaven?' He started rubbing my face with his palm. '*Ai-ya*, why you girls always cry for no reason?'

I sucked the mucus up my nose. 'I want to go both heavens.'

'Nowadays, you children are so spoilt. Always want both. Well you can't have both. You got to choose one. When you die, who do you want to be with – me, or your Uncle Cheong?'

I didn't say anything.

He patted me on the head and smiled. 'Never mind, don't cry, I know who you'll choose.' His golden tooth bobbed in and out of his mouth. 'You're not a bad person, like him.' He pointed to a man thrown from a cliff into a field of spikes. 'You're a good, filial girl.' Then he threw me a dark look, as if

24

any aberrant behaviour of mine would be punished by a fate too horrible to imagine.

Now, some people might think that gambling at your father's funeral would be a gross violation of taste and propriety, but not the Chinese. After all, my relatives reasoned, you need *something* to keep you awake. So, as darkness fell and eyelids drooped, my aunts and uncles clashed mah-jong tiles across the plastic table top, while hired mourners huddled round the coffin, wailing and weeping. For some reason, these two groups seemed to co-exist happily: the mah-jong players weren't put off by the flood of grief by their side, and the mourners weren't offended by the gaiety at the gambling table. Consequently, as at all Chinese funerals, sobs mixed peacefully with the triumphant cries of 'pong!'

A wave of murmurs rippled through the crowd. Heads twitched and eyes cast snide sideways glances – signs that always marked Uncle Cheong's arrival. Many years ago, he had offended everyone because of the funeral arrangements (or rather, the lack of) for his wife. My aunts always gossiped: 'After his wife died, he couldn't be bothered. Her funeral, just any how do, can already. He just put her in a coffin, dump in church, that's all. Then the next month after she died, you know what he did? Go world tour. Wife not even cold in her grave yet, he go London, India, China, go all over the place, enjoy himself. All these men are all the same, *so* useless. Their wife die already, they so happy, can do whatever they want. No more wife, can get a life.'

But no matter what they said, they couldn't poison my heart against Uncle Cheong. When he arrived, I ran to him, screaming, 'Uncle Cheong, Uncle Cheong!'

He grunted as I crashed into his chest. 'Woah, woah, and I missed you too.'

'Play Superman!'

'*Ai-ya*, girl, how come you got no taste, your grandfather's funeral and you still want to play?' He grinned. 'You know your mother not happy with me already, I don't want to upset her any more. Your mother see us playing – she'll scold us – then how?'

'I'm not afraid of my mother.'

'Well, *I* am. Your mother is the fiercest woman I know. They didn't make her a prefect at her school for nothing. Just one black look from her and I curl up in a foetal position.'

'But I'm so *xian*, this funeral is so boring.'

'Your *gong gong* so close to you, aren't you sad?'

'*Yah*, but you can be sad and *xian* at the same time. All I do here is sit and drink Fanta.' I dropped my head. '*Gong gong* love me so much, but I can't even cry at his funeral.'

'Sometimes we're so sad we can't cry. When my wife died, I never cried at the funeral, so everyone thought I wasn't sad. I looked at her but it didn't look like her. She was so white, so hard, it *wasn't* her. She was packed in this big black box, like something on display. It was like everyone was crying to this ice statue. So I couldn't cry. But every night I dream about her, dream about how she really was like, living, breathing, laughing, and when I wake up, my T-shirt is all wet.'

Uncle Cheong told me about his dream: he saw the coffin that his wife lay in, heavily draped. It had twelve escutcheons, and twelve locks with twelve different keys. He sought those keys, crossed the wastes of sea, made runes in the rainless sands. Finally, he came upon the black beach. There, on the dark water, the dead lake, was the black-browed boat man, the guide of shadows, his cold pale hand at the oar. He boarded the boat. The oarsman toiled, bending his body, climbing through the night and the water, beating the oar until they reached the other side. There, on the dark sand, she stood, all in white, pure as her mind. She opened her arms to embrace him, her voice echoed his call. Echoed like an angel dissolving in the air, like a shapeless flame. He woke, and the echoes became mere echoes, sounds shaking dust in empty spaces. He woke to absences, to air without angels.

After he told me his dream, Uncle Cheong didn't say anything for a long time.

'When I die, I want everyone to cry,' I said. 'I want everyone to really miss me. I want buckets, real tubs of tears, Niagara Falls. I want them to declare a National Day of Mourning, and make everyone hang a black flag outside their flat. People *better* be upset, if not I come back and haunt them.'

Uncle Cheong laughed.

'What are you going to do now?'

Uncle Cheong shrugged. 'Sit here and try not to fall asleep.'

'But isn't that bad?'

'Why?'

'My mother always tells me that *gong gong* loved me the most. Last time, he always bring me go out, go to Haw Par Villa, go KFC. He never did that for any of his other grandchildren. But I never did anything nice for him.' I was only a kid, and there was nothing I could give my grandfather that he didn't already have. 'And now he's dead. I have to do something for him.'

'But there's nothing we can do. We just have to leave him in God's hands.'

'But God will send him to Hell.'

Uncle Cheong spread his hands. 'You have to be willing to be helpless, and let God be your help. You can struggle with your own power, try and fix things with your own flawed schemes, but you'll find that it's useless in the end. Better just to surrender it all to God. His strength fills us when our strength is gone.'

A shrill voice pierced the air. It was my mother's. 'Mei, stop sitting around doing nothing and come over here and help these people cry.'

She dragged me to the altar. The King of Hades judged the deceased's popularity by the amount of tears shed for him, hence the professional mourners. Volume, not sincerity, counted.

I stood there, trying to cry, bashing my heart with images that would bring tears: my grandfather after his stroke, sitting on the bed, his brain gone, a recipient of Interact Club care. Now the Interact Club is a society at my school that visits old folks' homes every week. Bearing gifts that they made during their Art classes – wooden clothes pegs glued together into toy chairs, bookmarks made out of dried orchids stuck on yellow construction paper, lanterns stapled together from red *ang-pow* envelopes – the Interact members act as surrogate grand-children, chatting with the old folks. They always round off their visit by singing 'That's What Friends Are For', only they never ever complete the song because by the time they reach the middle of the chorus, the sopranos (that is, the girls) have become a blubbering wreck. In Moral Education class, the Interact chairman would always share the latest 'Granny Abandoned by Ungrateful Children' story, and my teacher would conclude with a lecture on filial piety, one of the core Confucian values found in the national curriculum. During these classes, my face had one of its mugshot moments, my features fixed in a vacant stare, emotionless, inscrutable, revealing nothing. I focused on the full stop chalked on the blackboard behind my teacher's head, hiding what I felt, hoping my classmates would never find out that *my* grandfather was an Interact Club charity case.

On the few occasions when we did visit my grandfather at the Evergreen Moral Home for the Aged Sick and Handicapped, I never wanted to go back. It's the smells that hit you first, the nauseatingly sweet smell of open sores and wet bandages, reeking of urine, saliva, sweat, pus – the stench of incurable sickness blanketed by the pungent odour of strong medicine. I stood at the doorway, gagging, my lungs fighting to adapt to the atmosphere. This wasn't the smell of death – that is bearable – no, this was the noxious smell of decomposition, when flesh and soul and heart and bone separate, then rot, deteriorate until all is reduced to a putrid pile of rubbish ready to be wheeled out. The syrupy smell of decay.

The Home popped all the nasty 'D' words into my mind – dark, dank, dungeony – it was like walking into a giant sewer. Blades of light slid in from the steel-shuttered windows, stencilling the emaciated silhouettes crouched on their beds, skeletons draped with oversized pyjamas. The room seemed semi-liquid, the floor wet, the walls sweating; a sick dampness infused the air. There was nothing to do here, just old people on beds in the blackness, and the occasional nurse in white marching down the corridor, a steel bedpan glistening in her hand.

I couldn't recognize my grandfather. His pyjamas were too big for him, something I never thought would happen. The pot belly I always rubbed for luck had melted away, replaced by sagging folds of helpless flesh. He didn't bark orders to his children, instead he just lay there nodding at their inane icebreakers.

'Look it's Mei Mei,' my mother would point at me, 'your favourite grandchild come and visit you. Don't you recognize her? Can you say the words – "Mei Mei"? She brought you some oranges to eat.'

Technically, it wasn't me, but my mother, who brought the oranges, but usually I was the one who offered the gift to my grandfather. My mother told me, 'Whenever your aunts and I give him anything, he always push our hand away, but he love you so much, he will take anything from you.'

So I held the oranges towards him and said, '*Gong gong,* eat oranges.'

The fruit hovered in his line of vision, but he didn't seem to see them, his watery grey eyes remained blank. After a while, he said, 'Oh!'

He didn't say anything for the rest of the visit. My Second Aunt peeled the orange and stuffed it in his mouth.

This was not my grandfather, not the man who raised me, but a stranger I couldn't connect with. It was like my grandfather had died, and this Stygian pit was the first level of Hell.

I thought about all this, standing in front of the altar at his funeral. God knows I didn't do enough for him while he lived, the least I could do now was cry for him, but I couldn't even do that. And I knew that because I couldn't cry, the King of Hell would think that I didn't love my grandfather and make him stay in Hell longer, which made me feel even more guilty. This line of thought dried me up completely.

Meanwhile, the pro' mourners wailed on, the Nile flowing down their faces. I don't know how they make themselves weep buckets, maybe it's because they're lamenting how Fate has been so cruel as to consign them to such a degrading occupation.

'Hey, you stand here so long, why you still don't cry?' My mother dug her sharp nails into my arm, drawing blood. 'Hurry up, pray to your grandfather.'

'Ouch,' I said. A tear finally trickled down my cheek.

Now came the time that I dreaded the most, the few hours before the body is coffined – the Death Watch. Boredom, I could handle, but dealing with the threat of turning into a lump of coal was another matter altogether. According to my mother, if a pregnant cat jumped over the corpse during the Death Watch, the deceased would jerk up and start a mad dash, running in a straight line, uprooting trees in his path and killing anyone within his reach. One touch, just one touch and the corpse would choke all breath out of you, turning you black.

Shoulders jerked at the unexpected clap of thunder, and a few of my aunts turned their heads from their mah-jong tiles to glare at Uncle Cheong, like it was his fault. Two aunts volunteered to stand over the corpse with paper umbrellas, to protect the body from the lightning.

I heard a miaow. I knew I was a bad person, an ungrateful, no-good non-crier. If a pregnant cat resurrected my grandfather, I'd be the first person she'd kill. I had to hide.

In the corner, two monks dozed at a table, the areas around their necks and armpits wet with sweat. I crawled under the table. Hidden by the thick tablecloth, I hugged my knees tight to my chest, but I could still hear it, the cat's long, cold miaow. Did pregnant cats sound any different from normal cats? I wasn't taking any chances. I shut my eyes but the vision wouldn't go away – my grandfather bearing down on me, black, demonic, his arms flung out, clawing for me, droning, *why you never cry for me? Now because of you, I have to stay in Hell. Why you never pray to me? Now I'm going to take you with me, for ever.*

The cold sweat soaked my clothes, made dark rings under my armpits and damp, freezing patches around the small of my back. It was no use hiding, my grandfather would find me anyway: the thump, boom, thump, boom of my heart filled my ears, drumming out my location to him. I didn't know what to do. Should I un-Christian myself so I could save my grandfather by my own power? But if I un-Christianed myself, what about Uncle Cheong? Who should I choose?

This phrase suddenly popped into my head – Christ took my sins and cleansed every stain. Of course I always knew this, Uncle Cheong always repeated this to me, but before today, it was nothing but a dry, empty slogan, Christian auto-pilot words, a mantra chanted so often in church until it became nothing but a hollow noise. Under the table that day, I suddenly realized what it really meant, and I don't know why I didn't understand it before then.

Everything which God sees as bad is not there any more. Now things which other people might consider bad about me, things which my parents and teachers always scolded me for – like abandoning my grandfather at the old folks' home, not crying at his funeral, crooked margins in my maths exercise books, forgetting to switch off the video – I still had these horrible flaws, but everything which *God* considered bad about me – that's all been removed. In His eyes, I can do no wrong. Can you imagine having a relationship with someone like that? Someone who sees no faults in you, who finds nothing offensive or deficient, who weeps and sings songs of adoration to you, because in his eyes, you are flawless. Nobody else I know can ever be as completely satisfied with me as God is. For other people, there will always be some flaw in me that makes me less than perfect in their eyes – maybe I'm too short, or too logical, or don't squeeze the toothpaste in the right way. Christ is the only person who loves me because I am perfect in His eyes. At that moment, it didn't matter how much my mother scolded me, or if my grandfather burned with anger at me from Hell – I'd found someone who would always love me to the point of near-worship, and I knew that that was the only thing I'd want for the rest of my life. All my guilt disappeared. My soul fed on Something, tasted the tears – were they mine or God's? – for each drop lighted my mind, altered my genes, turned me into something new, from soul to soul, from blood to blood. His spirit filled me until He became my very breath and my only desire: when I breathed I was using His breath and all I wanted to breathe was Him. Thus, panting after him and panting him, I opened my mouth and felt the unutterable kiss.

I opened my eyes. The thunderstorm stopped, and moonlight trickled under the tablecloth like silver water.

One of the monks stirred. His hand went under his robe, pushing it aside. Before this incident, I'd always wondered what priestly underwear looked like. Was it spotless? Was it holy? The monk's robe fell open, revealing – Levi 501s.

CHAPTER 3

Andy

'Your problem, Andy, is that you never plan,' my father said. 'When I was your age, I had a plan for the day, the month, the year and even the decade. And that is why I have always known where I wanted to go and no one has ever been able to stop me. Do you know why?'

I said 'Hmmmm,' which could mean a) 'Please tell me more' b) 'I don't care' c) 'Yes, I do know why. You've never been screwed because no one can find a dick that's big enough for your asshole'.

'Why? It's because I have a sense of direction,' he said, 'while you just drift along with the tide.'

I said, 'Hmmm' again in my best driftalong voice. Why didn't I defend myself? Why didn't I marshal my wits and let loose a Wildean riposte? Yeah, but that would like, require intellectual effort. And saliva. I had better things to do with my spit than to waste it on a goggle-face, bat-breath midget who had more hair on his butt than his head.

It's Saturday, it's summer and, outside, God's free tanning machine hangs in the air, shining its ultra-violetness on the good and the evil. It's the kind of day that's ideal for wandering around half-naked, scaring children with the sight of your hairy back and corpse-white skin. In other words, the perfect outdoors day. So what am I doing indoors, why am I in

Debenhams, squatting outside the ladies' changing room?

It's because Saturday is our Family Day, our official day for family bonding. Don't get me wrong. I've got nothing against family bonding. However, could someone please tell me how waiting for my mother to try on four blouses is going to bring us closer together as a domestic unit?

My mother got the idea for a Family Day after watching some slot on *Richard and Judy*. According to R & J's special guest, Dr Lilith Chambers, author of the *New York Times* bestseller, *Families are from Saturn*, you had to set aside at least seven hours a week to spend with your spouse and sprogs to save society from its imminent, apocalyptic demise. How could my mother not believe her? Dressed in a black Donna Karan suit, Dr Chambers had that all-wise, Athena aura – she looked like a Jewish Oprah. She smiled her more-soothing-than-Prozac smile and told us how divorce and single parenthood had led to a rise in teenage pregnancies, domestic violence, drug abuse and homelessness, accompanied by a decline in consumer confidence and SAT scores.

I agreed. As we all know, the deterioration of family values has also led to breast cancer, global warming, the Lockerbie air disaster and United's shock defeat against York in the third round of the Coca-Cola Cup. The happy family is the nucleus of civilization itself. So every Saturday morning, me, Mummy and Daddy had to do something Together, no matter how anal it might be. But hey, I could take comfort in the fact that my time in Parent Purgatory would somehow mystically contribute towards ensuring the advent of world peace and a buoyant British economy.

'Have you thought about which GCSEs you're going to take?' my father said.

'No,' I said.

'Now, I know that you may find the number of options

35

bewildering rather than liberating,' my father said, 'but from my experience, I've found that there's nothing that cannot be solved with a little foresight and a strategy for the future.'

You see, the problem with my dad is that we can never have a normal conversation about neutral subjects like the weather or TV listings. Every time he talks to me, he feels like he has to improve me. I mean, like hey, his time is precious. If our conversation had no utilitarian function, he would have wasted his time talking to me instead of doing something useful, like thinking of ways to increase the yield of pre-tax dividends under current accounting standards or something. So every time before he speaks to me, he thinks of something I might fuck up and gives me a long lecture about whatever stupid thing it is that I'm probably about to go off and do at any moment.

'You must avoid the temptation to follow the crowd,' he said. 'Don't choose a subject just because your best friend chose it and you want to be in the same class as him. Don't be a lemming. You have to base your decision upon a careful evaluation of your own personality. You have to ask yourself certain key questions, for example, what are your skills and abilities?'

I shrugged.

'What are your values and interests?'

'I'm not really into anything at the moment,' I said. It was July, post-FA Cup, weeks before the start of the new season, and most of the big clubs were off playing exhibition matches in Jamaica, Malaysia, Hong Kong or some other far off place. The summer is a nuclear winter for all football fanatics in Britain.

'I'm trying to teach you to ask the right questions,' my father said. 'The five "Ws".'

'Huh?'

'Not "huh?" That's not the right question. You have to learn how to ask the right questions. The five "Ws". For example, what do you want? Why do you want it? Where can you get it? et cetera.'

'Hmmmm.'

'Well, let's start with the first, basic question. What do you want to be?'

'I don't know.'

'What is your goal in life?'

'I don't know. I don't even know if I *want* a goal.'

My father gave up. 'Why don't you just take English, French, Literature, History, Geography, Physics, Chemistry, Biology and Maths?'

'Okay,' I said.

Before I went to university, my parents planned everything for me. I followed their lead, not because I liked it or agreed with it, but because arguing with them was too much hassle. I was never a rebellious teen. I was just bored. During adolescence, I wasn't a rebel without a cause – just a kid with no decent TV programmes to watch.

I come from Fallensham. Don't come here. It won't be easy though – many people don't plan to come here, but for some reason, they stumble into town and end up living here for ever. Fallensham is like Hell – to find it, all you have to do is follow the path of least resistance.

Fallensham has nothing apart from grass and cows, nothing but the wide, empty skies above the flat fields that spread out for ever. The only landmark near my home town is this sewage plant that looks like a giant white maggot, and a black water tower, a steel skeleton with spider legs.

In the city centre, there is, excitingly, one off-licence (which also contains the video shop, the cobblers, the dry cleaning service, and the Royal Mail), and the obligatory W H Smiths, Boots, a NatWest bank, and a Co-op. The proprietor of the Co-op has a major attitude problem. I remember a housewife going into the supermarket, clutching her new Delia Smith cookbook, and asking him if he had any sun-dried tomatoes. Judging from the look on the manager's face, you'd think she had just asked him for some peppermint-flavoured condoms. After he recovered from his shock, he said, 'We don't do sun-dried tomatoes, we just have ordinary tomatoes. We don't have any of those new foods,' as if sun-dried tomatoes were recently invented by some mad scientist in Geneva, with financial backing from Brussels. The supermarket only has the standard staple foods like potatoes, carrots, lettuce, cans of tuna, rice pudding and frozen chicken, none of that fancy 'new' food suggested by Delia, like cranberries and pesto sauce. Here, everyone eats bangers and chips. There are no Indian or Chinese takeaways, just a chip shop that serves cod, mushy peas and chips.

All the shops are completely utilitarian. Just enough shops for you to get by, providing all you need to live on, but nothing to make life worth living. No art, no entertainment, no culture. No computer game shops like Future Zone, no HMVs or Our Price or Virgin Megastores, no shop devoted to something that was just for fun, no frivolous yuppie specialist shops selling candles or cheese exclusively. The city centre enables you to buy your fags, crisps, and pick up some Spam and bread, so that you can go home after a hard day's work and switch on the TV.

Not that there's anything *wrong* with Fallensham. There's not an oppressed minority group in sight – no single mothers, no orphans, no Rwandan refugees, no gays, no blacks, no Pakis, we don't even have anyone who's fucking handicapped. Somebody must be doing something right.

I looked at my father. He stood outside the changing room, clutching my mother's handbag. For a horrible Mystic Meg moment, my future balloons into view: I will go to university, then wander into a job that pays me five figures, even though I don't Believe in what I am doing. I will spend eighty per cent of my life trying to help some MNC achieve complete and utter world domination of the chocolate biscuit market, and even though I know it is a completely pointless job, I cannot find more meaningful employment even if I tried. I will marry a girl, probably called Sara, have a blond son named Thomas, and spend my weekends in our house in Surrey gardening, cooking Delia Smith recipes and DIYing. I will become my father, the Husband-Waiting-For-Wife-To-Try-On-Dress, standing there with a glazed look, seeing nothing, bored, mindless, a living corpse, the man with the handbag. This is the best British life can offer. Death by domesticity, afternoons spent measuring out my life with coffee spoons.

I fled. I ran out of the store into the sun that glowed white death. It was a hot summer's day, hotter than it had ever been before and hotter than it has ever been since. The sun burned so intensely that it melted the car tyres, choking the air with the tang of burnt rubber. The glare of the sunlight upon the yellow brickwork of the houses hurt my eyes. The white light bounced off the pale pavements until the whole air was white with light. A broken bottle lay on the tarmac, flashed in the light, blazed like burning magnesium. I couldn't see a thing, nothing but white light, the rays piercing my eyes, so I closed them and opened my ears. I heard nothing. No roar of engines, no creak of bicycle wheels – it was safe. Eyes still shut, I started running, fleeing from Fallensham, trying to escape from what I was to become. I will not turn into the man with the handbag.

How long or how far did I run? I don't know. I just bolted

down the road, eyes shut, listening to my Nikes crunch down on the gravel. Finally, breathless, having burnt all the fear that fuelled my sprint, I collapsed. My knees cracked the baked mud.

I opened my eyes. I was by the bank of a river. I had no idea where I was, and I didn't know where to go. So like, what else was new?

I panted to the river and drank. I walked by the bank for, I don't know, ten minutes, and I got bored. I had no alternative but to go home. Where could I run to? It's so boring, everywhere, anywhere you go.

I set off in a random direction. I knew I would never find my way home unless someone helped me. But I wasn't going to get any help, not out here by myself, so I just kept walking. After a while, the sky turned red, then black. I didn't know what to do, so I started to pray. Sure I'd been to church and made all the right noises (after all, my parents were Church of England hatched and dispatched) but I had never prayed seriously before, never really felt that I really needed God to hear my words. However, at that moment, standing in the dark, I would have tried anything – telepathy, tracking duck prints, Indian smoke rings, sub-Saharan rain dances, anything really, just so I could get home. But none of the above worked, so I said – *God if you're there, give me a little direction.*

A bright, round light loomed towards me. I ran out to it and bam! – I flew. For a moment, everything went truly black, a darkness that was not just a mere absence of light, but one so thick you could choke on it – death descending.

Then the air turned into light, white and clear, transcendent, filling everything so I could see nothing else, nothing but brightness – God, the King of Kings, dwelling in unapproachable light. I sucked the liquid air and knew that this was what Heaven was going to be like, when you feel you could live like this for ever, a moment when you'd like to be frozen in time, in a photo, a portrait, a sculpture, a moment when you looked full at your desire. It was the only time in my life that I've felt any meaning. If I could have just captured that moment, kept it inside, I'd never have hungered for anything again.

A great fire blazed between four bronze columns. A gold cup stood right in the middle of the flames, but it shone so brilliantly that the fire lost its brightness, just as the stars do when the sun rises.

I reached for the cup. I wanted something I could take back, to prove that I had really met God.

An angel flew towards me with a lance. Though it had no flesh or veins, blood spurted from the white tip of the spear, flowing down to the angel's hand.

'Will you take charge of it?' the angel asked me.

'I will,' I said, and grasped the cup.

The angel raised the lance and drove it through both my thighs.

My body smashed the earth. I opened my eyes. With the side of my face pressed against the ground, I saw the sharp edges of the grass rise gently. The breeze blew over me, where it came from I did not know. And then it was gone.

After that, I blacked out again.

When I woke up, my eyes blurred and everything looked white again, only this time the smell of antiseptic hit me strong. When my vision cleared, I saw my father, my mother, and a doctor. 'What happened?' I said.

'We don't know,' my father said. 'We found you lying on the grass by the river.'

'Can't you remember what happened?' my mother said.

'Yeah. There was this big white light, it was really round. And then God and the cup and . . .' My legs hurt. A lot. I looked at them. 'Why are my legs hanging from the ceiling?'

'You fractured the bone in both your thighs,' the doctor said. 'We think you were in an accident.'

'He says he saw a big round light,' my father said. 'Maybe it was a motorcycle.'

'How did I get here?' I said.

'A motorist found you lying by the road,' my father said.

'But I saw . . . where's the cup?' I said.

'What cup?' my father said.

'Nothing. So it was just an accident?' I said.

What else *could* it be? I had no cup, no proof, no souvenir from heaven apart from two broken legs. How the hell could I ever convince anyone that I saw God?

'I guess you're right,' I said in my best driftalong voice. Father knows best.

CHAPTER 4

DAY TWO: MONDAY

Mei

I woke up to find myself suffering from a bad case of *fragilitas crinium*, or in layman's terms, split ends. Strands of hair stuck out of places in my head I never knew I had. It was a rebel hair day, a day when nothing on your head will submit to styling. I had only two options: chop it off or wear a hat. Andy always says that I make too much out of my bad hair mornings. I see them as a bad omen, a sign that the rest of the day will be damned. And I know I'm right – you know that the next twenty-four hours are going to be tough when the first thing you see in the mirror looks like Yoko Ono with a live porcupine on her head.

As I drove up the black hill towards the Central Police Station, the cuckling of motorcycle engines and the wheeze of buses faded away. I noticed a strange smell, strange because it was natural, not the fumes you expect to find in the Central Business District – the smell of fresh, dew-encrusted leaves. I could actually hear the crickets as my car cruised past the dense mass of vine-entangled trees.

Though I've been to the Central Police Station many times, it still shocks me. I'm addicted to *Cagney and Lacey*, *NYPD Blue*, and I keep expecting police stations to be dark and menacing, buzzing with mosquitoes, assaulted by grime, noise, cigarette smoke and paper blizzards. But police stations in Singapore are so clean and bright, so unexpectedly cheerful, it's unnerving. With pink floor tiles, lime green walls, air-conditioning, and an assortment of potted dumb canes and money plants, the station looks more like a civil service office than a sin bin.

The duty officer sat beneath a framed Snoopy jigsaw puzzle. I asked to see Andy. I waited beside the 'Charge Office' board, next to the fire extinguisher. Some resourceful person had created a makeshift container for the marker pens and duster by wedging a soap dish between the wall and the extinguisher. In the corner, through a Panasonic stereo system, Technotronic exhorted everyone to work their body. The duty officer took Technotronic's advice to heart and gently rocked his head to the beat. On the top of the left stereo speaker, a gold trophy proclaimed this station winner of the 'Most Courteous Report Room Contest'. I could see part of the lock-up from where I sat. I expected bars of steel, but instead, a wire mesh fenced in the cells, mesh reminiscent of the ones used for the chicken coops at my aunt's *kampong*.

I've always had my TV-fed fantasies about police stations, about how they must be centres of excitement, buzzing with blue cops snapping on their gun belts, the air frantic with the crackle of walkie-talkies. I mean, police stations are places where people *kicked ass*. But this place reminded me of a clinic. Sometimes I think my perpetual disappointment with real-life police stations, or with real life in general, is due to my overactive imagination – what I see with my mind's eye is always a million times better than what this grey earth can produce. But other times I think it's not my fault at all, and that the banality of this country is due to the authorities' desire to replace excitement with efficiency, passion with punctuality – their ability to turn everything into boredom.

Andy finally emerged from his cage, his shoulders scrunched, twisting his fingers.

'You're such a liar,' I said. A week ago Andy told me that he had become a Christian, that he had found God and that he wasn't going to let the punters use his flat as a betting house any more. 'You faked it all, pretending to have seen Jesus, giving up gambling. You only said that to trick me into going out with you.'

CHAPTER 5

Eugene

Oh right. I guess it's my turn now. Erm, what shall I say? At parties Mei always introduces me with the same line – 'Oh, come, meet Eugene. We've known each other since primary school. He's like the little brother I'm glad I never had.' Well, that's me – in Britain, I'm what you call a 'swot', in America, a 'nerd', and in Singapore, the '*kia su* kid' – the tiny child in the corner with the Asimov novel and spectacles face. I'm sort of like Jordan's brother, that dark, quiet and ugly member of New Kids on the Block whose name no one can ever remember. Mei's intro of me always gets a laugh from the guests, but it doesn't do anything for my confidence. In general, introductions have never done much for my confidence. When my mother brought me into the world, she made a *major* mistake. For starters, she named me Guo Xing, '国兴'. But then my uncle, who is some sort of fortune teller, calculated the number of strokes in my name and it was a bad number, or something, as it meant that I would die or generally catastrophise my life when I was in my twenties. He wasn't very specific as to what exactly would happen, but pronounced my doom in terms filled with terrifying generality. So my mother changed my name to one which had a more auspicious number of strokes – Ge Xun, '各讯'. But I always think, hey, I've already been named. My fate has already been set. I'm really going to fuck something up when I go past the big Two Zero. *Oh my God* . . . At this stage, Mei usually passes me a paper bag while I hyperventilate. But I hope this at least explains why I've spent most of my twenties in a state of constant neurosis.

When we were kids, Mei spent most of her time beating me up. We always played fighting, but according to the rules, I couldn't actually touch her, I could only feint blows in her direction. She, on the other hand, could punch me as hard as she liked. When I asked her why we played by these rules, she would just glare at me and say, 'Because I'm a girl and you're a boy, *stupid*. Boys can't hit girls.' Mei invented those rules, but to this day, she still insists that she's a feminist.

When we were thirteen, every time we watched a Bond video, we would pretend to beat each other up. Once, I jumped off the bed, spun and swung my right foot at Mei's head. She ducked, crouched on the balls of her feet, and leapt. Her right fist, propelled by the entire weight of her body, struck my chin like an ejecting spike. I crashed into the basket of laundry.

'There's only two things that touch me,' Mei said. 'My boyfriend, and soap.'

We spent the afternoon punching the air, bare feet swinging from the floor towards the ceiling, only stopping to peel our wet T-shirt collars from our necks. The thunder jerked us back to reality. Pins of water bounced off the window shutters, puddling the void deck with murky grey splotches. Though they were made of stainless steel, public opinion deemed that the shutters weren't strong enough and needed the protection of the green iron grilles. My mother told me this steel-iron barrier kept the burglars out, but I knew better. Anything exciting, like criminals, were in short supply on housing board estates. The labyrinthine metal outside our windows kept people in, not out, trapped them in their dinky two-bedroom flats, entombed them in Fortress Boredom.

I escaped through fantasy, transforming my bedroom into an adventure land, injecting magic into the mundane. A lot of our games involved nothing more than jumping on and off my bed, but in our minds we leapt out of trees to ambush aristocrats, or scaled Mount Everest with skipping ropes. We played Star Wars by switching on the fan to full power. When Mei spoke into the whirring blades, her voice went metallic – she became Darth Vader and droned chilling threats, while I made heroic noises as I waved my light-sabre/broomstick.

Sometimes, lying in bed at night, my stomach hurt. It was useless, all these games were just make-believe. My fantasies couldn't satisfy me, they only whetted my desire, lodged an ache like a balled fist in the pit of my stomach. The daydreams floated like vampiric phantoms, sucked the joy from my present existence, possessed me with the demon urge to morph into someone else, haunting, taunting me to get out, get out, go West young one.

'Why nothing ever interesting happen in Singapore?' I complained to Mei. On TV we always saw lots of shootings, car chases, bank explosions, but they all took place in the West. 'Why we don't have any guns? Why can't I get kidnapped or shot? I don't even know anyone who has been burglarized!' Raising my voice to compete against the loud rattle of rain against the shutters, I announced my goal in life. 'When I grow up, I'm going to go to England or America, and I'm going to catch a lot of murderers. I'm going to be like Arnold Schwazeneg, Schwitznegger, Shch – oh never mind.' How could someone be your role model if you couldn't even pronounce his name?

The West was filled with rolling hills, verdant fields, purple mountains, golden ponds and emerald lakes, full of opportunities to wander lonely as a cloud and chance upon a crowd, a host of daffodils. My English pen pal often wrote about the cute furry animals that would sneak into her house, wild squirrels and baby rabbits. Cockroaches and fruit flies were *my* household companions, creatures which have never been made into soft toys. Consequently, I am ashamed to confess that sometimes I do a Wordsworth and lie on my couch, wishing I was in some field in the Lake District, finding my blissful solitude in viewing that golden flash with my inward eye.

Hundreds of washing poles hung from the windows at the back of our apartment block, their wooden-clipped clothes swaying in the dark. Water plopped from the clothes to the pavement, scattering black, round rings on the grey cement.

Someone screamed. A woman crashed out of the window on the fifteenth floor, tumbling through the layers of wooden poles. The poles cracked, splintering wood on the ground. Clothes snapped from their clips, fell, and covered the twisted corpse like a shroud. These were the clothes that buried her: one pair of blue Giordano jeans, two cockroach-bitten singlets, four Triumph bras, a pair of green Crocodile briefs, a dark blue Raffles Girls' School track top, a faded Brownie uniform with badges for First-Aid, Tracking and Crafts, one green imitation Chanel T-shirt, three plain white shirts for the office, and one yellow-grey batik shirt for the trip to Bali. Then a child's T-shirt floated on to the corpse. Strawberry Shortcake smiled up at us from the T-shirt. 'I'm always smiling, cheerful, and very bright,' she said.

'Oh my God,' Mei said, 'don't look. You see this, afterwards the rest of your life you get nightmares, cannot sleep.'

She covered my eyes with her hand.

'Oh cool. Is it *that* gross? Let me see.' I clawed at her hands.

She let go, I saw the woman, and ran from the window. 'Oh yuck yuck yuck, so gross, so grosssss.'

'I told you so. Now you cannot keep the picture out of your head, they have to send you to Woodbridge mad hospital. Serve you right, who ask you not to listen to me?'

I returned, carrying a camera. 'Oh so gross, take picture, take picture.'

She snatched my camera.

I continued to make 'bleargh' faces. 'You see the head twisted like that. A hundred and eighty degrees. Yuck, yuck.'

'So yucky then you look for what?' Mei said. 'This kind of thing you also want to see.' She snorted disdainfully. Then she peeked at the body below. 'The corpse's eyes are still open. Hey, Eugene, she's looking at you. She's going to get you.'

'Shut up,' I said. 'Do you know who she is?'

Mei stared hard at the corpse. 'I think . . . she looks like . . . Marissa. Mrs Lam's maid.'

'You think she jumped?' I asked.

Mei shrugged.

'Hey, you know that Mrs Lam kept nagging her,' I said. 'She always shout at Marissa so loud – "You stupid girl, Chinese New Year how dare you sweep the floor? You want to sweep all my luck away? You continue like that I take away your deposit."'

'Don't be stupid, if a maid gets nagged, it doesn't mean that she'll go and commit suicide. If every maid that gets nagged, commits suicide, then there'll be no maids left in Singapore. Not raining cats and dogs any more – raining maids.'

'Hey, if the maid didn't jump then you think what – somebody throw her out of the window?' My eyes widened. 'You think somebody . . . *murdered* her?' I started humming the theme tune from *The Twilight Zone*. '*Wah*, wait till I tell the people on my school bus. "Hey, you know what? Yesterday somebody in my building got murdered."' I jumped and clapped my hands. 'Excitement.'

'Why you think somebody murdered her?' Mei said.

''Cos it'll be really cool if she was murdered,' I said. 'Then we got mystery to solve. Nothing ever happens around here. I hope she was murdered.'

'*Choi, choi*, don't talk rubbish,' Mei said. 'Mrs Lam is a very nice lady. She's not the psycho type.'

'You know what they say,' I said. 'It's always the quiet ones.'

Mei glared at me. 'Don't you have a test to study for?'

'Can't you stop acting like a prefect for five seconds?' I said. 'Even my mother isn't as strict as you.'

'Even my mother doesn't have tits as big as yours, you fatty bom bom.'

More insults were traded, followed by a spot of mutual hair-pulling, chest-pushing and shin-kicking.

After we exhausted ourselves, I said, 'Maybe we should go and visit Mrs Lam. To comfort her.'

'To *kaypoh* you mean, you big busybody,' Mei said.

'Hah, like you not interested,' I said. 'Don't you want to find who murdered Marissa? This is our chance to be real detectives, like the Famous Five.' I went to my school bag and took out my Whizz Kids' *How to Be a Detective*. 'Now according to this book we need fingerprint powder. Charcoal is the best.'

'Where to get charcoal?'

'Go to the kitchen, *girl*.'

'Stupid, we only have a gas stove and a microwave. Who cooks with charcoal any more? We can use Johnson's Baby Powder. It works better on dark surfaces than charcoal.'

'That's so un-macho. Why your kitchen so lousy, got no charcoal?'

'We can use pencil lead instead.'

We gathered all the pencils in the flat, and started scraping the lead tips with our pen knives. Black dust powdered the air, settling slowly into the jam jar.

I looked at my book again. 'It says here that we need a brush made from camel hair. You got one or not?'

'Singapore where got camel? We'll use my paintbrush.'

'Right. All we need now is to find an excuse to go up to Mrs Lam's house and dust her place for prints. Oh goody, even more excitement,' I said. 'I'll go put on my Scout uniform, and you go get your Guides uniform. We'll go to her flat, and we'll tell her that we got to do this good deed, clean her house, to get a "Helpfulness" badge or whatever those stupid things are called. You distract her, bring her to the kitchen, wash her windows, while I dust Marissa's room for prints. Ask Mrs Lam loads of questions about Marissa, and remember to switch on the tape recorder. If she makes a slip, we can use it as evidence. You get the picture?'

'Cheese.'

I hit the red button, filling the air with chimes from the first bars of the 'Blue Danube'. The door opened a fraction, then shuddered to a stop. Mrs Lam peered through the chained gap.

'Hello, we're from the Scouts and the Guides. Can we do a good deed?' I lifted my red bucket and cloth to show her that I had brought my window-cleaning apparatus along.

The door sprung free from its chains. 'Of course, come in, come in, you're so kind.'

Mrs Lam gathered us in. She looked at Mei. 'Why your face so white, you poor girl? You having your period now? I go and pour some ginseng tea for you.' Her back disappeared into the kitchen.

Mei stuck out her tongue. 'Ginseng.'

'Say you love ginseng tea, say she's the best ginseng tea

maker in the world. Drink as much as possible, keep her occupied while I do some snooping.'

Mei sulked towards the kitchen, while I ducked into Marissa's room.

Marissa's dressing table was buried under all sorts of chemicals — hairspray, lipstick, the usual stuff, but also some tubes and aerosols that did more subtle stuff that I didn't know anything about. I picked up a bottle of transparent yellow liquid called 'Eskinol Clear', and noted the Manila Import Services Pte Ltd's promise that it would whiten any Filipino skin 'in 14 days, Guaranteed!' Pencilled on her complimentary AIA Insurance calendar was a mysterious list of numbers: '4046 – 1, 8241 – 2, 8460 – 1, 0922 – 2, 5686 – 2, 8712 – 1, 0724 – 1 Quickpick $1'. The bottom of the drawer was filled with love paraphernalia, stuff like this packet of pink envelopes with loads of red roses on the front and the words, 'When we are together again, our relationship will be ♥♥♥'. Puke-inducing or what? Stuffed between the pages of her diary was a poem written in romantic doggerel, e.g. rhymes like 'flame'/'rain', 'see'/'me', professions that 'my own heart brims with tears unshed', like in a bad Michael Bolton song (is there any other?). The poem was signed 'Tom', plus a phone number and address. Who was Tom? A white American GI grinned from a black-and-white photo clipped to a McDonald's menu. Was that him? I scribbled in my notebook 'Tom. Boyfriend? Murderer?' Shading in all the empty spaces, I ensured that no gaps on the page could be filled with forged evidence, in case the book fell into criminal hands.

Time to dust the table for prints.

'Eugene, would you like some ginseng tea?' Mrs Lam walked into the room. Her eyes swivelled from the paintbrush in my hand to the black powder that smudged the cream table top.

'What are you doing, boy?'

'Nothing.' I chucked my equipment into my bag.

Mrs Lam snatched my bag. Rummaging through it, she found her card:

Criminal Record Card No. 1

Name: Mrs Lam
DOB/Age: 40?–50?
Place of Birth: Singapore
Occupation: Teacher

Distinguishing features: freckles, pimples, a mole on the upper lip and more wrinkles than Jabba the Hutt.

'Is that supposed to be me? she said.'

Under the 'mug shots – front and side' section were two crude sketches of Mrs Lam.

I nodded.

'You really think I weigh that much? Do I look that old?'

I gulped.

She gave me a hard stare and said, 'I don't like your manner.'

I knew what I should have said. I should have been cool like Marlowe, and said through the side of my mouth, 'You don't like my manner? That's all right, 'cos I'm not selling it.'

But I wasn't cool, I couldn't think of a single snappy wisecrack. I just stood there, thinking oh shit oh shit oh shit oh shit oh shit.

Back at our detective HQ, Mei had her mouth stuck under the tap, washing out the taste of the ginseng.

'Why you didn't distract her long enough?' I said. 'You know how much trouble you got me into? Lucky she so shocked, I ran away before she could catch me.'

Mei dislodged her mouth from the tap and sputtered. 'It's your own fault. Who ask you to be so slow? Did you get any fingerprints?'

'I didn't have time. I managed to get a bottle to dust at home.' I produced the 'Eskinol' bottle.

Mei gave me *such* a look. 'You're going to hell. I can't believe it. You *stole* something from a dead person?'

'It's not stealing, it's confiscating evidence.' What was the big deal? Detectives in novels always took stuff from crime scenes and nobody ever made a fuss. I drenched the bottle with talcum powder, all psyched up to find arches, whorls, loops, composites. I knew all the different categories from reading the Whizz Kids book, but though I zapped sticky tape over every inch of the glass I got nothing for my efforts.

'Did you get any useful info from Mrs Lam?' I said.

'She said she was away on holiday when Marissa fell. She thinks it was an accident. She say that whenever Marissa was hanging out the clothes, she always did it very dangerously. Like if a bird landed on the end of the pole, on one of the blouses, Marissa would try to shoo the bird away, stick her hand out at the bird to hit it. I guess that's what happened that night – Marissa leaned and leaned, then whooshed out of the window.'

I rubbed the imaginary stubble on my chin. 'I don't believe this accident theory. Marissa was a spy. The numbers on that paper were code messages.'

'Those were lottery numbers, stupid.'

'Maybe someone hypnotized her. I saw that on *Columbo* once. The murderer hypnotizes her, say that when she hears the phone ring three times, she'll feel really hot, and jump out of the window. We can go and ask Mrs Lam's neighbour if the phone rang three times before Marissa fell.' I clapped my hands together with glee. 'I'm such a great detective, the clues just fall in place like that –' I snapped my fingers. 'It's almost too easy. Everything is clear when you have the vision of a genius.'

'Rubbish. *Columbo* is TV. Life is life. Get real.'

'You got a better idea?'

'I'm not the one with the vision of the genius.'

I shut my eyes. 'Marissa definitely had a boyfriend, that's why she had so much make-up. But they split, that's why she put all the love envelopes at the bottom of the drawer.'

'So what do you think happened, O Wise One?'

'Maybe Marissa's boyfriend wanted her to run away with him to America. Maybe she couldn't because . . . because . . . she had to stay and work in Singapore to earn money for her family. Maybe her boyfriend got jealous, they fought, and he pushed her out of the window.'

'Marissa wasn't murdered. It was just an accident. She was just doing her job, hanging clothes, and she fell. She died doing a boring, boring job. That's how our lives are going to be like. Die after living a boring, boring life.'

'You're wrong, it was murder, I can feel it. I know what will happen – we'll discover too much, because people always think children don't know anything, but we *know*. We'll find the murderer, and he'll try to capture us, but we'll escape to the police just in time.'

'That kind of thing only happen on TV one *lah*. Or in England and America. Nothing exciting is ever going to happen to us. Face it, Eugene, you're too ordinary. You look exactly like all the other boys your age – durian hair, big owl glasses, brown oily skin. If they drove a bus down the pavement, they would hit twenty kids that looked exactly like you. You're not special. You're like me, you're just *normal*.' Mei said that the problem with this world is that nine out of ten people are so dull that no one would want to write or read about them, and the tenth person, their life is so bizarre that no one would believe it. It's this horrible, but necessary and inevitable imbalance that rules our lives.

But her words only made me burn to prove that inside this typically dorky-looking boy was a Rambo. Authority types like Mei hated me, because I was an unorthodox, fly-by-wire kind of guy, a renegade who would cut through red tape and regulations to get things done. I'd do whatever it takes to get justice, and if those pen-pushers at city hall can't take it, they can stick their biros and DA126 forms up their you-know-where. I flapped the photo of Marissa's boyfriend in Mei's face. 'I'm going to catch him, no matter what you say. Then they'll interview me on *Crimewatch* and I'll be famous.' I stuck out my tongue at her. 'And you'll be nothing.'

Mei snatched the photo from me. 'Wait a sec. I think I saw him.'

'When?'

'On the night Marissa fell, I saw this guy go into the flat.'

'You sure?'

Mei nodded. 'We better go tell the police.'

'No, I want to interview the guy before we go to the police. Search his flat. Now, if we . . .'

'What's this "we" thing? If you want to go talk to a murderer, you can go by yourself. You want to get killed – that's your problem.'

'You're going to desert me, chicken?'

'I'm leaving it to the police.' Mei opened my toy cupboard. 'Maybe we should play Scrabble instead.'

'Maybe you should go home, Judas.'

'Maybe I will.'

After receiving our information, the police raided Tom's flat. They found Marissa's purse and jewellery in his cupboard.

57

Faced with the incriminating evidence, Marissa's boyfriend broke down and confessed.

'Don't you think it's strange?' my father said.

'What?' I said.

My father shut the newspaper report on Marissa's boyfriend. 'According to the murderer, he had no idea how Marissa's purse and jewellery got into his cupboard. That's what really scared him. He thought that God or Marissa's ghost must have planted them there, so he confessed to the police to save his soul.'

'It's a miracle.' I shrugged.

As for Mei, because she was so nasty to me about the whole detective business, I resolved not to friend her for at least a week, to teach her a lesson. I decided that I wasn't going to speak to her unless she bowed down, made flapping worship gestures with her arms and addressed me as The Great Detective. But three days later when we passed each other along the corridor, we both said 'Hi', and everything went back to normal.

CHAPTER 6

DAY TWO: MONDAY

Andy

When I first asked Mei to go out with me, she told me that she couldn't be 'unequally yoked'. When I asked her what the hell she meant, she quoted 2 Corinthians 6:14 at me – 'Do not be yoked together with unbelievers' – which basically meant she wouldn't go out with anyone who wasn't a Christian.

'Last week, when you suddenly converted,' Mei said, 'at first I thought – hmmm, *very* suspicious, but I decided to give you the benefit of the doubt. I was so wrong.'

'What do you mean?' I said.

'I kept warning you but you never listen. Don't deny this. Ever since you came to Singapore, every Saturday night you had to bet with the bookies, and every Saturday night I kept telling you that you're going to get caught. You never learn, do you? You had to keep on betting, betting, betting until you got busted.'

'What do you think happened?'

'It's obvious isn't it? All week, you kept going on about Newcastle and Man U, how Saturday's match was going to decide the championship. So I guess your punter friends turned up as usual, and you just couldn't say "no".'

I shook my head. 'That's not what happened at all. There wasn't any gambling in my flat when I was arrested. I told you, I've turned to God. No more gambling. I'm a changed man.'

'So what really happened?'

'I was in my flat, on my way out to see you – just putting your gift in my pocket – oh, you'll love what I bought – it's this packet of diet chocolate bars. It's got all these cool centres – orange, apricot, mint, toffee, coconut – sugar- and fat-free, only a hundred and six calories each. I know how you worry about your thighs. Is that a good gift or what?' I looked longingly for approval.

'You were supposed to get me some shampoo.'

'Oh yeah, right. But anyway I was putting the chocolate in my pocket – no punters around me, in an absolutely non-soccer, non-gambling situation – when there's this knock on the door. The police raided my flat, they arrested me and everything, but I didn't do anything wrong. I was framed.'

I told her all about my arrest.

The fan hung above me like a chrysanthemum, its golden petals spinning from the ceiling. The swift blades cast dark strokes against the concrete above it, sent blurred, black stripes streaking around the orange ceiling. I'd never noticed it before. It's one of those moments when you casually glance at something that's always been there and suddenly you realize you've never seen anything quite so magical in all your life. I sucked in my breath and dropped on to the sofa. I had to get dressed to leave but I couldn't move – though this sight was a thing of beauty, I had to meet Mei, another thing of beauty, in ten minutes' time. Mei's beauty was unlike that of the pattern above me – hers was the steely, even caustic type, like mercury. She had an impatient energy, an attraction too powerful to be fixed. She hated everything that was late.

The flames from the altar next door licked the fumes of the 'Lucky Oil' into my flat. Smoke curled in through the steel shutters of the windows, sweet incense from the burning oil. A couple of months ago, returning home drunk and consequently, stricken with mad craving for chips, the bottle of 'Lucky Oil' was a dead ringer for Mazola corn oil. So I nicked some to deep-fry my potatoes. Fortunately, Mei popped by an hour later and sent me to the hospital to get my stomach pumped before anything lethal happened.

I know I was going to be late for my date, but I just lay there, transfixed. I had entered one of those rare moments in life, that maybe, if you're lucky, you get once – a moment when fantasy and reality merge, when you live out what you only usually dream through TV. I pressed the volume button on my remote and watched the chrome knob on the Sony wind upwards, drowning out the rattling rain. The bass bounced off the floor, knocking the breath out of me. But my body soon adjusted, my heart thudding along to the rhythm; I melted into the song, let the guitar riffs wind round my body. That's the thing with loud music – fight it, and it's like banging your head against the wall. You'll just end up with a headache and bleeding ears. Better to surrender to it, let the wailing waves carry you, ride the surf.

Spread-eagled on the sofa, wearing only black boxers, I felt like a model in an MTV video (dir. David Fincher). The scene I was in had all the elements of a Fincher video – the bass, the smoke, the fan, the acid rain outside. Everything was picture perfect – I lay there, my white skin pale against the black leather cushions, experiencing a mystical visitation, waiting – any moment now – for the face of Madonna or George Michael to appear projected on the ceiling, mouthing the lyrics to their latest Billboard Top 5 hit. Life could not get better than this.

A Chinese face peered through the shutters. The man tapped the window to get my attention. I stared at the ceiling. He waved a plastic ID in his right hand and flapped some paper with his left. His lips moved and it seemed like he was saying

– 'Shit is a Sioux warden' – but I knew that couldn't be right. I cut the music.

After I opened the door, the inspector did more paper-flapping in my direction. 'Inspector Koh, CID, Gambling Suppression Branch,' he said. 'This is a search warrant. Please co-operate with us. We will conduct the search in your presence.'

I'm shitting myself, thinking – they're going to bloody wreck my flat! You know, I've seen the movies and I know that when you get raided, the police splinter down your doors, yank down your cabinets, take out their knives and slit up your sofa looking for contraband.

'Where are they?' the inspector said.

'Who?' I said.

'Don't pretend,' he said. 'We've been watching your flat for the past month.'

I knew who the inspector was referring to. 'They' were the bookies. Usually, on Saturday nights, Loong ran his betting shop in my flat, but fortunately, not tonight.

'I'm not hiding anyone. You can check, you've got the warrant,' I said. 'I'm the only one who lives here, apart from the usual lizards and the occasional stray iguana.'

'Check the toilet,' the inspector told his junior officer. The junior officer was a skinny teenager. All I could think of was how young he looked – like hell, I was being busted by some kid who probably wasn't old enough to buy cigarettes yet.

The junior officer returned to the living room with a Filofax. 'It's all here, sir,' the officer said. 'Names and numbers.'

The inspector shot me a meaningful look, but I'm like 'Huh?'

'I've never seen the Filofax before in my life,' I say. 'And if I'd seen it, I never would have bought it.'

I mean – huuurgh, it was ugly. The cover had this blotch of yellow, brown, white squiggles, like someone shat on it, wanked all over it and then topped it off with a sprinkle of pond scum. It looked like something that dropped out of the Sphinx's nose. I knew that I should be worrying about jail and shit, but all the time, the only thing I could think of was – how the hell can they even think that I could own a Filofax like that? I mean, I'm a cool, hip guy. I'm always aware of what's in the UK Top Twenty, I know who's in, who's out, who's on the move. I mean, I'm the 'in' kind of guy who knows who's the smart one in *Beavis and Butthead*. So I say to the inspector, 'You don't *seriously* think that the Filofax belongs to me? You know, like I have more *taste* than that,' and he just gives me this look that says that, in his eyes, my cool quotient equals to zero. And I feel like a pile of cack. And I tell myself, 'Andy, you are one mind-fucked boy. You ought to be worried about spending the rest of your life in jail for a crime you know nothing about, instead of worrying about whether Inspector Koh thinks you're hip or not'. But you've got to see it to believe it – the Filofax was so ugly, it was traumatic.

The officer cuffed me and led me out, past the other flats. The corridor was filled with the noise of clanging swords and the flutter of kung-fu somersaults, the sound of twelve TVs all tuned to the same channel, everyone watching Chinese Cinema I: *Ming Demon*.

We reached the lift. The doors opened, revealing a Filipino maid with two children, a teenager in a dark blue pinafore, lugging a black Nike tennis bag that was half her height, and a housewife, carrying four big red plastic bags from Robinsons, probably on her way back from the Great Singapore Sale. When she saw us – the police officers, and me in cuffs – about to enter the lift, she nudged her nine-year-old boy with her knee and said, 'Let's go.'

'But not our floor yet,' the boy protested.

'Shut up. We'll walk up the rest of the way,' she said, and

pushed him out of the lift. The other passengers shot fearful glances in my direction too and scrambled out.

I've never felt so dangerous in all my life. It was *so* cool.

I thought I was going to get it when the police brought me to the statement room. I expected this dark room, pitch black with nothing but a huge hot yellow light blazing in my face, you know, those rooms you see in cop shows, the ones with two-way mirrors. I expected two detectives to play good guy, bad guy, both hunched over me, their hot breath down my neck, shaking me by the collar, trying to extract a confession, threatening to beat me. I was all psyched up to say stuff like – 'I know my rights, I want my lawyer. I'm a British citizen. Call the embassy. Call the British Council. I'll set Amnesty International on you if you so much as lay a finger on me.'

But the real statement room looked like the staff room in my school. It had all the usual office stuff – Biros in mugs, packets of Blu-tack, ring reinforcements, half-used wrapping paper, a family photo of a kid flapping around in a pool with a Jurassic Park dinosaur float, a huge Garfield tissue-paper holder, and on the wall behind them, a 'Mr Kia-su' cartoon calendar. I felt like I was being audited by an accountant, it was like being arrested by Coopers and Lybrand.

The inspector started making some pretty serious allegations – he's going to book me for being some triad, secret-society gambling honcho or something. He served me the notice and I read the charge.

'Do you wish to say anything in answer to the charge?' he said.

I'm completely gobsmacked. I work as a relief teacher at Dai Tang Secondary School, and earlier that morning, you wouldn't believe the crap I had gone through just to be able to bring the kids I teach to Fort Canning. My principal said it wasn't safe – like please, I'm bringing the kids to look at some cannons, it's not like I'm taking them bungee jumping over shark-infested waters or anything like that. I told my principal that, and he said, 'Fort Canning is a big hill. What if the children fall down and break their heads? Like Jack and Jill. Then the parents will come and sue the school. Then how?' My principal only agreed to the field trip after I got the parents to sign all these consent forms in triplicate, absolving the school of any responsibility 'in the event of any injuries (whether psychological or physical), damage or deaths'. Anyway the point of this story – and there is a point to it – is that this morning my principal treated me like I was some pea-brain git who couldn't even supervise a simple field trip, and ten hours later the police are trying to get me to admit that I'm this genius mastermind who's been funnelling millions of dollars in bets all around the world.

I told the inspector about the field trip but he didn't say anything. He just eyeballed me for a minute and said, 'I advise you to mention any facts you intend to rely on in your defence at the trial.'

'Don't I have a right to remain silent and all that TV stuff?' I said.

'*Yah*. You can tell us your defence for the first time in court. But it's better not to.'

'Why?'

'Usually the judge will think that you've made it up. You leave it so late to give your defence, he might not believe you. If you're innocent, then there's no harm talking to us right? All we want is a voluntary statement.'

The inspector passed me the Filofax. 'Look carefully at the names. Do you know them?'

I looked at the list of names – Ho Fat Foon, Yap Chin Chai, Kwok Wok Woon, but they didn't ring any bells. I mean, I could have been reading a Chinese menu, for all I knew.

The inspector started reading all this stuff from the Filofax – 'August 24, Liverpool versus Arsenal, two hundred thousand dollars', and I was like 'What?'

'Don't try and bluff me,' he said. 'We can verify all these bets. Three million dollars.'

'You know all about these bets?' I said. 'Good for you. Because I sure as hell don't know *anything* about them.'

'Well, I've got good news and bad news,' Mei said.

'Bad news first,' I said.

'The maximum sentence is a fine of two hundred thousand dollars and jail not exceeding five years.'

'Ouch. And the good news?'

'The minimum is twenty thousand dollars, and one month in jail.'

I jerked my head back. 'That was the good news?'

'Sorry, I lied,' Mei said. 'What do you expect – I'm a lawyer. I should have said – I have bad news, and bad news.'

'Twenty thousand? That's more than a whole year's salary. How am I going to find that kind of money?'

'Didn't you make a lot of money betting?'

I shook my head. 'Sometimes I win, sometimes I don't. It evens out. I'm about a thousand dollars in profit at the moment. Shit. Jail . . .'

'. . . Is mandatory,' Mei said. 'One month, minimum.'

When I first got arrested I wasn't too worried about it. Yeah, sure I got stressed, but only in the way people get stressed if they get done for parking on a double yellow line. You sort of think – 'Oh bollocks', but it's not like your life is over. When I got arrested, I thought the worst thing that could happen was maybe a big fine, a slap on the wrist. But now I saw my whole life evaporating before me. 'Five years?' I said.

'Don't worry, I'll visit you,' Mei said. 'I'll bring cookies.'

'I can't cope with jail. I'm twenty-two, I'm in my sexual prime, I can't spend five years in jail. And after I get out I'll be screwed. Who will want to employ a convicted felon? And if I can't get a job, how am I going to pay off a two-hundred-thousand-dollar fine?' I snapped my fingers. 'I know, maybe I can write a book. Don't you think this whole gambling/jail thing sounds pretty exciting? Maybe I can get loads of dosh for my story, you know, to help me pay the fine.'

'I'm sure your life will make a great alternative detective story,' Mei said.

'You really think so?'

'Yes, most detective stories would be about the protagonists' remarkable powers of observation. Your story would be about your remarkable lack of observation.'

It hit me for the first time – the whole big bag of shite, cosmic seriousness of the situation. They say that in moments of despair, staring at the dark night of the soul, you tap into pools of poetry that you never knew you had; a rare moment of eloquence grips you, as the Muse is moved by pity to visit you, enabling you to articulate the awful existential condition of man. Sitting there, contemplating my penalty, I had an epiphany, my lips moved to utter two simple, yet moving words that described my plight, something Hemingway might have said, a real literary statement in the dirty realism tradition.

'Oh shit,' I said.

'That is an accurate summary of the situation,' Mei said.

'Why jail? I didn't do anything *evil*,' I said. 'It's only gambling, it's just a laugh, you know. I didn't hurt anyone.'

Mei rolled her eyes. 'It's just a "guy thing", I suppose.'

'Exactly.'

'You expected a spanking rather than a kick in the teeth.'

'It was just a *game*.' I spread my hands. 'I'm just the victim of a cultural misunderstanding.'

In England, gambling is just fun: you have Dale Winter and Mr Blobby and lottery balls popping up on your screens every Saturday night and everyone thinks it's a right laugh. In Singapore, most forms of gambling carry a mandatory prison sentence. I was finding this a lot lately – things that you do in England in order to become one of the lads, those hard-men initiation rites – in Singapore, those exact things would get you fined, incarcerated and caned. That's like, well confusing. I mean, they can jail you for *two weeks* just for swallowing one tiny E tablet.

'I'm getting really paranoid,' I said. 'I keep thinking, any moment, I'm going to get done for something that I didn't even know was illegal. I'm scared that if I fart too loudly I might get hanged for polluting the environment.'

Every Saturday afternoon, during our university days, Eugene would listen to 'Sport On Five'. Every ten minutes or so, his mobile phone would ring and he would jabber frantically in Hokkein. At night, we would gather in the common room with our beers and our Salt and Lineker crisps, watch *Match of the Day* and jeer at Jimmy Hill. We also bet on the soccer results. The losers would have to buy a crate of beer or pay for a week's subscription to the *Sun*.

When I went to Singapore, Eugene introduced me to the punters he had jabbered to while he was in England. So when we ran the soccer-betting in my flat every Saturday night, it was like continuing the hallowed, male-bonding ritual that we had started at university. When Mei first told me that betting was illegal, I was shocked.

'It's so stupid. I mean, soccer-betting is perfectly legal in England. It's fun, it's like the lottery, it's like beer,' I said. 'Can you imagine if a government tried to ban alcohol? Can you imagine being only allowed to drink water?'

Mei did not look distressed at all.

'It's ridiculous,' I said. 'Every Saturday, on my way to do ECA with those kids at my school, I always get caught in the traffic jam at Bukit Timah Road. All these cars, buses, unloading hundreds of punters, all going to the Turf Club to bet on horses. How come betting on horses is legal, but betting on soccer is not? How can the Singapore government be so inconsistent?'

'It's not as simple as that. You can only bet on horses at the Turf Club, where the government can keep an eye on things, to make sure they don't get out of hand. It's illegal to bet on horses anywhere else, e.g. in someone's house,' Mei said, 'just as it's illegal to bet on soccer in your flat.'

'Why do you have such stupid laws in your country?'

'Andy, you're in jail not because our laws are stupid, but because *you* are stupid. Gambling is addictive, it's a waste of money –'

'I don't care. You have to fight this law. It's awful. I can't imagine not being able to bet on soccer. It'd be like – not being able to play Doom.' I lowered my voice in hushed horror. 'It'd be like banning the FA Cup Final!'

'For some reason, I'm not shocked by any of those proposals.'

I sighed and looked sadly at her. 'You are one culturally deprived woman.'

I guess I let the punters meet in my flat because I never had the feeling that I was doing anything *bad*. I couldn't imagine getting into trouble over it. It was all so casual. We were just a group of twenty guys, watching a 'live' soccer match on TV, drinking Tiger beer, smoking Camels, chomping on melon seeds and betting. Gambling in my flat was the same as all the boozing and drug-taking I did while at university, it was just fun, you never got the feeling that you were doing anything evil. It was just a good laugh.

*

69

'Your problem is that you're suffering from a chronic case of Peter Panitis,' Mei said. 'You keep acting like this perpetual Lost Boy.'

'I'm not immature,' I said, 'I'm just a free spirit.'

'Irresponsible.'

'Spontaneous.'

'Unprepared.'

'Fun-loving.'

'Andy, there's a difference between the fun that is funny – "ha, ha", and the fun that is funny – "weird".'

'What do you mean?'

'You have a distressing inability to distinguish between the brand of humour that is amusing and the type that is merely disgusting. Your ability to fart louder than is biologically necessary definitely falls into the latter category.'

Mei always treats me like I'm some toilet-trained pig. She always gives me so much stick. She's always so superior, as if she knows everything, while I know nothing. Sometimes, like now, I'd really like to have a go at her too, but I can't, because she's a woman, and if I point out her faults, it just sounds sexist and condescending. But there are things I could teach her, if she could only humble herself for once and admit that I am obviously right. Here is my Top 5 Lessons that Mei needs to learn:

5. 'How To Stop Whining and Nagging', or 'How To Act Younger Than Your Mother'.

4. Having happily and painlessly spent over *fifty thousand* dollars on a Certificate of Entitlement, road tax, sales tax, insurance, all that just to get a car, it does not make sense to park your car half a mile from Cathay cinema so you don't have to pay *three* dollars to enter the Central Business District.

3. You will not be emotionally crippled for life if you don't shop on the same day you receive your pay cheque.

2. 'How To Kill Cockroaches Silently'. Screeching and 'eeeeeek' noises have no deleterious effects on lizards and spiders. Yes, you, even you can learn how to exterminate household pests without having to make squealing pig noises!

1. Wearing the sexy bikini I bought you will not damage your brain cells.

Anyway, just then was probably not a good time to slag her off, because she was my lawyer and the only person who could get me out of this mess. So I just swallowed my indignation, nodded at her and agreed that I'd been a bad boy.

'How are we going to find out who framed me?' I said.

'Right, in order to draw up a list of suspects, we need to think of three things.' Mei stuck up her thumb. 'Motive.' Up came her forefinger. 'Means.' Finally, the index finger rose. 'Opportunity.' She put down her hand. 'Motive first. Revenge might be a motive. Did you offend anyone? Does anyone have a grudge against you? Who hates you?'

'You know me. I'm Mr Lovable himself.' I grinned. 'Who can resist my charms? Why would anyone hate me?'

'Didn't you ever offend anyone? Maybe when you were drunk?'

'No. I'm not that bad when I'm pissed. I'm not the type of bloke who gets *psycho* pissed.'

'What do you mean?'

'When I'm drunk, I don't get violent and hassle people or beat them up or anything. I'm not a yob. I just enjoy myself, puke and pass out.'

'But often you don't remember what you've done when you're drunk. Could you have done something to someone and just not remember it?'

'That's a really stupid question. If I can't remember what I did when I was pissed, how can I tell you about it?'

'What I mean is . . .' Mei put on the tone that I'd heard her use with stray dogs and wilting plants. '. . . in the past few months, can you remember *when* you were drunk? Maybe I could check up on any witnesses. Maybe they can remember something that you can't.'

'Well you're usually around, most of the time I've been really pissed. If I'm not with you, I'm usually with Eugene. Maybe you could ask him.'

'What about the punters? Did any of them have anything against you? Maybe something you said?'

I shook my head. 'Most of the punters spoke Hokkein, so I hardly even talked to them.' When I arrived in Singapore, Eugene told me that I could survive by mastering the all-purpose phrase, 'Is it?' (pronounced as 'Izzzit?' in Singlish) which could be used to express agreement or disbelief, or as an acknowledgement that I was paying attention, just two handy words I could throw in whenever there was an awkward gap in the conversation. 'I just said "Is it?" to the punters whenever they spoke to me. There was no way I could have pissed any of them off with that.'

'How did you place your bets then?'

'I would tell Eugene about what bet I wanted and he'd translate for me.'

Mei frowned. 'Well, I guess another possible motive might be money. Who stands to profit? Would some punter make more money if the gambling took place somewhere else?'

'I really don't know. They were always talking in Hokkein. Maybe you better phone Eugene and ask him about it.'

'How many punters met at your flat on Saturdays?'

'About twenty.'

'So you're telling me that there were about twenty gamblers, most of them with dubious backgrounds, meeting every week in your flat.'

'Uh, yeah.'

'And I suppose that all of them used your toilet at one point or the other?'

I nodded.

'Any one of them could have planted the Filofax,' Mei said.

I could see that things were not looking good. Twenty men, most of them pretty dodgy, and I remember some of them spent a *long* time in my toilet. They all had plenty of time to plant the Filofax. But I always figured that hey, a man's got to do what's a man got to do, so I never made a fuss about it.

'So when can I get out of here?' I said.

'Tomorrow,' Mei said. 'Maybe.'

'Why "maybe"?'

'Your offence is non-bailable.'

'What? You're kidding. Even shoplifters can get bail.'

Mei shrugged.

'You mean I'll be stuck in here till my trial starts?'

'The magistrate will usually grant bail if you apply for it.'

'What? So you mean I *can* go?'

'Not until maybe tomorrow. The sub courts don't open till then.' Mei paused. 'And that's if you can find a bailor.'

'What do you mean "if"? You're going to bail me out aren't you?'

'We'll see.'

'You're not going to leave me here! You can't!'

'It depends on how much bail is. Maybe I can't afford it.'

'Look, I swear I won't do a runner. You can trust me.'

'Since when?'

I searched my memory for a precedent, but found none. 'What if I don't get bail?'

'You'll be remanded in custody until the trial starts.'

'For how long?'

'A couple of weeks.'

'No way. I'm innocent. Why should I stay in jail for yonks for something I didn't do? I have a life to get on with. Responsibilities to take care of.'

Mei made a lip-farting noise. 'Like what? Playing level 3.11 in Doom for the eight-hundredth time?'

'No. For one thing, there is no level 3.11 in Doom. And another – answer me this – if I'm in jail, who's going to take the kids to Fort Canning?'

'I'm sure they'll survive the disappointment.'

'You are so mean to me. I don't think I want to go out with you any more.'

'Thank God. Another prayer answered.'

I stared at her for a while to see whether she was serious or not. I couldn't tell. 'You can't expect me to sit here, doing nothing.'

'You *can* do something very useful while you're here.'

'Such as?'

'Thinking. Now that might be a nice activity that you might consider picking up.'

'What do you mean?'

'You never think about anything before you do it. Andy, I know you think you've been framed, but the way you've acted ever since you arrived in Singapore, the way you've acted all your life, you were just asking for it. When bad things happen to you, they don't "just happen". You have to rethink your life, because at the moment, you're trapped in a cycle of destruction. You're going nowhere, just wandering around in this circle of chaos. I mean, so what if you're acquitted? If you don't change your basic ways, you're just going to get into trouble again. Things will never change. And you won't always have someone like me or Eugene to help wipe up after you.'

'But what's wrong with my life?'

'You'll have plenty of time to think about that now.' Mei

got up to leave. 'As for me, I have about twenty suspects to investigate. Enough of this idle chat, I have to go.'

The English Premiership is huge in Asia. Believe me, you have *no idea* how big it is. *Manchester United* ('The Official Magazine Of The Double Double Winners') sells fifteen thousand copies in Singapore and Malaysia alone. The magazine is so popular, they've even got some bloke to translate it into Thai, and this special edition attracts an amazing twenty thousand readers, month in, month out. If it wasn't for football, England might as well not exist. Mention major cities like Durham, Birmingham, Dover, Bristol and York, and all you'll get is a blank stare. Mention Chelsea, and it's like Christmas: faces light up with epiphanic recognition, grins flash around the room and voices chime in a single chorus – 'Ah, Gullit!' Okay, okay, so Chelsea's fame in South East Asia is due to a Dutchman, but that's the nature of the game these days.

I don't know why English soccer is so big here. Though the Brazilians are world champions, and Italy arguably has the best league in the world, Singaporeans only have eyes for the teams in England. Why? Why do they idolize players who couldn't even qualify for the last World Cup Finals?

Traditionally, in England, you support your local club. Football clubs are rooted in the community, so when the team wins a match, the whole city celebrates. Just look at the names of the clubs – Newcastle, Liverpool, Manchester City etc. (The only exception to the rule is Tottenham Hotspur, of course. I've been involved in *way* too many conversations with Singaporeans, trying to explain to them why Spurs don't play at Tottenham Court Road.) Okay, okay, I know that it's changing nowadays, as evidenced by the obscene number of Man U fans located miles outside of Manchester, in bourgeois southern outposts like Surrey. But the fact that Man U fans in Putney get stick for supporting Fergie's babes is evidence that there is still a widespread, deep-rooted belief that you should support the football club nearest to your home. London-based fans of the Red Devils often get taunted with the fact that they can't be real fans because they don't even *live* in Manchester – they're just 'jumping on the United bandwagon'. I guess it's this whole British thing about 'loyalty'. Local supporters are supposedly more faithful. Though the sky be pissing down, though the Wagon Wheels be stale, though the home side gets thwacked time and time again, the local fans will always be there, enduring the agony of defeat through the draws and losses, the replays and the play-offs. Soccer, for the football fanatic, has nothing to do with the quality of the game. Their local team might only score goals from accidental deflections off the butt, but the fans will still pay over fifteen quid to watch those gaffs, simply because it's *their* team. In fact, technically, their love for their team has nothing to do with soccer, but everything to do with these huge, abstract values – fidelity, passion, love.

Fans in the Far East are no less obsessive. I don't know why. They put their money where their heart is, and they sure have a lot of money. When the police read out the bets from the Filofax to me, going through a list of five-, six-figure sums, I knew they weren't bluffing. Five figures is a pretty average bet for a big Premiership match. The punters in my flat were always taking the piss out of me for only placing four figures at a shot, and I knew that if I couldn't prove that I wasn't responsible for co-ordinating those bets, my sentence was going to be as large as those numbers typed in that Filofax.

CHAPTER 7

Andy

Following Mei's suggestion, I decided to compare the Saturday I just had in Singapore with the Saturday I had in England a year ago, to see if I could spot any patterns that would expose my supposed cycle of chaos.

Saturday (Last Year)	Saturday (This Year)
Fallensham	Singapore
Late, late morning. Wake up in time to catch the closing credits for the 'X-men' on *Live and Kicking!* Annoyed with yourself for waking up too late, because you fancy Rogue, who is one of the cartoon characters (like Jessica Rabbit) who you find extremely snoggable. Resort to satisfying yourself by having perverted daydreams about children's	Late, late morning. Wake up. Switch on TV. RTM, the Malaysian TV channel, is unbelievably bad. They're running clips of flowers, with Richard Clayderman playing lounge lizard music in the background. It makes you fall asleep again.

TV presenter, Emma
Forbes:

Scene: Inside a personal limo

Emma (naked): Don't
worry about messing up
my hair and make-up. My
personal hairdresser and
make-up artist is waiting
for me at the BBC studios.
Oh Andy, take me now!
I've always wanted to make
love to an England
International striker.

Afternoon.
Remember it is Eugene's
birthday. Because he has
been so consistently nice to
you, you decide to do
something nice back, like
buy him a cool gift.
Mention casually to
Eugene that you are going
down to the city centre and
does he want anything in
particular? "We're out of
milk," Eugene says. You
decide to buy him a
chocolate cake. You go to
the bus stop at three
o'clock, but the bus does
not arrive until half-past
three. You arrive at the city

Afternoon.
Remember that Mei has
just been promoted.
Because she has been so
consistently nice to you,
you decide to do something
nice back, like buy her a
cool gift. Ring Mei up and
mention casually that you
are going down to the city
centre, and does she want
anything in particular? 'I'm
running out of shampoo,'
Mei says. You go to the bus
stop at three o'clock, but
the bus does not arrive
until half-past three. Three
No. 56 buses arrive at the
same time, one behind

centre at four, wander around looking for a cake shop, but somehow, manage to get *completely* lost and end up at the train station. By the time you find a cake shop, it is five o'clock – the shop has closed. The only shop that is open is the newsagents-cum-off-licence-cum-video shop, where you buy Eugene a birthday card. You have enough money to buy a Terry's Chocolate Orange, but then you remember that you haven't bought your Saturday quota of lottery tickets yet. You are convinced that if you *don't* buy your usual numbers today, this is the day they will win three quidzillion pounds and you will kill yourself. So you buy the lottery ticket. You feel a bit guilty, but you make a mental note to share the money with Eugene if you win the rolled-over jackpot.

Evening.
Lottery results come out –

another. You are getting used to this in Singapore.

Evening.
You decide to be a good

| you do not win anything. Sadness. Give birthday card to Eugene. 'Where's the milk?' Eugene asks. | Christian and not have any punters around to gamble tonight. You get arrested. |

Five lessons I learnt from the above exercise, in ascending order of importance:

5. I have a vivid, but rather disturbing, imagination.

4. I am crap at shopping.

3. I get lost easily. I am, as they say, 'directionally challenged'.

2. When I get lost, I get confused. When I get confused, I do stupid things. (Refer back to lesson Number 3.) This might explain why I'm often in trouble.

1. I am not a bad person, but bad things just seem to happen around me. I want to do nice things for people, but it never seems to work out. They say that the road to Hell is paved with good intentions. I am full of good intentions.

CHAPTER 8

DAY TWO: MONDAY

Mei

I unlocked my drawer and took out the title deed to the flat.

'Where are you taking that?' my mother said.

'To court.' I put the deed in my briefcase.

'What for?'

'Business.' I snapped the case shut and brushed past her. 'I got to hurry. The place shuts for lunch at twelve-thirty. If I don't make it before then, I'll have to wait until quarter past two.'

My mother grabbed my case. 'You can't take that.'

'Why?'

'You give away the flat, where am I going to live? I know what you're up to. You can't take the flat from me. I homeless, how? You want me to sleep in the drain?'

'Nobody is going to be sleeping in any drains. Why you always get hysterical for nothing?'

'Nothing? This is not nothing. You want to take the flat away from me and you say it's nothing?'

'I – am – not – taking – the – flat – away – from – you,' I said. 'You understand English or not?' I repeated the same thing in Mandarin.

'Then you take the title deed for what?'

'This morning I went down to the sub courts to get bail for Andy. The judge granted it, I'm going back to the courts to deposit the security. I need something to prove that I have the means to provide security for Andy, like share certificates, title deeds, jewellery . . .'

'I'm not giving you any of my jewellery.'

'I'm not asking for your jewellery. I'm not taking anything away from you. Why you go crazy for nothing? You act like I'm selling the flat or something. All I'm going to do is take the title deed and deposit with the court. As security. After Andy's trial is over, I'll get back the title deed. It won't affect us at all. You can still live in the flat, do what you like as usual. Why you make a big deal out of nothing?'

'But if Andy run away, then how?'

'He won't.'

'But if he does, then how? Will we lose the flat?'

'Maybe. But that's really unlikely.'

'Why you want to use our flat? So risky. Why can't you use your own money? You got so much in POSB, why you don't use instead?'

'Very troublesome. If I use my POSB account as security, that means I can't use my ATM card to draw money. And I'll have to cancel all my giro payments.'

'What kind of excuse is that?'

I didn't want to tell my mother this, but I guess I had to: 'Anyway, I can't use my POSB account. It doesn't have enough money to cover Andy's bail.'

'What? But you got so much money,' my mother said. Even though I only just started my career, just because I am a lawyer, my mother thinks I have giga-zillions stashed away in some Swiss account.

'What did Andy do? Was it so terrible? Why the judge set the bail until so high?'

'Andy's foreign.'

'The judge afraid Andy will run away?'

'Andy won't run away.'

'Why not? He got no reason to stay in Singapore. He got no family here. If I were him, I'd run away.'

I looked at my watch. 'Let go of me. I'm late, I don't have so much time to argue with you.'

'You can't take the deed.'

'Yes I can. This flat belongs to me and I can do whatever I want with it.' I took out the title deed and jabbed at it. 'Look – my name. It's written here in black and white. It's mine.'

'Just because your father left it to you, doesn't mean the flat isn't mine too.' My father left everything in his will to me, instructing me to take care of my mother, as she was absolutely terrible with her finances. 'Your father gave me nothing when he died. Where got any other wife like that?'

I rolled my eyes.

'All my other friends, all get richer and richer,' my mother said. 'They got progress. Last time they live in one-room HDB flat, then move to HUDC, now many of them live in landed property, got their own garden! But me? My life never get better. I born that time – got nothing; get married – still nothing; I die that time, you know what I will get?'

'What are you talking about? You have everything. The flat's under my name, but you always act like it's yours anyway. All the decor in the flat – it's all done by you. You think I like pink walls?' I made a face. 'But I let you do whatever you want with the flat.'

'You say only. I want to do *feng shui* but you don't let me.'

'That's different. That's just a waste of money.'

'Everything I do also waste of money right?'

'You think it's so great to have all the money? You want Daddy's money? Go ahead, take it. Then you can take charge of all the business – pay the bills, do the taxes – and I can relax. Why do you think Daddy left all the money to me? Tell me – the water bill – do you know how to pay that?'

My mother didn't say anything.

'No?' I said. 'You don't even know how to pay the PUB. You only want money so you can buy this, buy that. Money is not just for spending. It's a great responsibility. You know what would have happened if Daddy gave you the money?'

'What?'

'You would have lost it. You would have given everything to the temple priest.'

My mother shook her head. 'I'm always very careful with my money.'

'What about the time you tried to buy that "magic" stone from him? Ten thousand dollars to cure your rheumatism.'

'In the end I still didn't buy.'

'Only because I wouldn't give you the money.'

'You never give me money for anything.'

'Why do you always talk like I'm depriving you? You have food, clothing, a roof over your head. And what do you do? Nothing. You don't work. You don't do anything. You just sit at home and shake leg, play mah-jong all day and sing karaoke all night. You even have a maid to cook and clean for you. Why do you keep complaining that you have no money? What do you need it for? I take care of everything for you.'

'Last time, your father also said that.'

'Oh forget it.' I turned to leave. Then I stopped, and said, 'You think I care about all the money Daddy left me? I don't need it. I'm making enough on my salary. Daddy's money is all for you. I take charge of the money to protect you, make sure you don't waste it, make sure you got enough to last you until you die.'

'You really want to *protect* me then you don't take away the deed.'

'I really need the title deed. If not, I can't bail Andy out.' I put down my briefcase. 'But if you're really worried about the flat, I won't use it, okay?'

My mother took the deed from my briefcase, went to her room and locked the door.

Eugene answered the phone with a fancy BBC English accent – 'Hello, this is the Lee residence, Eugene Lee speaking,' but once he recognized my voice, he slipped back into Singlish – '*Wah leow* woman, you know what time it is now? We're not living in the same time zone any more. Why you call me so late?'

'Andy was arrested last night.'

'Hah, what?'

'For being the head of a soccer gambling syndicate.'

'Wha-what? Andy can't even buy *milk* without getting lost, how can he run a syndicate? No. It can't be. What about the other punters? Did anyone else get arrested?'

'No.'

'Can I do anything?'

'I need money for Andy's bail.' I told him how much I needed.

'Ouch. I want to help, but I got no money in Singapore.'

'You can transfer some to a local account.'

'It's, uh, a lot of money. What if he jumps bail?'

'He won't.'

'Erm, this is *Andy* we're talking about. Whenever there's a problem, he runs.'

'We can't just leave him in jail.'

'Can I do anything else?'

'Forget it.'

'I can't get bail for you,' I said. 'Sorry. Not enough money.'

'What am I going to do?' Andy said.

'Are you going to plead guilty or claim trial?'

'I'm innocent.'

'It's your word against the police's. Why should the judge believe a bookie?' Mei said. 'These are the facts. The police have been watching your flat for the past couple of months. They know you've been using it as a betting house. The only thing they needed was some written proof, something to link you with all the bookies. And now they've got it.'

'The Filofax.'

'Exactly. I'll be honest. If we go to trial, we *will* lose.'

'But don't you believe in God?' Andy said. 'I mean, I know things look bad, but if I plead not guilty, I'm sure we'll win. God won't let me go to jail, not after I've become a Christian. I can't believe that the first thing that's going to happen to me after I've turned to Him is to go to jail. You can't believe that He'll let a thing like that happen to me. He won't let me take the fall for something I didn't do.'

'Let me tell you what I believe. I believe in Jesus Christ. I believe he died for my sins and rose from the dead. I believe that he justifies the righteous and punishes the wicked. What I believe about the judicial system in Singapore is a different matter entirely.' I looked around the police station. 'And I intend to keep my opinions to myself, because my thoughts on the law might get me arrested under the Internal Security Act. Right now, I don't know how God figures in all this. What I do know, I'm telling you. I know that as things stand, there is no way you will be acquitted. All God requires to acquit you in the heavenly court is to look into your heart. That's the way God runs things up in the sky, but the judge down here requires more than your word. And that's all we have at the moment. Unless we can find out who framed you, unless we have concrete evidence – if not, as your lawyer, I'd have to advise you to plead "guilty".'

'I'm sure the jury can see that I'm innocent.'

'We don't have juries.'

'What? Why not?'

'It's a Western idiosyncrasy,' I said. 'The judge is the one who decides your fate. Him and him alone. We'll be going before District Judge Philip Ng. He sentenced four people to death last year. He could jail you for parking on a double-yellow line, and feel that he's doing society a favour. If we lose, you're looking at three to five years in prison.'

'What should I do?'

'If you plead guilty, I could do a good job in mitigation. Maybe if I do a lot of grovelling and snivelling on your behalf, who knows? You might get off with just a few months in jail.'

'What are you going to say?'

'I'll probably play the "innocent abroad" card. But you can use anything. You could say you were born prematurely. It worked for Michael Fay, it got him a few less strokes of the cane. Anything goes.'

'Five years versus a few months. That's a big difference. But I'm innocent.'

'It's up to you. What do you want to do?'

CHAPTER 9

Andy

The first time I laid eyes on Eugene, he was having this weird conversation on his mobile – 'How am I? Can do, *lah*. Classes haven't started yet so I'm very *eng*, just sit in my room and shake leg and eat *waffelstroop* . . . *Ja, lekker.*' When he saw me, he jerked out of his seat, and said, 'Uh, someone's here. Bye.' He fumbled the phone shut and hid it behind his back. 'Hi. I'm Eugene. I'm your room-mate. Unless you don't want to live with me. I . . . I won't mind if you want to change . . .' He punctuated every phrase with a violent nod, hoping (I guess) that I would nod along with him in room-mate-ish affirmation. I didn't think anyone could be more nervous about the first day at university than me, but here he was, right before my eyes, the poster boy for Neurotics Anonymous.

'Hey, no problem, you're cool,' I said. Then I nodded a lot. That seemed to pacify him. 'Who were you talking to?'

'My parents.'

'What language were you speaking?'

'English. And Hokkein. And Dutch.'

'In the same sentence? Wow.'

'I've been . . . around.' Eugene took out his mobile from behind him. 'You don't mind this, do you?'

I shook my head.

'I mean, I know it annoys some people. They think you're

showing off or something. I ... I was on the train and my phone rang and this lady just *looked* at me. I started talking to my parents and she just kept looking at me and I ... I ... I got so scared, I couldn't talk any more.' Eugene breathed deeply to calm himself. 'Where I come from – Singapore – we use mobiles all the time. It's really normal.'

'I didn't think you were trying to be flash.'

Eugene jumped and pointed to the ceiling. 'I installed a carbon monoxide detector. Don't you think that's a good idea?'

'I guess so.'

'You can't be too careful about these student digs. We have to check it every day. If it goes blue, we will too.'

We stared at each other for a while.

Awkward moment.

I asked him the usual Fresher's FAQs to break the quiet – we exchanged A level results and course details. When Eugene found out that I was doing English and Philosophy, he asked me about God and evil. He said that he knew someone who, literally, got away with murder. 'You know, why does a good God let good people suffer? Huh? Why doesn't he kill bad people?'

I shrugged. 'How would I know? I can't even figure out how to use the microwave in the kitchen.'

'But you're doing philosophy. Don't you think about good and evil – stuff like that?'

'I'm more into epistemology. Stuff like, "Who am I? What am I doing here? Is this really happening to me, or am I dreaming?" I think about things like that, usually after I've done a lot of drugs.'

Eugene laughed.

I was like – *ting* – roll the canned laughter, flash the 'Applause' sign. I'd said something right. I finally got him to calm down.

I asked Eugene why he decided to come to Fallensham.

'Well, the university has a really *progressive* education programme. Lots of emphasis on real life case studies and . . . and . . . "the flexibility of the modular system gives you the freedom to explore specialist interests without sacrificing core subjects."'
Eugene nodded. 'I remember that from the prospectus.'

I was impressed. Eugene really *researched* this place. I chose Fallensham because it was the university in the UCCA handbook that was closest to my football club.

However, Eugene would rather have gone to Oxford. He got a conditional offer, but screwed up his maths exam. He put the decimal point in the wrong place on his binomial theorem question. That's so typical. Eugene puts one decimal point, one tiny black dot in the wrong place, and that completely alters the rest of his life. Most of the other first-time conversations with freshers in my corridor were depressing in this kind of way. They spent their time exchanging lists of universities they would rather have gone to if they hadn't messed up their A levels or their interviews.

Tonight, I had only one plan in mind – go to my first Fresher's disco and pull. The disco was having this 'Traffic Light' theme, i.e. wear red if you were unavailable, orange if you were open to propositions, and green if you were – go! go! go! In particular, I was eyeing Clare. To make sure that she got the message, I drew a traffic sign on my T-shirt that said, 'Park and Ride'.

Now I know that a lot of guys go – 'huugh let's get really pissed tonight', but I'm not like that at all. You might find this hard to believe but I don't ever plan to get drunk. It just happens.

I mean, take the night of the Traffic Light disco. I know that a sure way to get pissed is to drink on an empty stomach. I did try to eat dinner beforehand, honestly I did. But this was my first time in the kitchen, and I didn't even know how to switch on the stove. The only other people in the kitchen were the girls, and I didn't dare to ask them how to operate the stove in case they got the impression that I was some useless eighteen-year-old who'd never cooked or cleaned in his entire life and was completely reliant on his mother. That described me perfectly, but that's not the point. So I tried opening a can of baked beans, only I didn't know how to use the can opener. I kept turning and turning the can opener but it just nudged the lid downwards, it wouldn't actually *open* the damn thing. I mean, they should call those contraptions can nudgers, rather than can openers. So I thought, oh sod it, I'll just have to cook the beans in the container. So I put the can in the microwave, and it's one of these really advanced machines. I stabbed all the buttons in sight, and all these numbers came up, they flashed, some in red, some in yellow. I kept pushing the buttons randomly, but all that happened was that the symbols on the display changed and the machine went beep! and boop! and I basically didn't know what the hell I was doing. But I persevered, I refused to succumb to the tyranny of this white box from Hell, and I pushed more buttons and the machine suddenly went eeeeeenh! and the yellow light blinked and the can started to rotate inside the microwave and I was like 'Yes! Victory is Mine!'

Clare screamed. She got all hysterical about me putting metal into the microwave. What's the big deal? Anyway, she stopped me from cooking my baked beans.

So the only alternative left was toast, and I thought – I can handle that, like I *have* toasted my own bread while living with my parents. So I put the bread in the toaster, and this tiny, and I emphasize *tiny*, as in minute, insignificant, barely discernible, wisp of smoke rose to the ceiling, and set off the fire alarm. It blasted the whole corridor with noise, and I decided that this would be a good time to make a quick, sharp exit.

So basically I didn't get to eat anything all night, which was what made me really drunk later on, but as you see, it wasn't my fault. I did try my best to eat something before I drank.

The LCR disco is probably one of the most anti-social social events ever invented. It's completely dark so you can't see anyone, with music so loud so you can't hear or speak to anyone. All I did all night was stand in the dark and feel the music beating me to death. The floor vibrated with the thumps, beats bouncing off the ground, smashing into my feet. The bass went duh, duh, duh, slamming against my chest, the physicality of sound, the music hit me in blocks, and I wondered, why the hell did I actually pay to do this? I could get the same effect in my room by turning on the stereo at full blast, switching off the lights, pouring beer on my carpet and puking, and I could do all of that for free. But here I was, standing on a damp piss patch on the carpet, and I thought – I can't believe I actually paid three quid to do this. Usually, if you have your mates around you, it makes the whole process bearable. But the worst thing was that it was Fresher's week, the first week at university, and I didn't know anyone.

Then I saw Clare and went up and offered her a fag. I followed up with some Fresher's FAQs, then Clare asked me, 'What sort of music do you listen to?' I thought hard about my answer, because I really wanted to pull. At this stage of the evening, I was willing to get into the knickers of anything that wouldn't give me a rash. So after much deliberation, I said, 'My taste is fairly eclectic. Indie, funk, New Age, R & B, jungle, swing, rock – though I hesitate to use the term "rock" because it has become a generic term for chart music that includes such a wide range of artists that it has lost its ability to define musical boundaries.'

Clare just nodded and refused the offer of another fag. Then she gave me the classic brush-off, waving cheerfully at some imaginary friend at the other side of the room, and said, 'Right, luv, I've got to go.'

So there was no one that I could talk to, and no one who seemed interested in talking to me. I stood there in the dark all night, panicking, thinking – I'm never going to make any friends, I'm going to be alone for ever, I'm going to die a virgin in a council flat, and it'll be five months before the neighbours notice the smell of decomposition coming out from the cat flap. So I just drank and drank and drank.

What *really* happened after I staggered out of the LCR I'll never know. My recollection of the events that evening are hazy at best. I can't confirm any of this – I only know this through the testimony of others – but I supposedly went to the loo and tried to turn the tap off with my head. I also allegedly puked at every other lamp post, like a dog marking his territory, before finally managing to navigate my way back to the halls of residence. Sometimes I think my mates are just taking the piss out of me, like I never did any of those things, but I can't remember whether I did it or not. One thing which people claimed that I did, which I definitely think I did not do, was to throw pebbles at Clare's window and shout – 'Oi! Fancy a shag? No. What about a tongue sarnie then?' I know I'm bad, but I'm not *that* crass. You believe me, don't you? I guess this supposed 'request for a little something' incident might explain Clare's rather cool attitude towards me through-out the autumn term. But I always think that it's got nothing to do with that, maybe Clare was just so traumatized by me putting the can in the microwave that she couldn't speak to me for weeks.

Naturally, when I got back to my block, I was starving. It's really funny when I'm drunk, 'cos I start believing that I have talents that I don't possess when I'm sober. When I'm drunk, I *know* that I can't even walk in a straight line, but for some reason, I suddenly think that I can really cook. And I also suddenly think that I can really sing. Whenever I'm really pissed, I'm Luther Vandross meets Delia Smith. I walked into our communal kitchen, and there was no lock on the fridge. Hah, the fools! They were just *asking* for the food to be stolen. I raided the fridge and started dumping everything in the frying pan – Findus crispy pancakes, fish fingers, eggs, mushrooms, 'Chicken Tonight' sauce, peanut butter, sausage rolls – and all the while doing an imaginary, but very loud 'Endless Love' duet with Mariah Carey. Then one of my neighbours started shouting at me, like 'Oi! What are you doing with my pancakes?' and wrestled me from the frying pan. I was too pissed to fight him off, so I just staggered to my room to get some of my own food. The only problem was – I couldn't open my door. I knew where the keyhole was, but though I kept jabbing my key at it, it wouldn't go in. The keyhole was about a millimetre long and wide, and my hand-brain-eye co-ordination was shot to hell, so I just stood there, stabbing my key randomly into the door. I kept swearing and squeaking – 'I can't get my key in. I can't get my key in', the pitch of my voice getting higher and higher. Then the drugs I took really started to kick in, and set off this panic attack and I was thinking, oh my God, I'm going to die. All the things I needed for survival, like my bed, my stereo, my cashpoint/Switch/Visa card, my jumbo economy packs of 'Snickers', they were all in my room, and I couldn't get in my room. Worse still, nobody was helping me, but all the people in the corridor were just standing there, pointing, *laughing* at me – 'Look at him, he's so pissed, he's *crying*.' My first night in college and I was homeless, starving, penniless, and the only people I knew were standing around me, laughing. Then someone prised my room key out of my hand, threw it down the corridor, and said, 'Go boy, fetch! That'll teach you to steal my pancakes.'

I crumpled to the floor.

'Hey – leave him alone.' It was Eugene. He picked up my key and opened the door. Then he carried me in, and laid me on the bed. He tucked my palm under my butt and turned me to the side, putting me in the recovery position, so that if I threw up, I wouldn't drown in my own vomit. He stayed up, watching me, until I fell asleep.

They say the friends you meet on the first day at university, you stay with for the rest of your three years. And they say that the best mates you have in college, usually stay your best mates for life. In Week 0, Fresher's Week, because of what Eugene did for me that night, he became one of those friends.

CHAPTER 10

DAY THREE: TUESDAY MORNING

Andy

'*Bangon!*' the Chinese policeman shouted, and waved his hand at me to stand to attention. It was so weird. Why did he shout the instructions in Malay? Everything else in the court was conducted in English.

Mei entered a plea of 'guilty'. She started mitigation by making the usual noises about me saving the court valuable time and money by not claiming trial, then continued, 'My client, being foreign, was unaware that he was committing a crime. To him, he was just letting a few friends meet in his flat to bet on soccer. Back in England, where he comes from, this activity is of course, legal.'

'Are you going to continue this line of argument?' the judge asked. 'Because if you are, I'll have to reject your whole plea. According to this, your client masterminded all the bets. Are you denying this?'

'Nobody masterminded anything. This is just a case of a few friends meeting casually to bet on a game.'

'What about the Filofax? It lists all the bets your clients co-ordinated.'

'The Filofax is just a record. There's no reason to suspect that it belongs to my client. It was probably dropped by one of his friends.'

The judge shook his head. 'That's not what it says here.' He tapped a piece of paper on his desk. 'According to this, the accused allegedly masterminded all the bets. He kept his records in the Filofax. But you tell me he wasn't involved in the actual betting. He only let the bookies use his flat. From your mitigation, the argument is a clear disqualification of your plea. I'd advise you to think before proceeding.'

Mei looked at me. I didn't know what the hell was going on, so I just spread my hands.

'Could I request an adjournment while I discuss the matter with the accused?' Mei asked the judge.

The judge looked at Mei like she had BSE. 'Court is adjourned until two-thirty,' he said.

'The judge wants you to concede that you masterminded the whole gambling thing,' Mei said.

'But I didn't do it,' I said.

'If you don't concede, he'll throw out your plea. You'll have to go to trial. And we know what will happen then.'

'What?'

'You'll lose.'

'What if I concede? What kind of sentence will I get?'

'I don't know. Maybe a year or more.'

'A year! No way. I am not pleading guilty.'

'But you've already pleaded guilty. If we change the plea now, if we go to trial, it'll look bad.'

'But I can't plead guilty now. My only decent excuse was sheer ignorance. And if I can't say that, then we have ... nothing. I don't even have the excuse of premature birth. This is all your fault. Why couldn't you see this coming?'

'It seemed like the best thing to do at the time.'

'How could you be so ...' I shut my mouth before I uttered the word 'stupid'.

'I've never done this type of case before. You called me, I

didn't call you. You can always hire another lawyer. What do you want to do?'

When we returned to court, Mei said, 'Your Honour, my client would like to withdraw his plea of "guilty" and claim trial.'
The judge nodded. 'I'll set the trial a week from today.'

DAY THREE: TUESDAY EVENING

Mei

I phoned Eugene to ask him if he knew who might have framed Andy. 'When Andy was drunk, did he ever do anything to upset anyone? Something he might not remember doing?'

'Well you know Andy can be a bit *xiao* when he's drunk, but most of the time he's sort of idiot-*xiao* rather than violent-*xiao*. Most of the time, people just laugh at him. Nobody really gets angry with him or anything. I don't think he upset anyone.'

'What about the punters? Did any of them have something against Andy?'

'No. Andy didn't even talk to them very much.'

'Eugene, why you so stupid? How come you let Andy get involved with those type of people in the first place?'

'What sort of people?'

'Bookies. Criminals.'

'I don't know. Maybe because it was illegal. Singapore is just so boring. You know how it's like. Remember when we were young, we were always out looking for crime, playing detectives. We were so desperate to get involved in something illegal, something thrilling. You know, crime equals excitement. I thought, maybe if I hung out with the bookies, there'd be loads of macho stuff. You know, I'd get to carry a switchblade in my back pocket and run down alleyways, chase cars, escape through secret trap doors. They'd have secret society rites, blood vows, tattoos, passwords, the works.'

'And did you get to do any of that?'

'No. Being a bookie is just like . . . business. You know, you make phone calls, count money, do sums, it was like being an accountant, it was like *work*. And so I thought, why get thrown in jail for this? If I'm in Holland, helping out my family's restaurant business, I'll get the car, the Rolex, the terrace house with the pond and the swans. I'll be making more money than I know what to do with. There's no point in staying in Singapore, running this betting business, running the risk of getting arrested. It's not worth it. It's not even *interesting*. But how did the police arrest Andy? Tell me. It must have been quite exciting.'

I sighed.

'But how come the police go and catch Andy?' Eugene said. 'He didn't go and write anything down right? If you've got nothing written down, they can't catch you. I told him so many times not to write anything down, but he never listened to me.'

'Andy didn't write any of his bets down.' I told him about the Filofax.

'Are the police going after the people in the Filofax as well?'

'I don't know.'

'How come Andy had the Filofax?'

'He has no idea. He says he'd never seen it before in his life. Someone must have planted it.'

'Why didn't they arrest the other bookies? How come they only arrested Andy?'

'When the police raided his flat, Andy was the only one there.'

'How come? The punters always go and meet at his flat every Saturday night. Why yesterday they suddenly didn't go?'

'Andy called off the betting house.'

'Why?'

'He's been born again.'

'No. As in "born-again Christian"?'

'Yes.'

'No.'

I didn't say anything.

'Since when?' Eugene said.

'Last week.'

'Shit. How did that happen?'

'I took Andy to Haw Par Villa. We had a long talk and he decided to become a Christian. I told him that he couldn't be a Christian and gamble at the same time, so he shut the betting house.'

'But why do the police think that the Filofax belongs to Andy? Didn't they dust the Filofax for fingerprints?'

'No.'

'Why the police so stupid? Isn't that normal police procedure, dusting for prints?' Eugene said. 'Even *we* thought of dusting for prints when we were detectives.'

I remembered Eugene throwing the lead powder all over Mrs Lam's furniture. 'Dusting for fingerprints might be really important in Enid Blyton books, but in real life, they don't actually do it that often. There wasn't any reason why they should have dusted for prints. Andy was the only one in the flat, the police found the Filofax there, and so they thought it belonged to him,' I said. 'Who would benefit if Andy was arrested? Would some bookie make more money if they set up the betting house at his place?'

'No.'

'Why would anyone want to frame Andy then?'

Eugene thought hard for a while. 'Uh, maybe one of the punters was arrested by the police. Maybe on another charge.

Maybe he cut a deal with the police – you know, set Andy up in exchange for a lighter sentence.'

'Do you have anyone in mind?'

'Loong. He got arrested in a raid along with a couple of other bookies.'

'When was that?'

'About a month ago.'

'I'll go to my office and see if I can dig up any clippings on his arrest. See if he got off with an unusually light sentence. If he did, then we'll have something to work on.'

CHAPTER 12

Eugene

My uncle was always telling my father to move to Holland to help him run his Chinese restaurant – 'Why you stay in Singapore for? GST, COE, CBD – everything you do, everywhere you go, you have to pay the government money.' Uncle always called the government – the People's Action Party – the Pay And Pay government. 'Here in Den Haag, I got three Mercedes and a house with a garden and a swimming pool. You still living in a HDB flat?' After my father received his brother's letter, he packed us up and moved us to Holland.

I was fifteen back then. I had always expected to spend the rest of my life wandering around the faceless white blocks in Singapore, but suddenly, one letter from my uncle and hey presto – I was standing in Den Haag Centraal. I blew smoke rings in the frosty air, fascinated by my own breath. The yellow trams sent crackles of blue sparks in the air. They whined along the network of black wires that snaked across the city, along streets named after birds and American presidents. Men cycled back from work, their cheeks puffed, peddling with effort, their heads bent against the wind, the edges of their trench coats flapping at their ankles. According to my uncle, you haven't had the full Dutch cycling experience until you get your bike wheels caught in a tram lane, and fall in front of an oncoming bus. The children enjoyed a more pleasant mode of transportation, skating along the frozen canals.

I bought a *bami* ball from a Surinamese guy behind the shiny metallic counter. A *bami* ball consists of grains of white rice cooked in a rich red tomato sauce, then deep-fried in batter until it became a golden ball. Never in my life had I tasted anything quite so repulsive. They served *bami* balls at my uncle's restaurant, which shows you how un-Chinese the restaurant was. No true, self-respecting Chinese would ever admit that the glooey gunk of cholesterol was invented by our ancestors. They didn't serve Chinese food at The Golden Dragon (unimaginative name, or what?) – they served what Dutch people thought Chinese food was supposed to taste like. The Golden Dragon was full of stuff containing what Dutch people thought being Chinese was all about, like being Chinese simply consists of having two stone lions outside your door, red lanterns, a few scrolls of calligraphy, chopsticks, and a tank of goldfish. My uncle brought us to the back of the kitchen and served some real Chinese food – Peking duck, shark's fin, beef tendon in a claypot, chicken feet – no chop suey, no fortune cookies, and certainly no *bami* balls.

While I was in Holland back then, I kept in touch with Mei all the time through e-mail. All her messages began with this long preamble – like 'whew I just pressed control-X just in time, and managed to send at least part of the message before my system crashed. Teleview is so *lau-ya* – which means "lousy", in case you've forgotten how to speak dialect – anyway, I can't wait till next month, when they're going to switch from DOS to a Windows-based system. ☺.'

Mei thought that living abroad gave me some marvellous multicultural insight. '*Wah*, I'm so jealous,' she wrote. 'It must be so exotic living in Europe, meeting people from all over the world.'

But the truth of the matter is, expatriates, or 'expats', lived in complete insularity. We subsisted in our own little ghettos. Even the British didn't socialize with each other – the English mixed with the English, the Scottish with the Scottish, and the Irish went to their own pubs. It was like living in a stagnant pond. We didn't have any Dutch friends. I couldn't speak a word of Dutch, nor did I need to, because most Dutch people can speak English. I didn't read the newspapers, or watch Dutch TV. I had no idea who the Dutch Prime Minister was. It was like everyone had this siege mentality, ganging up together with the people of the same race, resisting any contact with the host nation.

There was this guy who was a careers counsellor at the American School in Wassenaar. I asked him how he liked living in Holland, and he looked around his office, and said, 'It's like Little America here. I mean, I like this place, but it's difficult to get Holland in here, you know what I mean?' That's what living in the expat community is like, the complete insularity – it's difficult to get Holland in.

My parents had no non-Chinese friends, so my 'best' friend in Holland ended up being Loong. I didn't even like Loong, but I had to hang out with him because my parents did all their social activities with Loong's parents – Sunday *dim sum*, trips to Maudoradam, tulip shows in Keukenhoff, cheese-tasting trips to Edam.

Loong's father was an ambassador. Most of the expat kids, their parents were usually diplomats, or worked for the big multinationals like Shell or KLM or Phillips, and quite a few worked for the European space agency, ESTEC.

When I first saw Loong's bedroom, I couldn't believe it. It was full of stolen stuff. His bed leant against the wall, and on the wall were over fifty dark green cans of Diebels, a German beer. Loong got all of them in Dusseldorf. He broke into the different hotel rooms and stole the cans from the mini-bars. The cans were stuck to his wall with Blu-tack, like trophies. 'At night I lay in bed and count them to go to sleep, but I can never count them all. I usually get up to fifty-six, then I'm out. I like them, but sometimes they fall down in the middle of the night and hit me. Especially in the summer, when the Blu-tack gets soft.' Loong shrugged. 'Not that it matters. I usually have a girl over and make her sleep next to the wall, so if the cans fall down in the middle of the night, they hit her.' He laughed.

'Um, don't your parents mind?' I said.

'Mind what?'

'Mind that your room is full of stolen stuff. Don't they ever say anything?'

'No. As long as I'm doing well in school, they let me do whatever I like. Good grades are a sign that everything's heaven in my life. My grades are absolutely storming at the moment, so I can get away with anything.'

When I first met Loong, I wouldn't have dreamt of stealing anything at all. They had indoctrinated me too well in Singapore. Don't talk about shoplifting, I didn't even *chew gum*. But I guess Loong was different; though he was born in Singapore, he'd been an expat kid all his life. He never lived in any country for more than three years. And after I'd been an expat kid for a year, I started stealing too. When you're an expat kid, you get your kicks from smashing in headlights, lobbing rocks at lamp-post bulbs, and watching porno videos like *Driving Miss Daisy Crazy* and *Thunderballs*. Why did we do all that stuff? There was nothing else to do as an expat kid. Things were so boring everywhere. That's why I understood Michael Fay, that American expat. He acted just like any normal expat kid would, only it was bad luck that he was in Singapore, where they don't take any crap. It's just in the expat kid culture to go around stealing things, scratching cars – that's what you did with your life – you suffered through school in the morning, and at night you drove around, looking for beer, more outrageous things to steal, thinking of ways to wreak destruction, especially on the property of teachers, or MPs or the police. That was how you had fun, that was what everyone did, that was normal. So when the Michael Fay case came up, when he got the shit caned out of him for some minor acts of vandalism, and there was this unbelievable media hoo-ha all over the world, I couldn't understand what the big deal was. All this kid did was scratch a car.

The night before I left for Holland, I thought – goodbye Singapore, leave all the swots behind, I'm going to Europe! I knew exactly what Europe would be like, knowledge gleaned from reading Robert Ludlum and Jeffrey Archer. Holland, unlike Singapore, would be full of drugs, knives and prostitutes. Once I arrived there, my life would be full of mad and thrilling adventures – dodging bullets in windmills, canoeing down canals, chasing assassins down foggy, stone-cobbled streets. But the impossible happened – Holland was even more boring than Singapore. Everything closed at five, and at night, all you could do social-wise was go to the pub and get pissed. If you wanted excitement, you had to make it yourself. That usually meant stealing something, preferably a car, and going for a cruise looking for more beer.

I didn't have anything to live for, but I didn't feel bad enough about life to kill myself. Why was I unhappy? I ate well, drank well, there was MTV, and I had the latest game releases from i.d. software. I even played Doom on a computer network with guys in Hawaii, Pakistan and the Outer Hebrides.

But Mei was convinced that Holland could never be more boring than Singapore. She e-mailed me about how I was living the glam life; the movies come out earlier, I got to go to all the big pop concerts like REM, and the big musicals like *Cats*, things she'd never get a chance to see because those big entertainment acts never bothered going to Singapore. But I e-mailed her back telling her that was the problem with the people in Holland, the glitz, the noise, the lights, the fame, it's like everybody felt it was so important for them to do something all the time, to have something going on somewhere, some new play to see, some new record to buy, like a float, to stop them from drowning. If they had nothing left to do, then they would finally have to look at themselves and see that they were nothing.

If anyone was supposed to be happy, it was me. For one thing, I'd been to more countries than most people. We flew to Phuket, where we saw a show with queens. Later, as my father put in twelve-hour work days at the restaurant and made more money, we went to Hawaii, Gettysburg, Washington, but I only remember Boston – grey and rainy and the cab driver telling us that Texas Instruments had just gone bust. In Vancouver, we went to Chinatown. All the signs were in Chinese, everyone spoke Cantonese and Cantopop blared from the shopping malls. All the people in suits were Chinese, while all the parking attendants and cleaners were white. In Amsterdam, we visited a sex supermarket where they provided trolleys. I've been to all the Disneylands in the world – Orlando, Los Angeles, Paris, even Tokyo. I bet you didn't know there was a Disneyland in Tokyo. I've seen things none of my friends would ever see. Once-in-a-lifetime experiences. I can travel to any part of the world I want, I can buy anything I want, I'm at the top of the food chain, but I feel nothing.

'My friend has this theory,' I told Loong. 'Her favourite quote is from St Augustine – "O Lord, for thou madest us and our hearts are restless until we rest in thee." Her theory is that we're made a certain shape, and we try to stuff ourselves with all sorts of things, but we can never be truly filled, because ultimately only God satisfies.'

'Bullshit. You can never be happy if you follow God. All religion does is guilt people, make them repress what they really want to do. Look at me – this is the life: I see something I want, I take it. I want to do something, I do it. Nobody tells me what to do, what's right, what's wrong. *I* decide. I don't need a book, or some priest in a yellow dress, or some Jew in a white nightie to tell me what to do. Whatever I want to do, I do. Whatever I do, I succeed in doing. I'm completely spoiled, and doesn't it feel good? I don't need God, because I am a god.'

'But aren't you afraid of going to Hell?'

'I'd rather be a king in Hell, than a slave in Heaven.'

The day the ground caved in, I was up in Loong's room. Suddenly, we heard a great crack and screech. We looked out of the window.

'*Wah-leow*,' Loong swore in Hokkein.

Gone was the white flash of concrete in the sun. Instead, a hole exposed the grey jagged underbelly of the pavement.

'*Ai-ya*, I tell you if we were in Singapore this kind of thing won't happen.' Loong's father shook his head. 'All these Dutch pavements, so lousy.'

Spontaneously collapsing pavements were one of the many things you had to get used to if you were living in Holland. As a huge chunk of Dutch soil is reclaimed land, the earth beneath our feet used to be formless sea, and was thus liable to crumble at unexpected moments.

'What happened?' I asked.

'This cat was just walking along,' said Xiu Ling, Loong's sister. 'Then the pavement suddenly – pah boom! The cat fell in.'

We ran outside. Xiu Ling lifted the cat from the hole. Her fingers felt for the throb of its heart beneath the brown fur. 'It's not dead,' she said. 'Just unconscious.'

'I'll take care of the cat,' Loong said.

'You'll kill it,' Xiu Ling said. 'I'll take it to the vet.'

'Pa, tell her to give me the cat,' Loong said, 'I need it for my biology experiment.'

'Give the cat to Loong,' Loong's father said. 'It's only a stray.'

Xiu Ling pressed the cat against her chest.

Loong grinned. Then he told his father the magic words that would persuade any Singaporean parent to let their child get away with murder – 'If you give me the cat for my experiment, it'll help my biology marks a lot.'

Singaporeans are obsessed with grades. Take that fifteen-year-old, leukaemia-stricken boy who was in the *Straits Times*. In other countries, if you're a kid dying of a terminal disease, you do interesting things, like try to break a world record by collecting the most get-well cards, or meet Princess Diana. Does this Singaporean boy take this golden opportunity to do any of the above, before he snuffs it? No. Instead, he studies his butt off for his O levels. He achieves 6 A1s, but doesn't live to see it. What's the use of 10 O levels once you're six feet under? Our parents didn't understand that, for they believed in the positive correlation between moral fibre and good grades. So although Loong was a festering boil on the anus of humanity, when his parents looked at him – he was mainly glasses and freckles – they saw a cross between Einstein and Francis of Assisi.

Loong's father prised open Xiu Ling's arms, took the cat, and gave it to her brother.

Charlie Lim arrived in Holland about the same time as me. His father worked for KLM. He wanted to join the FBI or the

CIA when he grew up, thus he chose an appropriately American name for himself. I never knew anyone who wanted to be American so badly.

Charlie was a total Walter Mitty type. When I shared a room with him during our vacation in Vienna, Charlie woke up at four a.m. shouting, 'Battlestations! Buck Rogers reporting – Wilma, get those starboard lasers ready!' We all had our fantasies, but Charlie took his to a new level of neurosis. He told us how, one afternoon, when he was eleven, he had spent two hours tailing three cyclists.

'*Wah*, it was just like in "Hardy Boys",' Charlie said. 'You know those people who hire bikes from East Coast Park? They're not supposed to take bikes out of the park you know. I saw three boys riding bikes out of the park. Their bikes got the park logo on them. So I trailed them.'

Loong laughed.

Charlie smiled. 'I was good huh? They never knew I was behind them.'

Finally, Loong stopped laughing and slapped his lap. 'You know what?' Loong said, still smiling. 'That's the saddest story I've ever heard. Charlie, you're one pathetic motherfucker.'

However, Loong was the Head Prefect, and received at least four book prizes annually, so his words only made Charlie want to gain Loong's approval. Loong did everything to turn Charlie into a *gei ang mo* – a fake Caucasian. Europe, Loong told Charlie, was a place where academic excellence and ethics had gone out of style, where it was good to be bad. You cultivated decadence until it blossomed into sophistication. So like Loong, Charlie got his ears pierced. Like Loong, he wore torn Levi jackets, peered through his Ray-Bans, and slouched around with a Marlboro in his mouth. At night, they went to Loong's lab in the garden shed, where they tried to grow marijuana. They smoked pot, popped E, and got stoned on electric jelly and hash cakes. They were bad. They became European. Gone were the Singaporean, bespectacled, calculator-punching, aspiring engineer types. They became lean, mean, Continental machines.

Social-wise, Charlie's association with Loong paid off, because it got him an invite to the end-of-term party. It was a joint party between the American School in Wassenaar, the British School in Voorschoten and the German and International schools in Den Haag. This was *the* social event of the year. Not only that, it was a sixth-form party, and getting invited to a party by people a few years your senior was a sign of your complete and total coolness.

Loong, Charlie and myself were the only Chinese kids at the party. Getting invited despite being Chinese was a great achievement. The Orientals have never been considered a hip race. Japanese, Korean and Taiwanese kids never got invites to parties because the white kids who ran the gigs figured that the Orientals would much rather do their calculus homework than rock. But we were considered, in South African jargon, 'honorary whites'.

I collected my beer from the punch bowl and walked into the middle of a conversation.

'Can you believe that they send each other letters, telling each other how much they love each other and all that crap?' said Blond Boy. 'They stand on opposite ends of the lake and put their letters in little green bottles. They put the bottles on the lake and the messages float to the other side.'

'Jack is such a woman,' said Dark-haired Boy #1.

'Yeah, and when he kisses her, he even keeps his eyes closed,' Blond Boy said. 'Can you believe that? Kisses her with his eyes closed.'

'He's such a woman,' Dark-haired Boy #1 said.

'You know I watched this documentary on MTV, or was it Eurotrash?' said Blond Boy. 'No it was with Ray Cokes, so it's definitely MTV.'

'Ray Cokes is beast,' Pizza Face Boy said. 'Not like that fag Steve Young.'

'Yeah, that documentary was saying that there's no such thing as love,' Blond Boy said. 'Just this chemical thing in your body. You see this cunt and your eyes send all these signals to your brain and it starts pumping out chemicals and makes your body really hard. Endorphins or some shit like that.'

'No, that documentary was definitely on Eurotrash,' said Dark-haired Boy #2. 'They had clips of John Bobbitt's penis afterwards. Then some bit about lesbian body-piercing.'

'Jesus, who's in charge of this crap they're playing?' said the Black Guy. 'REM is great if I'm in my room and I want to get depressed, but you can't dance to it.'

An American girl staggered up. 'Hello, children.' She took a puff from somebody else's cigarette and said, 'I'm terrible, I don't even smoke.' She giggled. I remember somebody introducing her as a half-sister of the host. She was on holiday from Yale, visiting her folks.

'Hey look, it's your girlfriend,' the Yale girl said to Loong. 'She's waving at you.'

'She's not my girlfriend,' Loong said.

'Yes she is.'

'No, she isn't. We're not going out any more. It was a mistake.'

'Yeah, like Didi was a mistake.'

'Shut up,' Loong said.

'Who's Didi?' some Spic guy asked.

'Some girl in the junior school,' the Yale girl said.

'No shit,' the Spic said.

'Yeah, she's twelve,' the Yale girl said.

'It was a mistake,' Loong said.

'How could you make a mistake like that? She was only this tall.' The Yale girl raised her hand about a metre off the ground. 'She was only this tall.'

Loong was always doing that. Whenever he was caught doing something illegal, he would always pretend to go all stupid and naïve, like he didn't really know what he was doing. He topped the class in everything, he was probably the only guy in our school who didn't think that œstrogen was a kind of fuel additive. This was one smart guy, but whenever he was caught doing something bad, he would just go – 'Huh? Was that wrong?'

'Babyfucker,' the Yale girl said.

Loong threw a cushion at her.

She ducked and stuck her tongue out at him. 'I don't have time to play with you babies any more.' She looked round the room. 'Where's Catherine, where's my girl?'

'She's upstairs with Jorge,' Blond Boy said.

'Oh, he's gay,' she said, 'but he'll sleep with a woman anyway. So I'm not sure if I should go up or not. In case I interrupt anything.'

Catherine was a well-known slut. Her nickname was The Hole – her vagina was so big, you'd fall in if you weren't careful.

'I have a basic Yale belief that all men and women are bisexual,' the Yale girl said. 'Some are better at repressing it than others. I repress myself a lot.'

'I don't know about that,' Loong said. 'I must be *very* good at repressing any faggot tendencies.'

'Well obviously, you're Chinese. You repress everything. Just watch all these Zhang Yimou movies. They're full of oppressed women who are raped by their husbands and beaten by their mother-in-laws. I don't understand why these women just don't screw up their courage to the sticking point, and John Bobbitt their husbands.' She made a snipping gesture with her hand. 'I can't hang with Confucian ethics, and ancestral worship. It's obvious that those values are just the product of the oppressive authoritarian structure of the ruling class. Foucault. You heard of him, beer for brains?' She clipped the back of Loong's head.

One look at Loong's eyes and I knew there was going to be trouble. Just two minutes before, Loong's eyes had been hard and black, focused and intelligent. But now, annoyed with the Yale girl, he put on his act, pretending to be dumb and gormless. He blinked slowly, pretending to be pissed.

'Who you calling a fucker?' Loong pronounced it in the Dutch way, which pretty much sounds like 'Foucault'.

'Not fucker, you idiot,' she said. 'Foucault, the post-modern historian, the archaeologist of epistemes. Foucault.'

'You calling me a fucker?' His voice got louder. 'Who you calling a fucker? You calling *me* a fucker?' Loong broke his beer bottle against the table. He brandished the jagged edge. 'I'm going to cut you, you bitch.'

Loong chased the Yale girl around the house, trying to slash her face. She screamed bloody murder, but all the guys just whistled, clapped, stamped their feet – some even threw chairs in front of her path to try and trip her up.

Of course Loong wasn't really drunk. I know because he was sober enough to drive me home. 'Did you see her face? She was shitting herself.' Loong laughed. 'Serves her right, stuck up Ivy League bitch. That'll teach her to try and be post-structuralist at a party.'

A few months after Loong took the cat from the pavement, Charlie ran out of the garden shed, leaving a trail of vomit in his wake.

Loong laughed. 'Charlie's frightened about my biology experiment.'

'What happened?' I asked.

'Nothing. I just skinned the cat, took the flesh off and reconstructed the bone structure. Great experiment. I'll get an A, sure thing.'

'Make sure that you burn the carcass,' his father said. 'We don't want the neighbours to complain about the smell.'

A week later, Loong performed another experiment in the shed. After he finished, he ran into the house, breathless. 'Call the ambulance,' he said.

'What happened?' his father said.

'Charlie,' Loong said. 'Charlie – he's not moving.'

'What?' I said.

'In the shed,' Loong said.

We ran to the shed. Charlie lay on the ground. I touched his neck. No pulse.

'How long has he been like this?' I asked.

'Half an hour. I didn't know what to do,' Loong said. 'After he drank . . . I just sat there, he wasn't moving. I didn't know what to do. I just sat there, staring at him.'

'What happened?' his father asked.

'We were just mixing different drinks. Experimenting,' Loong said. 'Charlie wanted to get high.'

'What did he drink?' Loong's father asked.

'Orange juice and methylated spirits,' Loong said.

'What?' I couldn't believe it.

'I was mixing orange with vodka,' Loong said. 'Charlie said it wasn't strong enough. He asked me if I had anything stronger. I gave him the methylated spirits. He mixed the orange juice with that. He said, "I'm going to get *really* high." He drank it, then he just . . . Is he going to be all right?'

'He's dead,' I said. 'He's got no pulse.'

'Maybe he's just in a coma.'

'Why didn't you stop him from drinking that stuff?' I said. 'You knew it would kill him.'

'I didn't think it would hurt him,' Loong said. 'He's not moving. Is he dead?'

I couldn't believe it. Of course Loong knew that methylated spirits could kill. I mean, he was doing A level chemistry.

'I didn't know it would kill him,' Loong said. 'It was an accident.'

Loong let Charlie drink himself to death. He murdered Charlie.

'Call an ambulance,' Loong's father told me. 'It was an accident.'

Loong's father looked out of the window at the flashing lights on the police car. 'I tell you if we were in Singapore, this kind of thing wouldn't have happened.'

Loong told the police he was sorry. Again, he pretended to be stupid, and everyone bought his excuse. He was a victim of his environment, he said. He had been ripped from the shelter of Eastern values in Singapore, and thrown into a decadent Western society. In the big bad West, if you got good grades, you were labelled a 'dork', a 'nerd', or a 'swot'. In the West, you proved your masculinity through drink and drugs, through experiments. Loong had lived in the West for too long, and Charlie's death was the result. A tragic accident.

My parents swallowed Loong's myth completely.

'That's why I always try and raise you up with Chinese values,' my father said. 'You see Loong's father, big ambassador, never at home, never pay attention to who Loong's friends are. You see what happens when you're too influenced by the *ang mo*s. You start playing with drink, drugs. You do too much, you accidentally die.'

My mother nodded her head vigorously.

'His mother told me that she shouldn't have let Loong watch so many American TV shows,' my mother said. 'Loong is so young, so impressionable. They were a bad influence.'

Yeah, like the *Cosby Show* is really undermining the foundation of our state and shaking the psychopaths from the crevices of our social infrastructure. Loong didn't kill Charlie because of some bad Western influence. He *was* the bad influence.

Loong showed his parents his collection of American videos and heavy metal music, blaming his bad behaviour on violence in the media. Later that week, they built a fire outside the church, and burnt the tapes and the records.

I went to the police and told them everything. I told them about all the stolen goods in Loong's room, about how he skinned the cat and how he tried to slash the Yale girl's face. Surely that should have been enough to convince anyone that Loong was a psycho. The police searched Loong's room, but by then, Loong had removed all the stuff he had stolen. The cat, of course, was a silent, skinless witness. The Yale girl had returned to America, and had probably been too pissed that night to remember what really happened anyway. So nobody did anything about Loong. It was my word against his, and I guess that wasn't enough.

On the day that Charlie died, the red light from the police car flashed outside Loong's house. On the day the ground caved in, orange hazard lights had also flashed outside the same windows. Immediately after Loong's father reported the broken pavement, fix-it men had rumbled up with their cement truck, blocked off the hole with red and white striped tape, and surrounded the gap with the orange lights. They fixed the hole with the quick efficiency of the experienced – they were used to patching up spontaneously disintegrating pavements. When dawn broke, the hole was filled.

After Charlie died, Loong threw himself into studying for his A levels, and his parents never mentioned the incident again. He patched up his own 'accident' as quickly as the fix-it men patched the hole. On the morning after the men had repaired the hole, Loong's father walked on to the pavement, and stood there for ten minutes. I looked at him from the doorstep. 'Everything's okay,' he said. He stamped his foot on the ground. Solid.

I knew better. After the ground collapsed, stepping out of the house became a great leap of faith. But after a while I pretended that the ground was a firm foundation, a solid rock. Even if you couldn't trust the ground beneath your feet, you had to pretend. You couldn't think of how you could suddenly be walking on air. If you did, you would never step out of the house. Staying in the house wouldn't help either, 'cos God knows, the house could collapse on you. You couldn't live life with that kind of fear. Similarly, Loong's parents pretended that Loong was fine, that his good education gave him a concrete moral base. For Loong's parents, believing in their son's lame explanation was like filling the broken ground with straw, sticks and stones. Education was the foundation of every Chinese parent's philosophy. Education taught you how to get rich, and how to be a good person. In their minds, only lazy and stupid people committed crimes. If you were intelligent and hard working, you *must* be a good person. Loong's parents believed that as long as they gave their son a good education, as long as he pulled in good grades, that meant that he was a good boy, a moral boy, a boy who could do no harm, destined for greatness. If a good education couldn't guarantee a good life, they didn't know what could. They knew no other ground to walk on.

*

Charlie's death is lodged in me. Mei told me about her grand-father, how he suffered in hospital, and I guess Charlie's death is like my foreign body. It's one of those things that gets under your skin, and affects you for the rest of your life.

It was the anniversary of Charlie's death last month. Everyone here still believes that the boy who got straight As for his chemistry, physics and biology A level exams, was stupid enough to think that orange juice and methylated spirits would get someone high.

On my way to work that day, I bought five different publications. At the restaurant, I cut the first letter – a M, from *Haagsche Courant*, the second letter – a U – from *GQ*, the third, sixth and eighth letters – R – from *Der Spiegel*, the fourth letter – D – from *Rolling Stone* and the fifth and seventh letter – E – from *OK!*. I pasted four × 2 letters – 'mUrdErer' – on a postcard.

I sucked my cigarette. It finished burning, and I put it out amid the shells of some pistachio nuts.

I tore up the postcard and threw the shreds into the ashtray. I sent Loong lilies instead. The card attached said – 'Charlie's still dead. As always, I think of you.'

Loong sent me a card with Snoopy thanking me for the flowers.

After Mei phoned me to tell me about Andy's arrest, I went to the place where Loong used to live. Outside his old house, the pavement shone in the sunlight. I squinted at the ground, searching for cracks, but I found none. The light bounced off the ground that burnt as white, as solid, as concrete as it did the day before it collapsed.

CHAPTER 13

DAY THREE: TUESDAY EVENING

Mei

'Loong knows you think he's a murderer,' I said. 'Why doesn't he avoid you then? Why is he still friends with you?'

'We're not friends, it's just business. You know the betting? It's all word of mouth. If there's nothing inked in black and white, the police can't catch us.'

'Loong doesn't trust you, but he needs you.'

'*Yah*. He wants to bet on soccer, but only I got the contacts. You know the bookies that lot, they don't trust anybody. Only if I tell them – "Loong is all right", then they bet with him.'

'But if Loong's a murderer, why you still do business with him?'

'To keep an eye on him.'

'Hah?'

'I always hope that maybe one day, he won't be so smart. Maybe one day, he'll mess up.'

'Like how?'

'Uh, I don't know. Maybe some day I'll find some incriminating evidence – that hidden bloodstain, a smoking gun, some slip of the tongue. But it's never come. Loong's too careful. I don't know when, but I know that one day, it's going to happen – he'll make a mistake – and when he does, I'll catch him. I'll send him to jail.'

'Why you hate him so much?'

'He tried to kill me.'

'What? How?'

'When we first arrived in Holland, Loong brought me to his shed. He gave me this orange drink – "Drink it, it's very powerful. You'll see stars, visions, really cool shit. Very *shiok*." '

'Is that what he told Charlie?'

'Must be.'

'What did you do?'

'I tried drinking the orange, but it was so gross I couldn't – I just spat it out. Loong started making fun of me – "You *aqua*, even drink alcohol also don't know how. You're such a RI nerd. You better learn how to drink this, if not they won't let you into any of the parties here." I tried drinking it, I tried my best but it was just burning – I couldn't . . .' Eugene sighed. 'Loong just kept laughing at me, calling me "*hiao-hiao* sissy boy." '

'Did you drink it?'

'No. But I wanted to so badly. I was so embarrassed. My face so hot I thought I was going to spontaneously combust.'

'But if you took the drink . . .'

'I wouldn't be talking to you now. I'd be as dead as Charlie. Don't you see?'

'You think that's what Loong did to Charlie?'

'*Yah*. He gave Charlie the same drink he gave me. Charlie didn't mix the orange with the methylated spirits. Loong did the mixing and tricked Charlie into drinking it.'

I didn't say anything.

'Every night, I lie awake, and think – it could have been me. Loong could have tricked *me*. Charlie and me, we were so alike, with our fantasies about joining the FBI, playing detective games. We were both bored and naive, willing to do anything to get high, to get some feeling into our lives. If I had listened to Loong, been "strong" enough to drink that orange, I would be dead now, and nobody would do anything about it. Loong could kill me, and nobody would care, because nobody could handle the truth.'

'If Loong's so dangerous, why you let Andy be friends with him?'

'It was an accident. We went to the same soccer match together. Loong made a deal with Andy and once Andy got hooked on the whole gambling thing, there was nothing I could do. I warned him about Loong, but Andy only had eyes on the game, the money – you know how Andy is when he gets obsessed. He had that look . . .'

'I know what you mean. That slacked-jaw intensity.'

'Exactly. Once Andy got that look, I knew I couldn't save him. No matter what I said, Andy was always going to keep betting with Loong.' Eugene sighed. 'Andy just couldn't believe that Loong could do anything bad. That's the thing with Loong – just because he's got a first from Oxford, everyone thinks he's a great humanitarian destined to bring glad tidings of tax shelters to the middle class. But I want Loong to pay for his crimes. I want people to know that PSC scholars are not synonymous with moral virtue. I want the world to see that Loong is evil.'

CHAPTER 14

Andy

Sitting in this cell, I wonder – why did I put myself in such a dodgy position? Why risk getting arrested over a football match? I must have been mad. And maybe I am, but it's all due to the obsessional nature of soccer. For you, the discerning reader, the casual bystander, my barminess must be completely incomprehensible. So I'll try and explain it as best I can.

First, let me establish that usually, I'm a perfectly rational, sensible person. I brush my teeth regularly, work from nine to five, and eat three balanced meals every day. But when it comes to soccer, I go all weird. Soccer turns me into a statto, an anorak's anorak, a trainspotter's trainspotter, the complete git. Soccer was not just a game, it was my life, because I didn't have a life. Too mediocre to ever achieve anything great in life by my own merits, I latched my personal identity on to something which could achieve greatness for me: a football club. This was my dream: one day, the club captain would lift the European Cup 'live' on ITV. On that day, I would turn to my mates, point to the cheering crowds and say, 'That's *my* team.' On that day, I would finally be part of something significant.

When you consider how one's psychological well-being is so intricately tied up with the choice of one's soccer team, you would think that I would automatically have supported a club like Manchester United or Liverpool or any other big, rich, commercial, shirt-manufacturing club. This would ensure a lifetime of victories. However, instead of choosing a team with an inspiring nickname, like 'The Red Devils' or 'The Gunners', I chose a team dubbed – 'The Pigeons' – a team whose strip was a dull grey, white and black, much like the weather in Fallensham. It was another typical act of soccer dementia. Considering the fact that football supporters sign their souls away when they choose their club, you'd think that they would ponder their choices before they made the plunge. When you think how men swot up on the specifications of hundreds of cars before settling on a purchase, you'd think they would do the same when choosing a football club. And considering the popularity of the consumer car guide, *Top Gear*, you'd think that men would watch *Top Team* and compare speed, power, skill at handling corners and difficult weather conditions, before deciding which club to go for.

But I chose Fallensham FC simply because they were the first football club I ever watched. I know it sounds bonkers but it's true for so many football fans all over the world. They chose their team simply because, when their folks brought them to a soccer ground for the first time, there were two teams, one red, one blue, and they decided they quite fancied blue, and thus the blood commitment was made. It's a bit like that Donald Duck cartoon, when the baby crocodile hatches from the egg, and it thinks that the first thing it sees is its mother. The baby sees Donald, so it goes around following Donald, even though Donald spurns its advances, and does everything to try and disappoint the crocodile.

Supporting a football club is like falling in love with a woman. You know she only wants you for your money, but you stick with her anyway, irrationally. Why else would some clubs change their strips four times a season? The chairmen know that no self-respecting fan would wear an out-of-date strip, and so they shamelessly exploit a level of brand loyalty unrivalled in any other product. Here is a breakdown of a Fallensham fan's expenses:

Fixed Costs

Replica shirt = £35.99
Add £2 if you want your favourite player's number ironed on the shirt.
Add £0.80 per letter if you want the player's name on the shirt as well. (I am convinced that our club's chairman only bought my favourite player – Mikhailichenko, because with a name that long, he could make us fork out £11.20.)
Scarf = £5.99

Total = £55.18

Variable Costs

Ticket = £25
Programme = £5
Beer = £5
Cornish Pastie = £1.20
Fine for causing Grievous Bodily Harm = £1,500

I'm just kidding about the last one. I'm not a football hooligan. The closest I ever got to hurting someone at a match was when I waved my scarf in the air, and the prat behind me shouted, 'Hey, you nearly took out my eye with that.' I touched the edge of my scarf, and said sarcastically, 'Ouch, I nearly cut my finger on those woolly tassels, they're as sharp as Ginzu knives.'

But the point is that soccer is synonymous with high spending. It engenders a mania that makes you willing to stake your life savings on a single match. My devotion to Fallensham FC is completely futile. I watched *Hoop Dreams* a couple of months ago, and you can understand why the family of the players are going apeshit during the basketball match: it's because of the $$$$ involved, it's because winning and losing makes the difference between living in a drugs-and-death-infested ghetto, and a mock-Roman mansion in Beverly Hills. But for ordinary soccer supporters like me, Fallensham's results will have absolutely no material impact on my life. It's only the players who benefit, only the players who get the five-thousand-pound bonus, the BMW, the mock Tudor house, and the profile in *Esquire*. Whether Fallensham wins tonight or not, the average fan would still have to go back to his hovel and eat his regular dinner of baked beans and pasta.

For the chairmen and the sponsors, soccer is about money. But for the poor obsessive fan, even though a lot of money is involved, it isn't about money. It's about backing a team, staking a bit of your life on them. It's about loyalty. Maybe that's why I got involved with the whole gambling mess. Once you're hooked on that vicarious lifestyle, where the soccer team becomes you, you can't escape. But it's not our fault. It's the system, the rules set by greedy corporations and stupid law-makers – that's what turns the love of supporters into something exploitative and, in Singapore, illegal.

I shall not bore you with an elaborate history of the eight hundred and ninety-two matches that I've attended. Instead, I shall restrict myself to telling you about the biggest match in my club's history, Fallensham versus Amstelbruge. Two years ago, Fallensham miraculously spurted to a series of wins late into the season, and qualified for Europe. In the first round, they faced Amstelbruge, unbeaten in Europe for their previous eighteen matches.

Millions of fans around the world would die to watch the

match 'live', but only I – me! me! me! – could obtain this privilege, because I had fulfilled all the meticulous requirements, completed all the expensive initiation rites in order to Get A Ticket: a) I was a club member; b) I held a season ticket; c) I'd collected programmes from the last fifteen matches and faithfully pasted the tokens on to my token sheets; and last but not least, d) I successfully completed the tie-breaker on the match application form – 'Fuji film is the best film for capturing sporting events because _____'. So through hard work, perseverance, faithfulness, and unflagging loyalty, I had something that millions of others could only dream about. I could watch Fallensham versus Amstelbruge live, see history in the making, experience this titanic battle between English grit and Continental elegance in the flesh, while others could only view the thrills through their dinky fourteen-inch screens at home. Due to Fallensham's small ground, with a limited capacity of fifteen thousand, for that night, I sat in the bastion of exclusivity; for one night, millions of soccer fans around the world wanted to be me, a Fallensham supporter. For once in my life, I had something that everyone envied. They all wanted to sit where I sat. On that night, the Fallensham stands felt like Oxbridge, the Groucho club, and the Royal Box, all rolled in one.

I managed to get seats in the 'family enclosure'. I had never understood the concept of a family enclosure, which the club supposedly created in order to foster a 'family atmosphere'. I guess this stand did have a family atmosphere, in the same way *King Lear* has a 'family' atmosphere – it's filled with curses and sour faces, heavy with an aura generated by bickering, bitterness, and constant disappointment. I sat between two teenage girls. One pointed at a photo of Ryan Giggs in *Smash Hits* while the other squealed. A row of eight housewives sat in front of us, carrying a banner that said, 'Our husbands think that we're at home doing the ironing.'

Imagine my shock when I saw Eugene seated in the tower above the pitch. Eugene had never been to any of Fallensham's home matches – he wasn't even a card-carrying club member. How the hell did he manage to get a ticket, let alone entry into the deluxe directors' box? I stormed through the crowd to that exclusive enclosure, and demanded that the ushers give me an audience with Eugene.

'Real posh.' I looked around the box.

'Do you know him?' this Chinese bloke asked Eugene.

'Uh, yes. Loong, this is Andy.'

'How the hell did you manage to get in here?' I asked Eugene.

'Loong's father works for diplomatic service,' Eugene said. 'He got some spare tickets for this match that he didn't want, so Loong gave one to me.'

'You lucky bastard,' I said. 'You know how much I had to suffer before I could get my family enclosure tickets, sandwiched between the Giggs girlie brigade?'

'You a Fallensham supporter?' Loong asked.

'Yeah.'

Loong snorted derisively. 'Why? The only thing that would set your heart racing during one of their matches is the coffee you get from the chip van outside the ground.'

'Don't slag us off. Our trophy cabinet is absolutely bulging.'

'Yeah, that's because it's so undernourished,' Loong said. 'I don't know why you're putting yourself through this agony. Fallensham are definitely going to lose.'

'That's why an estimated four million viewers will be tuning in to watch the match,' I said. 'All the neutrals will be rooting for Fallensham.'

'I have never understood this strange English delight in killing giants, this "may the crappier team win" philosophy,' Loong said. 'Why does everybody here get so ecstatic when a team from a lower division defeats a Premier outfit, when Bolton beats Liverpool, and York topples Manchester? It's like this sick socialist fantasy – the rabble overthrowing the rulers, the giftless beating the gifted, rubbish overwhelming genius. The nation rejoices when a bunch of poor, unfit, drab amateurs defeat the brilliant, the creative, the deservedly highly paid. I'm with Nietzsche. Victory to the mighty! Kill the underdogs! Salute the Superman! Destroy the weak and helpless, get rid of those useless runts! If there's any justice, Amstelbruge will run Fallensham into the ground, crush them like the pathetic cockroaches that they are.'

'I know you're trying to wind me up, but it won't work. We're going to annihilate Amstelbruge.'

'Bollocks. Why don't you put your money where your mouth is?'

'Sure.'

'I'm going to make you an offer you can't refuse. I bet one season ticket against whatever you have in your wallet, that Fallensham are going to lose by at least three goals. What do you say?'

'You mean, if Fallensham wins, I only have to hand over my wallet to you, but if Fallensham lose, you're going to buy me a season ticket?'

'You got it.'

'What if Fallensham lose by less than three goals?'

'You'll still get the season ticket,' Loong said.

'Deal.' We shook hands.

The match started, and I made my way back to my seat. Everything began in the best possible manner. Amstelbruge played terribly. Casagrande ran through the centre circle, he was looking for either Snelder or Bechastnykh, but they weren't there. He reached the edge of the penalty area, crossed to the striker, but Fuchs was nowhere near it. Goal kick to Fallensham.

The fans greeted this display of incompetence with gleeful venom.

'Casagrande! You're shit!' I screamed so loudly, my phlegm hit the woman in front of me. 'You couldn't put a cross in a pools coupon!'

The woman didn't notice my spit, because she too was busy abusing the Amstelbruge winger. 'Casagrande! I'd buy you a pair of new boots,' she shouted, 'but I couldn't find a shop that sold shoes for players with two left feet!'

Amstelbruge's winger, Snelder, started a mazy dribble, but oh – foul! Fallensham's Jones threw himself in the challenge, Cantona kung-fu style, two feet in the air. He wasn't even looking at the ball. The referee reached for his pocket, and was it a red? – no, a yellow card.

Snelder walked past our stand, and everyone in the enclosure booed. Many chanted – 'You fat bastard, you fat bastard.' To Jones, we shouted encouraging things like – 'Kill Snelder! Break his fucking legs!' I guess you're wondering why I suddenly became a mental pygmy. I am normally not the Class A-type personality with homicidal tendencies, but at that moment, nothing would have given me greater pleasure than to have all the Amstelbruge players slip on the grass, break their spinal cords and spend the rest of their lives paralysed from the neck down.

Mikhailichenko, our Eastern European import, turned on his midfield magic. He flicked a simple pass to our full back, the return ball looped over the top of the Amstelbruge centre backs and Mikhailichenko ran after it. The defender trailed behind, chasing him with the angry expression of someone who realizes that the bloke in front of him has just got into the cab that was rightfully his. Mikhailichenko reached the corner flag, turned and the full back flung out his right foot to block the anticipated cross, but Mikhailichenko bounced the ball off his opponent's shins, skipped past him and bombed the ball into the penalty area. The ball arced over the goal, and Varney – the target man, our overweight, balding, thirty-three-year-old striker who hadn't scored in the previous five games – rose above the two defenders, and crashed his head against the ball. It was an unforgettable noise – the furious thump of bone on leather. The ball billowed in the back of the net. For a moment, there was a stunned silence. Then it came – the small ripple that triggered the tidal wave of cheers.

Wyatt, our manager, went off on a snowy sprint. Jiggling his arms in the air, screaming, 'Unbelievable!', he tried doing a victory run, but he was fat and unfit. He huffed and puffed with great effort as he ploughed through the snowy edge of the playing field. He soon decided that it wasn't worth the effort running, so he started jumping excitedly, but that soon exhausted him as well.

The home crowd sang – 'It's not over till the fat striker scores!' and – 'Varney, Varney, he's got no hair but we don't care.'

The referee blew for half time.

During the break, I took out my transistor radio and tuned into Radio Five. The men in the press box were also enjoying Amstelbruge's incompetence:

'So what do you think, Ron?'

'It's looking bad for the European champions. They're ceding possession, very much so. That's football's cardinal sin, if you like, giving the ball away. At the moment, they're playing like the football equivalent of Pamela Anderson. Too much up front and dangerously uncovered behind.'

'Great piece of skill by Mikhailichenko though. That boy's a bit useful, isn't he?'

After the break, Amstelbruge still didn't look like scoring. Our players hassled their attackers, crunching in those tackles, harried and snapped so that Amstelbruge didn't have time to complete a fluid move. Fallensham weren't out to play good football, they just wanted to make the opposition play as badly as possible.

Only ten minutes to go. Ten minutes to the next stage in Europe – who would we draw in the next round? I fantasized about travelling away with Fallensham to play in the San Siro against Milan, or maybe the Camp Nou in Madrid.

Fuchs dispossessed Jones. He skipped one challenge, brushed off another defender, and chipped the ball over the goalkeeper.

Complete silence. That's the sign of a brilliant goal. An attack so swift, so sudden, it catches the opposition by surprise, and before you know it, the ball is at the back of the net. For two seconds, the stadium was silent, a two-second gap of disbelief – you didn't even see the run, it was so quick; did the ball really go in? Everyone held their breath in hope. The visiting fans looked to the referee, he pointed to the centre circle, and they erupted. I sat down and swore.

Eighty seconds into extra time, Snelder ran down the left wing to the edge of the forty-yard box. Our full back, Bradshaw, raised his right arm, as if daring Snelder to shoot from this impossible angle. Snelder unleashed a pile-driver and the ball hit the net. The crowd 'oooohed' for a near miss. The players trotted on as if nothing much had happened. Everyone thought the ball had hit the side netting. The scoreboard still said 1 – 1. Then something strange happened. Our goalkeeper, Johnson, walked into the goal and picked the ball out from the back of the net. Suddenly, everyone – the players, the crowd – realized at the same time, what had really happened. Snelder had scored – from a twenty-degree angle! Unbelievable. Everyone had suffered from the same visual distortion. The shot was so tight that we all believed the ball must have whistled past the wrong side of the post. Snelder went off on a belated goal-scoring victory run. The Amstelbruge players jumped on top of him in ecstasy. The stadium fell silent. The crowd just stared at the goal.

That was it. We knew. Glory days for Fallensham were over – it was back to provincial obscurity. We were out of Europe.

After the match, Loong found me and slipped an envelope into my coat pocket. 'It was good doing business with you,' he said. 'If you ever want to bet on anything, just give me a call.'

'I will,' I said. I'd won the bet, got tickets for the whole season, but I still felt shit. Losing does that to you. I've heard it all – 'What doesn't kill you makes you stronger'; ''Tis better to have loved and lost, then never to have loved at all' – but I don't care what the poets or philosophers or pop psychologists say. That night, when we lost to Amstelbruge, real life proved those theories wrong. There is no dignity in defeat, no nobility in pain, just a wound that burns again and again. Failure doesn't make you wiser or more mature. Losing isn't romantic, life-enhancing or artistically inspiring. Losing sucks.

CHAPTER 15

DAY FOUR: WEDNESDAY

Mei

I went to my office to look up the records, to check if Loong
might have cut a deal with the police in the last six months. I
stepped into the glass elevator. The view from the lift makes
Andy go wow!, but the city skyline just makes me yawn. Ever
since I was a kid, one look at the skyscrapers, and I want to
emigrate.

I blame this malaise on watching too many episodes of
Lifestyles of the Rich and Famous. This appears on TV every public
holiday, providing the local huddled masses with vicarious
enjoyment of Jamaica, Beverly Hills and the Cayman Islands.
Mr Leach has yet to stop over at Singapore, and I don't blame
him, what can he say – 'With its flyovers, four-lane asphalt
highways, modern industrial parks, oil refineries and first-class
airport, Singapore is, um, um – maybe we should do another
location, Bob.'

Two hundred years ago, Singapore had nothing going for it,
zip, apart from trees, grass, thirty-seven fishermen and the
occasional outbreak of malaria and yellow fever. When Raffles
founded the island as a free port in 1819, everything was
torn down and built from scratch. And that's the problem.
Everything is so *modern*. It's been designed by architects who
believe that joy and beauty have been annexed from the universe, designers taught to respond to the untrained bystander's

comment, 'but it's just so ugly', by chanting the mantra, 'Form follows function.' The URA designed the city to be commercial and utilitarian, rather than exciting and exotic, with all the charm of a cement mixer. In the Eighties, they went ballistic with skyscrapers, so that future generations could say to their Western rivals, *neyeah-neyeah, my Daddy can build a bigger hotel than your Daddy*. Nowadays, new buildings sprout and spurt like exploding popcorn. Constructed with chrome and black glass, these buildings give a post-modern wink to Asian and Western traditions, i.e. they have green roof tiles like dragon scales, which are supported by Roman pillars. The new buildings also make no attempt to hide the huge pipes and taps, but exult in showing the plumbing system in all its sanitary glory.

To be fair, there is something exotic about Singapore. The only problem is it's all manufactured by the Tourist Board. They bulldozed all the old colonial, Peranakan shop houses to promote commerce and maintain cleanliness. Then they built new replicas of the condemned buildings, so you've got all this historical stuff that's so quaint, just like in the olden days, but with all the dirty and dangerous bits taken out. But a house that looks like it was built in the age of Raffles, only it's shinier than a hot waxed Ferrari and reeks of fresh paint – it's just not the same.

Anything alluring and exotic in Singapore is fake and sanitized. Singapore has the best man-made everything – it has the tallest man-made waterfall, one of the world's best zoos, a great bird park and underwater world. It's what Nature is like after it's been dry cleaned, mass-produced and sold in shiny pink plastic vials. Everything's been scrubbed down, made childproof, and pre-packaged for public consumption. Like the cleanest theme park in the world, trash on the Singapore streets has a lifespan of thirty seconds.

When Andy arrived in Singapore, like all first-time visitors, the first thing he said was, 'This place is so clean.' But what's so great about cleanliness? It's a grossly over-valued virtue. Nobody visits a place just because it's hygienic, you don't hear men saying to their wives, 'Hey Margaret, we just *have* to go off to Gleneagles Hospital this weekend, I just love that antiseptic ambience.'

Singapore is like Disney World minus the giant rodents and the fun.

Going Abroad was the core motivating principle of my life, and my mother knew it. When I was a kid, my mother inspired me by setting the Holy Grail before me – Going to Disney World. 'If you get four A stars for your PSLE,' she said, 'then Mummy and Daddy will bring you to Disney World.'

When I finally attained those stars, my mother bought me a Mickey Mouse lantern instead. I was a sobbing wreck. 'I don't want a lantern, I want to see the real Mickey Mouse.'

My father told me to stop whining, or he would smack me and give me something really worthwhile to cry about.

When you're young, you forgive your parents for lying to you. And throughout secondary school, my mother regained my trust and successfully dangled the old carrot of the Chance to Live Abroad. Whenever I got lazy – 'Ma, I don't want to read any more of the dictionary, it's so boring,' she would say, 'If you don't memorize five pages of the dictionary every day, how are you to improve your English? And if your English not good, then you cannot go UK to study. Mummy and Daddy got save up enough money for you, so you can go to any university you want. But you have to get good results first.' When I was eighteen, I got those good results. I got straight As, fulfilling the entry requirements to read law at University College, London.

We went to Ah Kow's coffee shop to celebrate. We sat down

on the wobbly stools at our usual table. Even though Ah Kow was filthy rich – he had a Rolex and a Mercedes – he still wore his cockroach-bitten singlet. He slammed dirty plastic plates and glasses against each other, and lifted them to his body with a sweep of his right arm. His left hand, armed with a dirty grey tablecloth, slid around the wooden table, brushing the stray bones and strands of noodles on to the pile of dirty dishes.

'What you want?' Ah Kow said.

'Shark's fin soup. Sweet and sour pork. Fried noodles. Braised beef in claypot – no chilli. Five bowls of rice. Almond jelly dessert,' my mother said. 'My daughter got four As today.'

'You going to study what?' Ah Kow said.

'Law.'

'Go NUS, is it?'

I shook my head and told him that I wasn't going to the National University of Singapore. 'I'm going to London.'

After I said that, my parents remained quiet for quite a while. I chatted on, talked about going to Harrods, and told them to make up a list of things they wanted me to buy for them in England.

Then my father said, 'You're not going to London. You're going to NUS.'

'Why? But you promised.'

'I say it's okay for you to go, but your mother say cannot. She *bu she de*.'

So that was the line. *Bu she de* – my mother wasn't willing to pay the cost. I should have seen it coming all along. My mother *bu she de* a lot of things. It was difficult to get her to spend large amounts of money on anything – like when we tried to get her to buy a microwave, she just said, '*Wah*, so expensive, I buy, make my heart painful, I *bu she de*.'

'But you always told me that it wasn't too expensive,' I said. 'You always told me that you could afford to send me abroad.

You always said that as long as I got good results, you would send me to any university I wanted. Why do you think I studied so hard?'

'It's not the money,' my father said. 'We're afraid that if you go abroad, you'll never come back.'

'But I will. I promise.'

'That's what they always say,' my mother said. 'That's what Mrs Lam told me, she said, "Once you let them go, they never come back. They say they will visit you, or phone you, but they bluff. You'll never see her again."'

Mrs Lam's daughter, Lisa, went to America to study, where she met her husband. Now she's living in Chicago.

'What if you're like Lisa?' my mother said. 'Go abroad, marry a white man, an *ang mo*. Now Mrs Lam only see her once every five years, only see her grandchildren once every five years. Mrs Lam always come to me and complain, "*Ai-ya*, I never get to see my Lisa, it makes me so *gek sim* – make my heart so pain." Why you think Mrs Lam got so many grey hairs? You want me to look like her?'

Considering that Mrs Lam looked like Jabba the Hutt, I could hardly have said yes.

'But I *will* come back once I finish studying in England,' I said, 'I won't make any *ang mo* boyfriends. I promise.'

'You're only saying that. I know you, you're like your Uncle Cheong,' my mother said.

'What do you mean?'

'Banana,' my father said. 'Yellow outside, white inside.'

'I see your room, all English books, your posters – all English singers, American movies,' my mother said. 'You always complain to me, "Singapore so boring." I know, once I let you go, you'll never come back. I lose money, lose anything else, never mind, but I cannot lose you.'

I didn't say anything. I just sat there, and at that moment, all I could see in my mind was the Mickey Mouse lantern.

Ah Kow stood in his cooking cubicle. He splashed water on to the noodles, shook the three dark bottles, the holy trinity of Chinese cooking – sesame oil, black sauce, and soy sauce – over the wok. The air crackled as steam spurted from the wok and enveloped the room.

'The smoke is getting to me,' I said, and left the table.

My mother followed me. 'Why you angry with me? I only don't let you go to England because I love you.'

'It's not that. You lied to me. If you didn't want me to go to England to study, why didn't you just tell me?'

'But it was for your own good. Don't you see? Now you get so good results, four As. If we told you – you can't go to England, then you wouldn't study so hard, wouldn't get good results, wouldn't get a good job.'

'But you always lie to me. Like when I was twelve, you said if I got four A stars, you would bring me to Disney World. Instead you got me that stupid lantern.'

'Stupid lantern? That lantern not stupid. Remember you wanted it so much? It was a *battery* lantern. So expensive. Last time, people never *buy* lanterns. When I was young, I always *made* my lantern. A candle lantern. During that time, you were the only child in our whole estate with a battery lantern. You were so spoilt.'

Every Mid-autumn Festival, parents gave their children lanterns to celebrate the Chinese victory over the Mongolian occupation. During the mid-seventeenth century, the Manchu troops ravaged Yangzhou. The soldiers hacked through doors, spraying splinters across the room. 'Drop your sword, and we will spare you,' the sergeant would tell the man of the house. The cleaver clanged against the floor. The sergeant snatched the cleaver, sliced it through the air repeatedly, each slash glinting in the light of the flaming torches. Soon the screams of the man, wife and child faded. The hut remained silent but for the rumble of the torches, and the heavy breath of the soldiers. The Manchurians took all the weapons – spears, swords, axes, and clubs, but our Chinese ancestors secretly made their own weapons. The only problem was – how could we get the villagers to attack at the same time? During the Mid-autumn Festival, the Chinese hid messages in the mooncakes passed on from neighbour to neighbour. 'When you see the lantern,' the message said, 'rise and fight!' That night, all over China, match sticks spurted, filling the villages with glowing dots of red lanterns.

'The lantern reminds you,' my mother told me, 'Snatch back your weapons, fight for your freedom.'

During the Festival, children walked around the playgrounds, beating time to the crickets' chirps, their red paper lanterns swinging on their wooden sticks. The candles flickered inside the lanterns, spreading the ground with pins of light.

My mother always made me a candle lantern, but they weren't good enough for me. I would run around our housing estate, pigtails flying, my pink flip-flops slapping against the concrete, and then the wind would puff out my candle. 'The candle is so inconvenient,' I said. 'Mummy mummy buy me that plastic Mickey Mouse lantern. It was a battery light bulb. Then I'll have no problem with the wind.'

My mother bought the lantern and I ran with it to the playground. My mother waited for me at Ah Kow's coffee shop. When I finished playing, I returned to the coffee shop. 'I'm thirsty,' I said.

My mother ordered coffee for herself and Ovaltine for me.

Ah Kow poured the coffee powder into the sieve above the coffee pot. Steaming water poured through the sieve. Ah Kow separated the coffee into two large copper mugs. Raising one mug above his head, he poured the coffee into the lower mug.

He repeated this four times to cool the coffee. The golden brown liquid flowed like silk from one mug to the other.

Ah Kow didn't cool the Ovaltine because he only did that trick for coffee. Ovaltine is a kid's drink. My mother poured the steaming Ovaltine into the saucer, then rippled the drink with her breath. Her tongue dipped in the saucer.

'Cool enough,' she said.

I lowered my head to the saucer.

'Where's your Mickey Mouse?' she said.

'Sandpit.'

'Idiot! Tell you to always keep it with you but you never listen.'

My mother ran to the playground. Her arms plunged into the sandpit. 'Someone stole your lantern! Your new lantern!'

'Mummy, don't be sad, can always buy new one.'

'*Ai-ya*, so *gek sim*, my heart so painful.' My mother put her hand against her heart. I was afraid she was going to have a cardiac arrest. Losing money always had that effect on my mother. When she finally got her breath back, she said, 'New lantern – just bought today. So *gek sim*.'

Ten years later, when my mother told me that I couldn't go to England, she asked me – 'Can you remember where you lost that lantern?'

I shook my head. 'Forget the lantern. Why won't you let me go to England?'

My mother brought me to the playground. 'Here.' She pointed to the sandpit. 'You lost the lantern here. Remember?'

I made a desperate, last-ditch attempt to change her mind. I ended up sounding like a character in some women's magazine story – 'Ma, you know how much I love you. You know I won't leave you for ever. I will return.' I nearly gagged when I said this, but at that point, I would have said anything.

'You remember that song you used to sing me on Mother's Day?' she said.

I nodded. It was a Chinese song that went, 'In the world, only Mother is good; she who has a mother is like a jewel . . .', followed by more soppy, vomit-inducing lyrics in that vein.

'You remember what you said when I gave you the Mickey Mouse lantern?' she said.

I shook my head.

'You hugged me when I bought the Mickey Mouse lantern. "This is my bestest gift ever," you said. You switched the lantern on and off, on and off, on and off, I was so scared the bulb was going to explode. But when you lost the lantern, you just said, "Forget it, never mind, can buy new one." Those are your favourite words. Nowadays whenever I ask you to do anything, you're always say, "Forget it." When you were young that time, you told me that I was like your jewel, that I was your best gift. But once you go away, when I'm not with you any more, I know what you'll say. "Forget it, never mind."'

CHAPTER 16

Mei

I took out the file of clippings to check which bookies had recently been arrested. My Nokia rang. It was my mother – 'I got something very important to talk to you about.'

'I can't talk now. I'm working on something important.'

'You always say that. You're always doing something *so* important. I always try and talk to you, but you always give me excuses – "I've got to watch the news, it's very important. I'm trying to read *Asiaweek*, got important article. I'm eating my dinner, I don't like to talk. Talking while eating is bad for my digestion." You think I can't see they're just excuses?'

'This *really* is important. I'm at my office, I really am working. I've got to check some files for Andy.'

'I also got something very important that I have to do today.'

'What is it?'

'I can't tell you on the phone. I want to see your face. You stay in your office, I come and see you.'

My mother put down the phone before I could say no.

I took out a file that contained the previous month's news clippings. Two weeks earlier, the police had raided a betting house in Kallang.

I phone Eugene. 'Problem. I've a list of bookies who were arrested last month. Loong isn't on the list.'

'Wha-what? I'm sure Loong was arrested last month. He must have done something to keep his name out of the papers.'

'Our whole theory hangs on the fact that Loong cut a deal with the police. But if we've got no proof that Loong even stepped in a police station . . .'

'Who else got arrested in raid?'

'Ho Kim Keck.'

'No.'

'Chia Tok Huang.'

'Never heard of him.'

'Yap Meng Kee.'

'No.'

'Kwan Heng Siew.'

'Yes. Yes. He was at Andy's flat,' Eugene said. 'Maybe we can get Kwan to testify that Loong was arrested in the same raid as him.'

'Do you have his phone number or address?'

'Oops. I left all the addresses in Singapore.'

I sighed.

'Sorry. I didn't think I'd need them here in Holland.'

'How can I find Kwan?'

'Maybe there's a soccer match on tonight?'

I checked the New Paper. 'There's going to be a match on at Jalan Besar Stadium tomorrow. Geylang versus Tiong Bahru.'

'Great. All the bookies will be there.'

'You sure? It's a pretty trivial match.'

'It doesn't matter. Gambling's got nothing to do with how important the match is. Bookies will bet on anything. I guess it's just a Chinese thing.'

That was true. When I was in secondary school, my classmates used to bet on the hundred-metre relay race. They shouted their lungs out during the race, and the teachers would grin with pride and say, '*Wah*, their school spirit so good.' But it had nothing to do with school spirit, and everything to do with having bet our ten-dollar weekly allowance on our runners beating the girls from the Convent of the Holy Infant Jesus.

'All the regulars will be at the stadium,' Eugene said. 'As long as there's something to bet on, Kwan will be there.'

'How will I know who Kwan is? How does he look like?'

'Chinese. In his forties. Very bad perm.'

'Um, excuse me, Eugene, but there are going to be a few hundred people in the stadium, all looking like that. You expect me to wander around going "Kwan? Kwan?" It'll take me for ever. I'll never find him.'

'Why don't you go to the police station? I'm sure they got his record there, his photo.'

This was a great suggestion, but I realized that I had to stay in the office until my mother came. 'I can't go there. I've got to wait for my mother. I agreed to meet her here.'

'You mother? Ah, don't care about her,' Eugene said. 'If your mother got problem, she can wait until tomorrow.'

'I can't stand up my mother. She'll kill me.'

'Hah, that's the problem with all you Nanyang girls,' Eugene said.

When I was young, in order to cure me of my infatuation with Western culture, my parents sent me to Nanyang Girls' School, hoping that this very traditional Chinese school would indoctrinate me with the core Confucian values, like filial piety. During assembly, my principal would make speeches about how it was important that we girls, when talking to boys, should not appear to be more intelligent than the male sex – 'or else you will never get married'. I resisted such propaganda, but I guess some of it must have filtered through my defences.

'They psycho you so much at that school,' Eugene said, 'make you think you have to obey your parents in everything.

Don't care about your mother, you have to help Andy.'

'I can't.' I put down the phone.

I stared out of my office window, waiting for my mother to arrive. I could see the Singapore river from where I sat. Fifteen years earlier, refuse from the Clarke Quay hawker centre had bobbed along the river – plastic cups, straws, half-eaten noodles, Coke cans, the *Straits Times*, the Yellow Pages and other sheets of oil-stained paper used to wrap food. But today the river was as clean and green as the rest of the country. Five-hundred-dollar fines and the threat of community service (an afternoon spent picking up rubbish at the beach, wearing a yellow fluorescent vest) deterred potential litterbugs. A wooden dinghy floated under the bridge. Beneath its brown canopy sat a wizened sailor, tapping his dark fingers against the tyres on the side of the boat. On the edge of the harbour, the Merlion, a white statue with the body of a mermaid and the head of a lion, roared clear water into the blue sea. Cars crossed the bridge, boiling grey clouds of dust and fumes behind them. The day was hot and the air was heavy. A tourist leant against the white rail of the bridge, his partner snapping photos of him from the other side of the road.

A few hundred metres from the bridge, I could see two men in long red robes fighting on a stage. They were doing '*wayang*', performing Chinese opera to entertain the spirits. They wailed songs, and fought battles with swords, spears, and acrobatic flips. Women danced to the clangs of gongs and cymbals, their long pink sleeves trailing behind them.

From my office, I could see the Westin Stamford, the tallest hotel in the world. The other skyscrapers towered above the green waters, white light bouncing off dark windows, a labyrinth of mirrored citadels, a city of glass. This was Singapore, the centre of information technology in South-East Asia; this was Singapore, a place where people still bowed down to idols, burnt joss sticks, consulted mediums, exorcized demons and walked on coals.

My mother finally arrived, bearing gifts. This was a bad sign – it usually meant she wanted something major in return. For my mother, being a typical Chinese woman, believed that balance underpinned all relationships. During Chinese New Year, I would get red packets of money from my aunts. In return, my mother would give her nieces and nephews red packets. Though nobody ever knew how much money was in the red packets – and this is where all my mother's cunning skills came into their own – it was absolutely essential that the money exchanged in those red envelopes was roughly equivalent. If you gave less money than you received, you lost face. If you gave more money than you received, you lost face because you made the other person lose face. I'm not sure which Oriental philosophy created this monetary system. Maybe it's some weird yin and yang thing, balancing good and evil, darkness and light, to attain some sort of cosmic harmony. My mother always taught me, that when it came to gifts, you never gave or accepted anything unconditionally. If someone gave you something, you would have to give him something equivalent at some later point, to absolve the debt, to maintain the balance in the relationship.

Today was the Mid-autumn Festival, the fifteenth day of the eighth lunar month, the night when the moon shone at its brightest. People celebrated this celestial festival by stuffing their faces with mooncakes. My mother placed a big red box on my desk. 'I got bake mooncake for you,' she said. She took the soft, round golden biscuit out of the box. 'Inside got red bean paste, sunflower seeds, and *two* salted duck egg-yolks – high in cholesterol, but I know you like them.'

I hated mooncakes. Like the lantern, they brought back bad memories, things I have never told my mother. Once I tried telling my mother that I hated mooncakes, but she just said, 'The mooncake, if don't eat, must throw away. But like that waste money, very *gek sim*.'

I didn't want to hurt her heart, so I ate the cake.

My mother watched me eat the mooncake. 'Do you like it?'

I grunted. 'You must want something. What is it?'

'I need to borrow some money,' she said.

'How much?'

'Three thousand dollars.'

'What for?'

'Cost-Plus got a "Mid-Autumn Madness" sale today. They're selling a laser-disc player, thirty per cent off. Offer ends today. I need the money now.'

My mother was a sucker for sales hype. She would go for anything which said 'Offer ends today'. She was the type who would mass-buy toothpicks – 'Five thousand toothpicks, only five dollars, so cheap, we'll never have to buy toothpicks again.' We also had lifetime supplies of paper plates, toilet brushes, and Aloe Vera shampoo.

'Why do you want a laser-disc player?'

'We only got a cassette tape karaoke machine at home. If we buy a laser-disc, then we can do proper karaoke, sing along with the pictures on TV. The machine also got the white dot that jump from one word to the other.' Her finger bounced around in the air. 'So we can follow which word to sing, can follow the beat.'

'But why do you want to do "proper" karaoke?'

'I got a very good business idea. You remember last Saturday night?'

'Unfortunately, yes.' It was the first time my mother ever had so many people over to karaoke, and if I had my way, it would be the last.

'It was so popular that I thought, why don't we have karaoke *every* Saturday night?'

When my mother made that announcement, I nearly died of shock. It was the closest I've ever come to a near-death experience. For a few seconds, my heart stopped beating, things went hazy, dark around the edges, I saw white spots before my eyes – believe me, for those three seconds, it was touch and go.

I finally managed to choke out a 'No.'

'But it's such a good idea. Can make a lot of money. Every Saturday night, all your aunties, all the neighbours can come. I can charge them five dollars, maybe also take the chance to sell them some cakes. Very fun. We can have different nights: A Carpenters night, Cliff Richard night, Boney M night – even a Filipino night. We can get all the Filipino maids to come, charge them five dollars and maybe even sell *them* some of my cakes. A very good business idea.'

'Forget it.'

'Why not? It's such a good idea. All of us love to sing, want to karaoke, but we're women, alone, we don't feel safe going to karaoke lounges to sing. Those bars, they always got a lot of men, drunk, men like . . . Andy. Is he still in jail?'

'Yes. Which is why I have no time to talk to you now. I've got to go find the man who framed him. I need to go to the police station to look up a photo.'

'How long is Andy going to be in jail?'

'I don't know. It depends. It could be up to five years.'

'Five years is a long time to wait. To get married.'

'I'm not going to marry him.'

My mother looked relieved. 'You know, it's good that you're not going to get married to an *ang mo*. I read in the newspaper, that scientists found that the Chinese IQ is higher than the *ang mo* IQ. If you get married to an *ang mo*, it might make your

children more stupid.' My mother's greatest phobia was that I
would get married to an *ang mo*, like Mrs Lam's daughter, move
abroad and leave her alone in Singapore. She was always trying
to put me off Andy. 'You know, I got sixth sense. I knew
something bad was going to happen to Andy. He's twenty-two
right? Master Chou say, age twenty-two not good, just past
twenty, just turn the corner. When you turn the corner, you
cannot see clearly, always have accident, always have bad things
happen to you. If you're around him too much, you're going
to have a lot of bad luck also.'

'Ma, I'm really, really not going to marry him.'

'But Mummy is worried. You're nearly thirty, and Andy is
your only male friend. Why you not like other girls, not like
Aunty Lim's daughter Jocelin? Jocelin went to Pulau Ubin with
the S D U, go picnic, play pass the parcel, met a nice doctor.
You always stay at home do *nothing*.' She wrung her hands
vigorously. 'Why?' Her waving hands slowed down as her tone
became more sympathetic. 'You got problem, you can tell
Mummy one you know.'

My mother always tried to get me to go on trips organized
by the Social Development Unit, the S D U, hoping that I would
meet a nice *Chinese* Singaporean graduate man.

'You know what they say about the S D U – Single, Desperate
and Ugly,' I said. 'Now I've got to get back to work.'

'But why you're always working? You need to have friends
too.'

'I have friends.'

'But I never meet any of them. Why you don't invite them
home?'

'There's nothing to do at home.'

'You can play Monopoly.'

'You're joking.'

'You always liked Monopoly.'

'Yes, when I was *twelve*.'

'So what? The Monopoly box says – "For children aged seven to Adult."' My mother slapped her hand to her forehead. 'I got it, I got it. Sudden inspiration. Light bulb flash above my head. You can invite your friends to our flat to sing karaoke.'

'Forget it. You are not turning our flat into a karaoke lounge, and that's final.'

My mother was always coming up with crazy ideas every month. Like last month, she wanted to adopt a baby from China. 'Mrs Lam showed me this video, all these babies so skinny, starving, the hospital so dirty, the government so bad to them.' My mother showed me the brochure from the adoption agency. 'Look at all the babies in the –' (and my mother actually used this word, I kid you not) 'catalogue, they're all so cute.'

'You're not buying *furniture*, mother. You can't just look at the catalogue and say, "I'll have that, it'll look very cute next to the TV." You'll have to take care of the baby for at least eighteen years. And you're over fifty already.'

'But I can take care of it. You let me borrow a few thousand dollars to buy the baby, can or not?'

'Forget it.'

After I weaned her out of the adopt-a-baby phase, my mother suddenly decided that her *real* dream was to become a hairdresser. She wanted to borrow ten thousand dollars to set up her own salon. 'I always wanted to open a salon. I can hire all these hairdressers, have a girl who washes hair called Suzie. Then I can also put stickers on the glass door that say, Air-con. If there's any customer I don't like, I can just play with their hair and say, *Ai-yoh*, why your hair so rough, you never heard of conditioner? So fun.'

I figured that she was just bored. My mother was always coming up with these supposedly great ideas, great enterprises she never quite thought through. She never counted the cost.

So usually I would put my foot down, and she would sulk a while. But she always got over it quickly, and the next day, she would come up with yet another ill-conceived idea. I thought this time would be the same as all the others. I would simply say, 'Forget it,' she would frown, go home silent, mope for a day or two, then recover. But this afternoon she said something she never said before, something I never expected.

'You're just like your father,' she said.

As far as I was concerned, there could be no worse insult. 'What do you mean?'

'I never told this to anyone before, because I always feel so *pei seh*. It makes me feel so embarrassed when I think about it. I feel so stupid.'

'What is it?'

'Once, when you were twelve, I wanted to run away.' My mother told me how, when I was a child, she made her own money by baking cakes and selling them to the neighbours. 'I didn't make much money, but after five years, I saved a few thousand dollars. Then your Daddy said, "Don't put the money in the bank, if you invest the money in property, can make ten times more, collecting rent." So I trusted your father, and he told me which property to buy, and I bought an apartment in Kuala Lumpur. I thought I very smart, I made sure the flat was in my name, so it was still my money.'

'So what was the problem?'

'When you got good results for your PSLE, when you got four A stars, I thought I could sell the flat and use the money to bring you to Disney World. But your Daddy said, "No." I asked him why. I said, "The flat is mine, I can sell it if I like," but he said I could not.' My mother said that my father had tricked her into signing some papers. They gave him power of attorney, so even though the flat was under her name, she could not sell it without his permission. 'When he gave me those papers to sign, I still saw my name as owner of the flat. How could I know he tricked me?' She remembered exactly where she was when my father told her that she couldn't sell the flat. She was hanging out the washing. She stuck the pole on the holder outside the window. Overhead, our neighbours had their washing poles out. When my father told her the news, she just stood there, watching the water drip from the clothes above to her own clothes. Then she ran out of the flat. She wanted to leave everything, make her own money, get a new job, a new life. As she left the building, she passed beneath the washing poles. She saw me at the window.

I remember that night, when I was twelve, my mother running from the flat. I didn't know why she was running, but I knew that she was going to leave me for ever. I ran to the window, and as she passed by, I just screamed and screamed and screamed.

'I looked up,' my mother said. 'The water drops on my neck. I thought they were your tears. I looked at the ground, so many round, brown water marks. I thought – no, it's not tears, just water from the dripping clothes. But it felt like your tears raining down on me. So I went back upstairs.'

I leaned back in my chair.

'After that you know what your father did? He sold the flat in KL. He used the money to buy the flat we have now. He bought it in his name, but when he died, he gave it to you. But it's my money. He bought the flat with my money. The flat is mine.'

'I didn't know.'

'Now you're the same as your father,' my mother said. 'I want to run the karaoke business, so I can have my own business, make my own money. But you don't like that, because once I make my own money, I can do what I like. I won't have to beg you any more. You always want to keep all your money to yourself. Always make me beg, beg, beg. Everything I want to do, you always say "forget it". I want to do *feng shui* for our house, you say "forget it". I want to buy a baby you say "forget it". I want to be a hairdresser, you say "forget it". I'm sick of always hearing that. I'm your *mother*. Why I have to ask *you* for permission?'

'It's not like that at all. It doesn't work that way.'

'It does. I was so angry. But then I thought – maybe if I open the karaoke lounge, make my own money, then I can do what I like. I don't have to ask my daughter for permission any more. If I want to get a *feng shui* expert, I'll use my own money. I won't waste *your* money. But you're like your father. You don't want me to make my own money. You want to control me.'

'No I don't.'

'Then why you don't lend me the money? You're so rich, you're a lawyer, I know you make a lot of money. A few thousand dollars to you is nothing.' She waved her finger. 'Nothing. Like air. But why you never lend me the money? Because you want me to always depend on you.'

I shook my head. 'You know that isn't true.'

'It is. I only need to borrow a few thousand dollars today to buy the laser-disc. When I make enough money, I'll pay you back. But you never want to lend me any money, so I'll always have to rely on you. You love it, that I always have to beg you before I can do anything.'

Before I could make a speech in my defence, the phone rang. It was Eugene.

'I . . . I just got a brainwave,' Eugene said. 'I'm so smart, I'm so in love with myself. I'm hugging myself right now.'

'What happened?'

'I thought of a way we could save Andy.'

'How?'

'Have you seen the search warrant?'

'Not yet.'

'I was thinking – maybe you should check who's listed as the owner of the flat.'

'Why?'

'Because the flat doesn't belong to Andy. But the police don't know that. When Andy went to Singapore, housing so expensive, he knew it was going to be hard for him to find a flat. Loong's parents had an extra flat, and Loong got his parents to rent the flat to Andy. The flat is still registered under Loong's parents' name.'

I knew what Eugene was getting at. If the search warrant listed Andy as the owner of the flat, instead of the real owners – Loong's parents, that would invalidate the search. 'If you're right, if the police made a mistake with the warrant, the Filofax would be inadmissible as evidence.'

'That's what I thought.'

'I'll go check the police records right now.' I put down the phone.

'I have to go to the police station,' I told my mother.

'But what about the karaoke machine?'

'Why don't you start baking cakes again, and selling them? After you've saved up enough money, you can buy the laser-disc player yourself.'

'But then, the laser-disc will be so expensive. Today, Cost Plus, selling it thirty per cent off. Offer ends today. If I buy the machine six months later, I'll keep thinking, if only Mei let me buy the machine earlier, I could have saved a few *hundred* dollars. You know me, whenever I lose money, always make me very *gek sim*. I have to buy now.'

'All right, all right.' I gave her my DBS Nets card, which only had four thousand dollars on it, so I knew she wouldn't go overboard with my money. I told her the PIN number for the card. 'Now I really have to go.'

'How long will you be at the police station?'

'I don't know. After that, I still have to go look for this Kwan man. I'll be back very late.'

'But you promised to visit your grandfather with me this afternoon.'

'He's dead, Mother, it's not like he's going to go anywhere. I'll visit Grandfather next week.'

'You always say that. And every time I go to his grave, I look at his picture and I say, "Your favourite granddaughter too busy to visit you. She's a big lawyer. Always busy, busy, got important case here, important case there. Always helping other people but never care about her own family. She promised to see you this weekend but she changed her mind. She says she's a Christian but she break promises and she doesn't care."'

In times like these I can only regard my mother with loathing admiration. Whether it came to borrowing money, or hassling me to get married, she knew exactly which buttons to push. 'All right, all right, but I'll have to go to the police station first,' I said. 'You go off and buy your karaoke machine, and I'll meet you at the crematorium later today.'

'Good, then we can also *soon pian* on the way, see your father,' my mother said. 'You also long time never visit his grave.'

'Correction. I have *never* visited his grave, and I'm not going to start now.'

'Why you hate your father so much?' my mother said. 'Sometimes I think it's my fault, I always tell you the bad things he did to me, maybe that's why you hate him. That's why I didn't want to tell you about the flat in Malaysia. I didn't want you to hate him because of anything he did to me. It's between me and your father.'

'Don't worry, I have my own, very personal reasons for hating him. It has nothing to do with you.'

'But why? Your father always loved you a lot. Always buy

157

you presents, soft toys, books. He never spent any money on me. When he died, he gave everything to you. With me he was always very *giam siep*, very stingy, but he loved you a lot.'

'You really love this don't you? It makes you feel so special, to pretend that he never did anything bad to me. It makes you feel so special, that you were the only victim. *You* were the only one who ever suffered,' I said sarcastically. 'You're so strong, you wonderful self-appointed martyr.'

'What bad things did your father do to you?'

'As if you didn't know. You saw it all. I told you about it but you never did anything to stop him.'

'Oh, you talking about that thing,' my mother said. 'But your father said he was just playing with you only.'

'And you think it's all right to play like that?'

'He said he didn't mean to hurt you. He said he was really sorry later. He said if he knew you so upset, he wouldn't have done it.'

'And you believed him? What about what he did at Red Hill? Was that just playing as well, just fun?'

'What happened at Red Hill?' My mother leant towards me, and took my hand.

That was too much. I was sick of her pretending. She must have known what had happened at Red Hill. I never told her about it, but she *must* have noticed that there was something very wrong with me when I came home that night. Even if I never told her with words, she could have read the events in my eyes, my cracked lips, my hands, my muddied skirt. It was so *obvious*. That night altered my life completely. My mother must have noticed the difference. How could she *not* know?

I got up, and left my office. Slamming the door would be an extremely childish and clichéd thing to do. I slammed the door. Hard.

CHAPTER 17

Mei

I never told anyone about what my father did to me. It was a family matter, an internal affair. And you never talked about internal affairs.

During my fourth birthday party, even though they gave me my presents already, for some reason, my aunts sat around me, all twelve of them, their eyes mesmerized by mine. The oldest aunt asked me, 'Is it true that your Mummy and Daddy always argue?'

Now this was before I learnt that important lesson about family secrecy. I couldn't see the danger signs. I didn't know what was going on, but I felt great. When you're a kid, it's not often that everybody is really interested in what you say, paying attention as if it mattered. So I puffed out my chest and said, 'Yes.'

My aunts got such a kick out of that single word, some clapped their hands, while others let loose their held breath. I never had such an amazing effect before. I had arrived. I was an equal among adults, it was like graduating from the small to the big screen, from being Waitress No. 3 in *Falcon Crest* to landing the lead in a Spielberg flick.

'What they argue about?' my aunt asked.

'My Mummy complain that my Daddy never buy her anything. She say when I want something, Daddy always buy, but when she want something, Daddy always tell her – "Don't waste money."'

Later that night, my mother brought me to her bedroom, shut the door and held my hand. I was confused, because my mother only sat me down if I did something terrible.

She said, 'Why you tell your aunties bad things about Mummy and Daddy?'

I kept quiet. I didn't understand what I did wrong. My parents argued all the time, it was a normal family activity. I didn't think it was anything important. I was just giving the facts, and surely the facts couldn't hurt anyone.

'Next time don't tell your aunties what Mummy and Daddy talk about,' my mother said. 'They only want to know so that they can say bad things about us. Laugh about us. They only want to gossip.'

From that day onwards, it was branded into my psyche never to talk about my family. If anything went wrong, we acted like it never happened.

My father dropped a pile of books on the table. 'See, Daddy love you or not? I bought all this from MPH.'

'I don't want them,' I said.

'I bring you to MPH tomorrow and we can exchange it for something you want.'

'I can get everything I need at the library.'

'Rubbish. MPH is the biggest book shop in the country, got all the newest books, how to compare with the library?'

'I'm never going to MPH again.'

'Why you like that? Last time you love MPH so much, we had to drag you out there crying.'

I used to always beg my father to take me to MPH. Once, when I was five, my parents left me there to shop at Yaohan. When they returned, the store had closed. They panicked, but finally got someone to open up. I was so small, sitting between the shelves, that nobody had seen me when they shut the shop. My parents said it was time to go home, but I wouldn't budge. 'Ah, girl, you know MPH used to be the Japanese Secret Police HQ,' my mother said. 'They used to torture and kill people right here, right where you're sitting!'

My father nodded and added, '*Yah*, last time, they got hang people's heads from the front door. Last time, war that time, if you sold things in the black market, the Japanese would cut off your head and hang it right outside MPH. We better go before the ghost heads start flying around.' My mother took my arm and said, 'Very scary. Flying heads.' She made 'whoo whoo' noises, which (I think) were supposed to be scary ghost sounds. But I simply told my parents, 'Five more minutes, I got only two pages left.'

But now, ten years on, things had changed. I didn't want my father to take me to the book shop any more. 'You know I love MPH, so every time you do something bad, you think you bring me to MPH, I'll feel okay again,' I said. 'I'm not going to play that game.'

'What you talking about?' my father said. 'I never did anything bad to you.'

'Why else would you go on this book-buying binge? Why this sudden surge of concern? You're just feeling guilty after what you did last Thursday, so you suddenly go and spend all this money on books.'

Last Thursday, my father taught me maths. He drowned me in his whirlpool of noise, all this screaming — *what do you get when you differentiate 3x+2y+7?* and I knew the answer, but all that noise, his hand rose above me, his spit on my face, I went dumb and he hit me.

'Why you always think the worst of me?' my father said now, 'I went to the "Good Parenting" seminar at the Community

Centre. They told me that I had to be supportive, be interested in my child's work. So many other parents can't be bothered with their children, but I try everything to help you win in life.' My father was a self-help programme addict. He believed that everything could be solved via positive imaging, in twelve simple steps. 'Good parenting can sow the seeds of life in your child's future. I just want to help awaken the giant within you.'

'My giant is quite happily napping at the moment. If you wake her from her beauty sleep, she'll be in a really bad mood and probably beat the shit out of you. Why don't you just leave her alone, and practise all that self-help bullshit on yourself.'

'Can't I get you anything? Any book you need, I can buy for you, even if I have to order it from England. Money no problem. I never regret any money I spend on my child.'

'I just don't want anything from you, nothing you can buy will make me feel good about you.'

'Why you learn from your mother to be so petty, so *xiao pi chi*? Sometimes I do a little thing wrong, then a whole week you just sulk, sulk, sulk.'

'Shut up and leave me alone.'

'You talk to me like that and I'll punch you. Why you treat me like that, no respect?'

'It's because you're a cancerous polyp on the penis of humanity.'

'Why? I do everything to help you. Who made you hate me so much? I've done nothing bad to you. I don't know what made you like that.'

'That's your problem,' I said. 'It's never your fault. If anything screws me up, it's because of the church, or TV, or the English education system. I've got nothing to say to you if you keep pretending you've never done wrong.'

'But what else can it be? I've done nothing wrong. It's your church. Ever since you started reading the Bible you've been like this. I got read in the "New Paper" today. All these cults they teach you to follow Jesus and forget about your family. This cult leader even quote the Bible, say whoever does not hate his father and mother cannot follow Jesus.'

My father blamed the church for everything. He went to a charismatic church once and during worship, people lifted their hands and spoke in tongues. One look at a grown man singing, dripping with tears, and my father freaked. My father kept frowning, muttering – 'Obsessed. Cult.' – that was his mantra throughout the service.

Hysteria controlled my father.

      —entrap your soul
      —suck all the money out of your bank
      —turn you against your father and mother
      —make you a zombie
      —are the root of all evil

Some people filled in the blanks with 'drugs', 'witches', 'communists', or 'foods high in saturated fat'. For my father, it was 'cults'. The Bible, church and prayer were the religious equivalent of soft drugs. You should never touch pot because it will invariably lead to a crack addiction that will vacuum all your cash, leaving you a brainless mess licking your own vomit and turning tricks, giving blow jobs to any john to get money for your next fix. Likewise, if you love Jesus with utter devotion, this spark of zeal can only lead to the furnace of culthood – a life spent selling flowers at the airport, wearing electronic headsets, performing multiple sex with monks in saffron robes, living in an underground nuclear shelter, cut off from family and friends, convinced that now is the time of Armageddon, time to drop toxic gas canisters on all the sinners in this evil world.

The media feeds this hysteria. When was the last time you heard a positive cult story? 'Lisa Chew escaped her abusive family to join the Light of the Holy Vision, and she has now found peace, love and endless bliss. She is a shining example to us all. And now to Michael for the weather.' I can't talk to my father about Christ without him going ballistic. He doesn't want to be convinced, doesn't want to realize that fervency doesn't necessarily suck you into mindless fanaticism. He fanatically avoids fanaticism.

'I got better idea than going to MPH,' my father said. 'Why don't we go East Coast Park? Or Sentosa? Go see the new Underwater World, can see real sharks. Anywhere you want to go, I bring you. A lot of fun.'

'I'm never going on any trips with you,' I said.

'There must be something I can do for you.'

'You can't do anything. You can't buy my forgiveness.'

He shook his head. 'Why you don't let me help you? I just want to help you be the best you can be.'

'You know nothing about what I want.'

'Anything you want, I'll give it to you.'

'You always get me the wrong thing. I tell you I want something, you give me something else.'

'So test me. Tell me what you want me to do and I'll do it.'

I thought for a while.

'I want to be,' I said, 'an orphan.'

My mother came into the room. 'I want to talk to you about something.'

Everything inside me suddenly went cold. During these talks, even though my mother starts by saying that she loves me, the conversation always ends up revealing some *hamartia* of mine.

I clenched my stomach, prepared to mutter 'uh-huh' or 'yeah' at the appropriate junctures.

My mother sighed. 'Your father told me to talk to you. You know how he's like, always going on about the same thing until you go mad. If I don't talk to you, he'll keep nagging me.'

'Well, just say your bit and leave me alone.'

'He just wants to get involved with your life, buying the books. Why don't you *chin-chai*, anyhow? Just pretend that you like the books. He just wants you to let him love you, that's all.'

I lip-farted. 'If he loves me, I won't like to see what he does to people he hates.'

'Got which other father love their daughter like your father? He spend so much money, brings you on all these trips to *educate* you. I young that time, my family so poor, we go Malaysia very good already. Sometimes I think it's maybe we spoilt you too much. That's why you're always so rude to your father. So ungrateful.'

My mother thinks I'm spoilt because I never appreciate anything my father gives me. My grandfather never gave anything to my mother, he was so stingy, he wouldn't even buy *clothes* for her. She had to sew her own school uniform. My father, on the other hand, lavished luxuries on me.

'Every time we go on a trip, whether it's Malaysia, or just going to Orchard,' I said, 'whenever we get lost, he hits me.'

'Your father just got a bad temper sometimes,' my mother said. 'When he's in a bad mood, don't go *ca jiao* him. Don't disturb him, just leave him alone.'

'Don't you see he's psychoed us into thinking it's our fault that he hits us? It's not up to us to find a way to endure. He's the one who needs to change.'

'If we didn't have to go in the car, everything would be okay. That was on Oprah Winfrey once – couples who argue – and the professor from Michigan said that most arguments take place in the car. Once your father in the car, he go mad.'

'Yet you make me sit in front with him.'

'I can't read when I'm in the car. I look at the map and I want to vomit.'

'You make me navigate so I get hit instead.'

'I sit in front, he drive me mad, but you could always cope.'

'I've been coping for you since I was *ten*. You're my *mother*. How can you always leave things to me?'

'Your father listens to you. He thinks I'm stupid, but you read all these books, you can talk so well, you can reason with him.'

I started to say something but couldn't. My feelings rose and stuck in my throat like a hard red ball, choking the words. I flung the can away, but missed the bin. The cola trickled on to the green marble tiles. Usually my mother would go mad about the mess, but she didn't say anything this time.

'I sometimes think compared to your father, I'm such a bad parent. He works all day, so tiring, but he still go MPH and shop for all those books for you. He loves you the most.'

Words still stuck in my throat. I spat each one out slowly. 'Don't – ever – dare – say – that – again.'

'Why you hate him so much?'

She knew, she always knew, and yet she still gave me all that love shit. She saw everything, watched what happened when I was six. On that sunny Saturday morning, she had been standing there beside the shadow of the door, a silent witness.

That Saturday morning I had been lying in bed, my blanket covering me from the sun's glare and the marauding mosquitoes. Determined to sleep in, I lay there despite the heat, ignoring the sweat that slicked my neck. Upstairs, Mrs Lam was renovating her flat, cutting tiles, filling the block with the screech of metal on marble.

My father came into the room and said, 'Wake up, sleepy head, the sun shining on your backside already.'

I ignored him.

'C'mon, Daddy take you to MPH,' he said.

I did not move. Then he lifted my shirt.

I don't know why it made me feel so bad. It was nothing much, just touching. His hands weren't rough, they glided lightly over my back and down my pants. But I could feel it all, my nerves pricked, cold, alert, the hairs on my skin erect.

What really got me was his voice, full of insinuation, the same voice he used when he was drunk at the restaurant and told the waitress, 'The buns you gave us very nice to eat, I want to eat your buns.' He touched me and said in the same playful voice, 'I know you're awake, huh, huh.'

I said nothing, did nothing, just lay there, frozen, each stroke paralysed me with shame.

Why did he do it? Maybe if he was drunk, I would understand. But he wasn't drunk, his breath didn't smell of alcohol. It smelt of mint, Colgate mint.

I heard my mother's voice, 'She doesn't want to wake up, just leave her alone.'

All the time she had been there, as usual, like when we were in the car, watching and doing nothing. I knew what she did after that, what she always did. She would sit on her bed and rationalize. My father was only trying to wake me up. My father was only playing with me. Nothing bad had happened, really.

When my father left, I locked myself in the bathroom. Crouched in the bathtub, biting my nails, I couldn't do anything, nobody could do anything, not my friends, my teachers, my mother. The tub was damp, it soaked my pants, my butt turned cold, but I didn't move, even when the mosquitoes landed on my leg, sucked my blood, I just sat there, my head bowed, eyes shut and hands clasped. I prayed that God would kill my father.

Later that evening, my father came into my room and said, 'Your mother told me you thought I molested you this morning. I never molested you. I was only playing with you. Molesting, only evil men do that.'

'I didn't imagine it,' I said. 'I wasn't dreaming.'

'I know how you feel. Children, they always think things worse than they actually are. You play with them, they think you're molesting them. I young that time, my parents always fought, I was always angry with my father because I thought he made my mother upset. But after my father died, I saw my mother missed him a lot. Then I realized their arguments weren't so bad.'

My mother believed his explanation. She never did anything more about my father, and I never told anyone about our family's internal affairs. Case closed. After that Saturday, I decided not to tell my mother about what happened at Red Hill. She wouldn't be able to handle it. What happened that Saturday was nothing compared to what happened at Red Hill. And if my mother couldn't deal with something so 'small', how could she cope with something like Red Hill?

When God didn't kill my father, I thought about doing it myself. I thought maybe I could hack him to death in his bed. But that would wake my mother, she might try to stop me, and I didn't want her to get in the way of my chopper. Murder is never convenient.

Another time, I tried punching my father into a messy pulp, but I was six then, and he just stood there, laughing, put his arms under my armpits, swung me in the air, while all the time my palms slapped his face. He just kept laughing. Later, at the swimming pool, we played 'Monster'. I held his head under the water for as long as I could, kept clutching his hair, but he clawed my fingers off his head. I stamped my feet against his shoulders, kept pushing him down but he flipped me off and burst out of the water, gasping. He sputtered, shook the water from his eyes, and laughed. 'I'll be the monster again,' he said.

That's what they always think – 'Everything children do, they do for fun.' Why did he laugh at everything I said? Why was I so cute whenever I said I hated him? He wouldn't stop when I told him it wasn't fun, it might be great for him but it wasn't for me, I hated it, it hurt, but he laughed, he was having so much fun with playing with me he didn't see it wasn't fun for me.

CHAPTER 18

DAY FOUR: WEDNESDAY

Mei

After I left the police station, I rang Eugene. 'Bad news,' I said.

'Why?' asked Eugene.

'I checked the search warrant. The police got it right. The flat's listed under Loong's parents.'

'That proves it. Loong set up Andy. He must have told the police that the flat was under his parents' name.'

'Did any of the other bookies know that Loong rented the flat to Andy? What about Kwan?'

'No. Only three people knew who really owned the flat – Andy, me and Loong,' Eugene said. 'It's so obvious. Loong's the real mastermind of the gambling syndicate. He tricked Andy into letting him use the flat as a betting house. Loong's the co-ordinator, he knew who bet what, he's the only bookie who would know exactly what to write in that Filofax.'

'But if Loong's the real boss, he'll be the one making the most money out of the betting house. Why would he get the police to raid the flat? It'll just destroy his business.'

'You said that Andy's just become a Christian?'

'Yah.'

'Maybe Loong was afraid of that. I don't know, maybe he was scared that Andy, in a fit of religious zeal, would turn him over to the police. He'd gotten into trouble with the police, after being arrested for horse gambling, and he knew he couldn't risk another arrest. So Loong thought, maybe if he framed Andy, it'd stop Andy from fingering him. Loong set Andy up to protect himself. Sort of pre-emptive strike.'

'Makes sense. If Andy is convicted, Loong's safe. No one's going to believe Andy if he says anything bad about Loong. Once they convict Andy for being the boss of the syndicate, the police aren't going to look for another boss.'

'Case closed. The police won't even *think* of trying to catch Loong, and Loong will remain free to enjoy all his illegal earnings.'

'But we can't prove that.'

'Why not? I can testify against Loong,' Eugene said. 'I've seen him make loads of illegal bets.'

'But you're Andy's friend. People will say that you were making all this up just to help Andy. If we're going to get Loong, we need to find another bookie to testify against him.'

'Why don't you talk to Kwan? See if you can get him to admit that Loong cut a deal with the police.'

CHAPTER 19

DAY FOUR: WEDNESDAY

Mei

My grandfather's ashes were stored in a big white concrete building. The crematorium looked exactly like a housing board block, tenements for the dead. Outside the building, my mother waved to me and handed me a packet of ghost money she had bought from the temple. They were square sheets of paper the size of a handkerchief, with red and gold patterns printed in the middle. My mother would light each sheet of ghost money one by one, then drop the burning paper into a big flaming container. Each sheet burnt meant extra money for my grandfather to spend in Hell. We burnt enough money for my grandfather to buy new clothes, a car, and a condominium.

We entered the crematorium. Inside, the crematorium housed the ashes of hundreds of people. Each of the deceased had their own little grey square, with their passport photo stuck behind a round glass cover. Some squares had elaborate red calligraphy; others just had the photo of the deceased and their date of passing. Small metal tubes were stuck next to the photos, for relatives to stick their joss sticks, or lilies in.

My mother chatted merrily to my grandfather's photo. 'See, I promised you right? I finally managed to drag your favourite granddaughter to see you.' She took out a styrofoam cup and two manila packets from her NTUC plastic bags. 'See I got bring your favourite food for you to eat—Bee Hoon, hard-boiled eggs with soya sauce, Kentucky Fried Chicken, coffee.' She took out a saucer and poured the coffee from the styrofoam cup. She blew at the coffee to cool it. 'Your granddaughter very good girl, very *kwai*. Today she got let me borrow money to buy karaoke machine. The machine very good – got surround sound, got super bass, got big, big mike.'

I just stood there.

'Why don't you pray to your grandfather?' my mother said.

I did nothing.

'Tell him you do so well in your law firm, got promotion.' My mother pointed at my grandfather's photograph. 'Look! I've been to your grandfather's grave so many times and I swear this time his photo is different. I've never seen him so happy. He's so glad to see you. Why won't you talk to him?'

There was so much I needed to tell my grandfather, but it was too late now. Like a few weeks ago, during the Hungry Ghost Festival, my mother had reminisced about my grandfather's final days. 'The doctors told me your grandfather didn't have long to live. He had cancer. When he choked on the fish bone, and it took him a month to die, I see him suffering like that, so *gek sim*, it hurt my heart. But maybe suffering from fish bone for one month better than suffering from cancer for years.'

The pieces fell together. Before that, I hadn't known that my grandfather knew that he was dying. My mother's words reminded me of the time when, months before he died, my grandfather gave the waiter at the coffee shop a hundred dollars for a bottle of Guinness. 'Keep the money,' he shouted. 'I can't take it with me.' Before I knew about his illness, I had always thought that the trip to Haw Par Villa, and the endless retelling of the story about the grave-hugging boy were just typical manifestations of senile sadism. Now, for the first time, I realized how scared he had been. In those last months, he was looking for a way out of Hell, an escape from an eternity wandering an ash-filled wasteland.

'You come all the way here, you're not just going to stand there and do nothing?' my mother said. 'Why waste your time? At least talk to your grandfather.'

I looked at my watch. 'I'm late. I have to go.'

'Your *gong gong* love you so much,' my mother said. 'Now he's gone, you have to do *something* for him – that's what visiting your grandfather is about. Never mind if you're a Christian or not. Just be *xiao xun*, show some filial piety. You have to do something to repay his love.'

'But he's dead. There's nothing to be done. If there was, I would do it. Once you've crossed the line, that's it, finito, closing credits. What's the point of doing all these rituals? They're just a waste of money, they can't help him, it just makes *you* feel better. It's like you didn't treat him so well when he was alive, but now that he's dead you can send him cars, shirts, a semi-detached house, and an endless flow of Guinness just by burning paper. You visit him now that he's dead so much more often than when he was alive.' It was so easy here, my grandfather smiling out of his passport photo, wearing that starched white shirt. It wasn't like the Home, where she had to wipe the spit off his chin. Why didn't she take care of him while he was alive, instead of letting him die alone under the blank stare of a wash basin?'

'We all actually wanted to hire a nurse to stay at your grandfather's house to take care of him,' my mother said, 'but your grandmother said no. She told us to send him to the home. She couldn't cope with him around. She's so old herself, and you know your grandfather was so fat. She had to help him go to the toilet. She couldn't cope, he was so heavy.'

'Why don't you just admit the truth? Admit that we treated

him like shit. We let him die all alone. We're scum. We deserve to go to Hell.'

'You hear what she say?' my mother said to the photo. 'She's so sorry.'

'He can't hear you.'

'Yes he can,' she said. 'See? He's crying.' A drop of water trickled down my grandfather's photo. It must have fallen from the wet flowers above.

'Why can't you just admit your guilt?'

My mother took out a fresh hibiscus and stuck its stalk in a red metal holder next to the slab. She took out a tissue, wet it with her saliva, and wiped the dust off my grandfather's photo. 'You see your grandfather's slab is so clean compared to the other slabs. The other slabs so dusty, you see – hardly anyone comes and visit them. But your grandfather's slab is always clean. We always come and see him.'

'It's too late.' But I knew my mother would never believe it. She couldn't. If it really was too late – too late to make amends, too late to redeem herself from the way she neglected her father – there was only one place where she would end up. The joss sticks, the ghost money, the visits – these rituals were the only thing that kept her from Hell.

My mother lit a joss stick, and waved it three times towards my grandfather's photo. 'Your turn.'

I shook my head. All that was in front of me was a photo stuck to a piece of rock.

My mother stuck the joss stick in the red metal holder. The amber glow burnt down the brown stick, leaving a trail of grey ash that teetered in its wake. The wisp of smoke brushed my face. My mother began to pray, 'My dear father . . .' but her breath blew the ash away. The ash floated; stayed still in the sky for a moment. Then the wind dropped, and the grey flecks fell to our feet.

CHAPTER 20

Mei

Admission was free, so I just wandered in. Nobody would pay to watch Geylang and Tiong Bahru. Who would be mad enough to give good money to see amateurs mis-kicking shots at the corner post? Only eight hundred people turned up at the Jalan Besar Stadium, most of them single men – single, not as in 'unattached', but single, as in sad and alone. They sat by themselves, each spectator at least two metres away from the next. Most of them weren't even concentrating on the match, but did other things, like reading the *New Paper* to find out the results of the Arsenal versus Newcastle match (a match that actually mattered), or eating their Nasi Lemak dinner or looking at their pinkie finger, admiring what they had just dug out of their ear. On the few occasions when their eyes did turn towards the pitch, they viewed the proceedings with the same disinterested expression one finds on security guards and parking attendants.

I finally spotted the stand where Kwan would be. It stood out from the others. One look, and you knew something illegal was going on. The stand was full of 'helmet heads' – men with all-over hair perms. You see, any poor man could get a straight back and sides from a cheap Indian barber shop, but perms were *very* expensive. And if you could afford to perm your whole head, well, that showed that you were in the big time.

The bookies dressed in typical 'Ah Beng' fashion – Yves St Laurent polo shirts with brown bermudas, gold Rolexes and Testoni loafers – co-ordinating their outfits to create a rich, greasy tackiness that was unique to Singaporean culture.

I spotted Kwan. He was thick in the action, wheeling and dealing, five-figure numbers rolling off his tongue. The referee glanced at his watch, and the bookies knew. Only a few minutes left, time for final bets, last chance for any transactions.

Beepers vibrated against belts, spurred their owners to death leaps, taking four steps at a time, down the stairs, racing for the three empty phone booths. Handphones rang their frantic rhythm above the shouts and crackle of Hokkein. Kwan activated his black phone with a slick snap – 'Geylang win 5, I give you half a ball. Okay, one hundred thousand dollars. I on you.' One hundred thousand dollars, that's half a year's salary. Those unequipped with modern telecommunication equipment used their hands, flicking fingers in the air, shouting over shoulders.

The market closed, the trading floor wound down. Everyone sat down on the yellow benches, jaws clenched, tapping the *Lianhe Wanbao* newspaper on their knees. The stand became a shrine, as prayers rose with cigarette breaths, that grey incense, pleading favour from all the major deities, from Guan Yin to Jesus, from Buddha to Vishnu. After all, Singapore was a multi-religious society.

The match ended. Geylang lost. Kwan threw his newspaper to the ground. The bookies streamed down the grey steps, chattering loudly as they headed for the South Exit.

I ran up to Kwan and spoke to him in Hokkein – 'I'm Mei. You know Andy? You always go to his flat and bet on Saturday night?'

He nodded.

'Andy's been arrested.'

Kwan looked shocked. 'That's terrible,' he replied in Hok-kein. 'How did that happen?'

'The police raided his flat, they found a Filofax, with all the bets in it.'

'Was my name in the Filofax?'

'Oh don't pretend,' I said.

Kwan looked confused.

'I know you planted it.'

'What do you mean?'

'The police arrested you last month. You cut a deal with them – you planted the Filofax in Andy's flat, so that they would have enough evidence to arrest him. You betrayed Andy for a lighter sentence.'

'I don't know what you're talking about. I don't know anything about a Filofax.'

'Andy says the Filofax doesn't belong to him. He's never seen it before. Someone must have planted it.'

'Why do you think it was me?'

'You're the only one who had a motive. Why would any of the other bookies want to frame Andy? Who else could have planted it?'

'I don't know.'

'See? You were the only one arrested by the police. You're the only one who has a reason to betray Andy. Everyone else was making a lot of money from the betting house. Only you would profit if the police arrested Andy.'

'I wasn't the only one who was arrested. There was another bookie who went to Andy's flat. He was arrested in the same raid as me.'

Yes! I'd hooked him, and all I had to do was wheel him in, get him to admit that it was Loong who was arrested in the same raid.

'You're just making that up,' I said. 'If there was another

bookie who was arrested, it would have been mentioned in the newspaper.'

Kwan shook his head. 'This bookie – his father's very important. He was arrested, but his father stopped the newspaper from printing his name. His father is a good friend of the newspaper editor.'

'You're saying that the other bookie cut a deal with the police?'

'I don't know.'

'Who is this other bookie?'

'I can't tell you. His father is very important. I don't want to get into trouble.' Kwan wriggled away from me and melted into the crowd.

CHAPTER 21

Andy

You wake at noon. (You don't do mornings. If there is a lecture in the morning, you miss it. You just don't believe in mornings.)

It is only 1400 GMT but you already feel drunk. 'I hate it when I feel drunk in the afternoon,' you say.

'You shouldn't have eaten all that electric jelly for breakfast,' Eugene says.

You didn't have a choice. You'd had your twenty-first birthday party last night, and some bastard had stolen all the food from your cupboard.

'I don't know which is worse,' you tell Eugene, 'the fact that he stole all our food, or the fact that he left a note saying "I'm sorry" and *two pence*.'

Anyway, the jelly was from the party. You make electric jelly the same way as normal jelly, but you substitute half the water used with vodka. It's amazing how much the jelly masks the taste of the vodka. Four blobs of electric jelly just tastes like jelly, but you've actually swallowed half a pint of vodka.

You can't believe what happened to you later that day, but it could have happened to anyone. Anybody (well, any student) would have done the same in your place:

Two hours later, in the seminar, you feel really drunk. This is a bad time to be drunk because the inspectors are in. The whole English department is suffering from anal retention because of the teaching assessment, because they desperately want to get an 'Excellent' rating. Your tutor even sent slimy, personalized, handwritten notes begging all the students to speak up during the seminar.

Your tutor is droning on about D—, one of the most incomprehensible, and hence the finest, writer of his generation. Your tutor distributes journal articles explaining D—'s work, journal articles arguing why one shouldn't try to explain D—'s work, and journal articles exploring the differences between arguing, explaining and responding to D— (with cross-references to Kant and Snow White).

'The analysis that I am about to present is based on a chapter in my new book, *The Egg in English Literature: sui generis and the Ego*, which is due to be published by Yale University Press in April.' The professor goes on to interpret the chapter in D—'s novel, where the transvestite eats a hard-boiled egg for break-fast. 'This passage is an acidly satiric critique of the fall of the House of Windsor. The transvestite, the fictional queen is obviously an allusion to the real Queen of England. Now we know, through Freud, that the egg is a symbol for female sexuality, representing fertility, and thus, creative genesis. Now the Queen's orb, the symbol of her power, is also in the shape of an egg. The Queen, by eating the egg, shows that she feels that her sexuality and power is under threat, and by eating the egg, shows that she intends to consume her sexuality and power, to make it part of her body politic, not sharing it with anyone else. Metonymic surface disguises metaphoric depth. Narrative transparency works together with symbolic depth.'

The professor asks you a question.

Now the beauty of doing an English degree, is that you can answer any question without actually having studied for it. Now if you chose science, you would actually have to know the *facts*. In a science class, your professor would ask you – 'What is pyridinium bisretinoid?' and if you can't give the one and only correct answer – 'It consists of two retinoid molecules, which are chemical cousins of vitamin A, joined by a positively charged pyridine ring, containing five carbon atoms and one nitrogen' – you're screwed. Literature is different, because unlike science, the professors make a living out of disagreeing with each other's theories. So, if you're in a Literature class, and he asks you what you think *King Lear* is all about, why, it's like, hey – option time! You might never have read *King Lear*, but if you say that it was about the Oedipus complex, or the rebellion in Scotland, or the rise of the middle classes, the tutor would nod at you and look really impressed.

The professor asks you, 'Which seminal author do you think D— alludes to in his work?'

You say, 'Shakespeare' – which is always a safe bet.

'Which play, specifically, was D— alluding to?'

'*Much Ado About Nothing?*' Now of course you haven't read the play, but it's the only Shakespearean movie you've watched. It's not a film you would watch voluntarily, but your sister insisted on dragging you along because she wanted to see Keanu Reeves' naked chest.

The professor bombards you with questions about the play, but you just sit there. You can't answer any of the questions because you suddenly realize that you don't know the names of any of the characters! You only know the characters as 'that Kenneth Branagh bloke' and 'that Emma Thompson woman'.

Anyway, the professor starts asking you about the treatment of Hero, and you're panicking, so you stammer – 'Uh, is that like the Denzel Washington guy?' and immediately *everyone* knows that you've only watched the film.

The professor shoots an embarrassed look at the bearded bloke who's doing the teaching assessment.

Since you are drunk, you figure that sitting still and keeping your mouth shut is the best form of damage control. However, the spirit is willing, but the flesh is weak. Your problem is that the alcohol has broken the chains that restrain your hormones. At the moment all you can do is stare at Clare. She is the most gorgeous woman you have seen in your life, and you have been perving her every week in class. You find her every feature fascinating. You want to say something absurd, just to see how her face would respond, how her eyes would move, her gestures. You want to see her laugh.

Looking at Clare, all you can think about is her naked in a lab with all her scientific equipment, test tubes, pipettes, tongs, the blue copper sulphate dusting her fingernails.

'I want to be your bunsen burner,' you say loudly to Clare. 'Hey, honey light my fire.'

It would be a good idea never to go to that seminar again. And like all good ideas, you know you will never follow them. You know that, because you are scheduled to do a class presentation on 'D— and Post-modern Poetics' with Clare next week, and if you don't do your share, that will piss her off and you will definitely not get into her knickers after that.

As Clare is a science student, unfamiliar with current critical approaches to literature, she is relying on you to guide her through the maze of '-isms'.

'I need someone older and wiser,' she tells you.

Is that quote from *The Sound of Music* a come-on or what? This is your big chance, an opportunity to make a big impression, to bail her out, to guide her, to be her saviour. Who knows what favours she may bestow upon you once you win her undying gratitude – the sky's the limit.

This train of thought peps you up, and you set about preparing your bit of the presentation. One look at your texts and you immediately become unpepped. The 'Introduction to

Post-modernism' book is so difficult, you don't even understand the pictures.

You spend an hour in the library photocopying articles from journals like the ELH, MP, SEL, TLS and S & M. The graffiti on the wall behind the photocopier says, 'Copying from one person is plagiarism. Copying from two or more people is research.'

The photocopies sit on your desk, unread, and are likely to remain perpetually in that state of non-usage. This approach to learning is based on an old student superstition that states that as long as you have the text in your bedroom, somehow the information will filter through to your brain. Sort of like learning by osmosis.

You cannot concentrate on your work because Eugene is playing his CDs too loudly. You wonder if he is sick. He's been playing Take That's 'Babe' continuously for four hours. When he isn't playing Take That, he's playing Sean Maguire or P.J. and Duncan. You understand why Eugene plays music loudly, you have no problem with that, you are a student, all students play loud music, you're cool with that. What you don't understand is thy Eugene has the musical taste of a pubescent female. You are convinced that Eugene is a twelve-year-old girl trapped in the body of a twenty-one-year-old Singaporean man.

You look through your seminar notes. The bits of your handwriting that you can actually read, you don't understand. You understand the words. I mean, individually, the words, you get them. It's only when you string them together that they become like @"£%^& to you:

discovery of Unconscious and environmental determinism de-centres autonomous self.

fragmented communities produce competing discourses, pressurizes gendered subjectivity

intertextual ironic play/self-formative canon

deconstructs binary opposites

transcendental signified absent in semiotic environment –
>~~hermetic~~ hermeneutic (sp?)

freeplay and multiplicity

self-reflexive fictionalized construct of the fictionality of fictional representation/anti-representation

The only thing in your notes that you can understand are the
final lines:

death of novel, author, God, Self, Freud. Everything.

Randomness. Chance. Chaos.

LIFE HAS NO MEANING

So it is official. Life is meaningless. The intellectuals have
debated it, and produced conclusions that your feeble brain
cannot understand, but only accepts. If only you were smarter,
then maybe you would grasp the logical reasons underlining
the inevitable pointlessness of existence, but all you can do
now is accept your fate.

You parrot these concepts in your essays because you want
to get a good grade. The next day, in your 'Re-Inventing
Lesbians: Be/coming Wo/men' seminar, you say – 'Good and
evil are authoritarian and repressive categories imposed by the
ruling caste.' You don't understand what you've just said, but
you know you've said the right thing because the phrases give
your tutor a joy-gasm.

Life used to be simple. Raised on a philosophy gleaned from
Saturday morning cartoons, you believed in good and evil,
believed that things happened for a reason, and in doing
things for a reason. The world was divided into heroes (cheers,

whistles), villains (boo, hiss) and victims (usually women or children or pets). God or His agents, e.g. Spiderman, always beat the bad guys, and everyone lived happily ever after. Behind every episode in life or TV, a moral message could be extracted and conveyed in ten words or less, such as 'crime doesn't pay' or 'regular brushing with a fluoride toothpaste helps prevent tooth decay'. But higher education has proved that such a philosophy is outdated. Maybe they believed in all that stuff in the nineteenth century, but now after Darwin, Freud, Nietzsche, behaviourism, and moral relativism, no post-war intellectual could believe in those things and keep a straight face. Life used to be based on abstract words like love, honour and peace, but now all that matters is what you can smell, taste, touch, feel, things like . . . paper clips and Big Macs. Your university course has taught you that your future contains nothing but a dark abyss of emptiness.

You stare at the blank page. You have to write down some-thing, anything. You scribble:

'From my extensive survey of primary and secondary sources, I have observed that a lot of the key words underpinning post-modernism and post-post-modernism start with "D", for example, Derrida, deconstruction, de-centre, discourses, death, Donald (Bartheleme) etc. Western society seems to be going through a "D" phase at the moment. Are we in the Decade of "D"? When posterity looks back on our age, will they call us "D"-ians?

From the previous lines, you might surmise that I am currently undergoing a state, which is absolutely apposite to this presen-tation, a state known as complete and utter Desperation.'

You crumple the sheet into a ball and toss it at the wastepaper basket. You miss, and the ball of paper ends up on the carpet along with the other balls of paper.

*

One day, when Loong was visiting Eugene at Fallensham, he asked you what job you were going to get.

'I don't know. Maybe journalism.'

Loong hoots derisively. 'Journalism? You've got a better chance becoming the first bisexual belly-dancing president of the Rotary Club. A survey in the "Independent" shows that seventy per cent of all graduates want to be journalists. Consequently, a degree is insufficient, in order to work in the media you need that *je ne sais quoi*. Employers want proof that you have a genuine interest in the field, but so far you've done nothing, you haven't even written for the college newspaper.'

Loong is Mr Super-Preparation. He plans everything. He even decides what he wants to eat for dinner a day in advance, like if he's having beef for dinner on Tuesday night, he takes the meat out of the freezer on Monday and marinates it for twenty-four hours. Now that's *preparation*. If he does that much work for beef, imagine what he does for his essays.

So what if you survive your next seminar? So what if you graduate? What next?

You'll never get a job, not in the current economic climate. You are educated enough to know all the logical reasons for why you have no hope. The uninformed, unwashed masses simply *feel* that they have no hope, a feeling gathered from the things they see around them – the 'Closing Down Sale' signs in the high streets – but for you it's different. Out of all the students in the country, you're in the top five per cent, you're an *Economist* reader, you *know* the economic statistics, you've got the macro view, the hard facts – Britain runs a deficit on both its visible and invisible trade, the poor are caught in the employment trap, sterling is losing almost five per cent of its trade weighted value every three months, the Confederation of British Industry report says that manufacturing output and retail sales growth is slowing, an index of business confidence compiled by IFO fell in November for the seventh time in eight months, half of the population receives means-tested benefits, and an IMF study shows that real long-term rates show an imbalance between desired investment and the supply of capital, suggesting that marginally profitable profits have been squeezed out by a scarcity of savings.

You have no future, and a university education has given you the concrete arguments to prove it. British businesses are doomed to fail; you know because you've tried – last week, in an attempt to save money on your grocery bill, you started planting potatoes in your garden, but the venture failed due to a breakdown in the existing infrastructure (your spade broke) and also due to the lack of government incentives for small-scale farmers like yourself.

What are you going to do with an English and Philosophy degree? You can write essays and take exams, and that's it. You're not trained to do anything *useful*. You'll probably end up shelf-stacking or waitering. What job do you want? What do you want to do with your life? How should you know? You can't even decide whether to watch the new Scorsese or the new Tarantino movie.

You're not like your housemates. Their lives are sorted. Take Asman, he's a Malaysian scholar doing accountancy, and once he graduates he's going to be bonded to the national water company for ten years so he's got his future pre-determined. Or Chin See, she's from Hong Kong, and even though she doesn't have a bond, her parents and culture dictate that she either be a lawyer or doctor or scientist, and she is chosen to be a lawyer. But no, you're different, you're from the West, that bastion of freedom and democracy. Your parents have always told you that you can do whatever you want, as long as it isn't illegal. They've always been supportive of all your decisions, and once you hit eighteen, they never dreamt of telling you what to do. You can do whatever you want to do, and you have no idea what that is.

What is your problem? You are a white Anglo-Saxon middle-class heterosexual male. Out of all the social categories, yours has the most freedom and opportunities. Every door is open to you, you are not oppressed or disadvantaged socially, mentally, economically, or ethnically. Nothing in the world discriminates against you; the system, the status quo is designed for your benefit, you have no excuse for failure, no one to blame but yourself.

Why are you doing a degree in English? You don't know. It belongs to a long list of things that you've done for no good reason. All your life, you've drifted from one thing to another, from GCSEs to A levels, with no fervent convictions, without any Master Plan, the same way that you drift at night from the King's Arms to the Mitre, the same way you spend your Saturday afternoon watching crap on TV, *Knight Rider*, then *Baywatch*, then *Gladiators*, then *Blind Date*, not paying attention, just lying on your bed as the white light from the tube flickers against your pale face, pondering questions like why Kitt's tyres always screech and kick dust even when Michael Knight is doing a simple left turn.

How did you get this way? Back in the sixth form, flipping through the UCCA handbook, you decided that out of all the courses listed, a BA (Hons) in English Literature sounded the sexiest. A science degree would have consigned you to a virginal and chaste existence with the other skinny geeks with taped up glasses. Poetry, on the other hand, turned women into quivering blobs of sexual jelly. So you spent many a night evaporating your thoughts in a sonnet. With your flaming red hair, blue eyes flecked with grey, a natural ear for rhyme and rhythm, and a fragile profile that gives you an aura of sensitivity, you considered yourself a seducer in the grand Romantic tradition. So you signed up for your English degree, confident that if you were lucky enough to catch tuberculosis or consumption, armed with your collection of lyrics, university was going to be one big sex-fest.

But the undergraduate terms fly past, and Valentine's Day is still a cardless affair. You whinge to your housemate about how no girl sent you anything for Valentine's, and she looks at you, surprised, and says, 'Oh, but I thought you were gay.' You are really shocked. Back in your room, you scrutinize your image in the mirror. Maybe you look *too* sensitive. Maybe your poetry ought to have fewer references to leafy glades and daffodils, and more on blood, body bags, exhaust pipes and MK-57s. Tomorrow, you will go to the gym to pump iron. You are going to be well hard.

You meet Clare at Americana, the campus fast-food joint. It is painted in red, white and blue, with the usual cliché pseudo-American accoutrements like traffic lights, pinball machines and a jukebox shaped like a gas pump. It reminds you of the moon – it has no atmosphere.

The jukebox is playing even though no one has put any money in it. It is playing Jive Bunny, Kenny G, Take That and Michael Bolton. You know the cafeteria owner's devious scheme. The jukebox is programmed to play tunes which give as much pleasure as having your wisdom tooth taken out, so that inevitably, some student, unable to stomach such drivel any longer, is compelled to pop in some coins to get Bob Marley to replace Kylie Minogue.

This may be the most important breakfast meeting you'll ever have. You, in the words of the immortal Baldrick, 'have a cunning plan': you will give Clare the poem you wrote for her, a poem that will surely make her swoon straight into your arms.

She shows you her notes. 'What have you prepared?'

'I couldn't really get into it.' You light your cigarette, inhale and look moody. You have spent many a night perfecting the art of the profound cigarette. 'If what D— says is true, if life is meaningless, the universe is governed by chaos and chance, what's the point of doing anything? What's the point of going to this seminar?'

'You didn't prepare anything for the presentation did you?'

'Of course I have. This is a genuine philosophical question that needs to be answered. Why study? Why live? Why this?' You wave your hands around. 'I'm sick of D—. I'm sick of everything about this seminar, sure, all the authors are terribly clever, and I'm sure they're right, even though they won't say they're right, because they don't believe in the concept of "right". I'm sick of it, I want to chuck it all, but I don't know what else I can do apart from what I'm doing now. I don't know what I want, because that's what they taught me – "You can't know anything any more".' The cigarette smoke spirals. 'What do you want?'

'I want to be able to do our presentation this afternoon,' Clare says.

'No, no, I mean, what do you *really* want? What are you willing to die for? 'Cos if you don't have anything you would die for, you don't have anything to live for.' Jesus, why are you quoting Malcolm X at nine in the morning? You're not even *drunk*.

'I don't know,' she says, looking bewildered. 'Maybe we should talk about the presentation later today. Perhaps after when you've actually done some preparation.'

'You know, I *do* know what I want.' You slam your fist on the table. 'I want good and evil, truth and lies, right and wrong. I want to know what the right thing is for everyone; and not just the right thing for you, but maybe not for me, binary oppositions, black and white, and not shades of grey, no ambiguities. I want things to be simple again – a life where all the clichés are true, where Jesus saves, justice will win the day, every cloud has a silver lining, tomorrow will be a better day, where love is all you need and all you need is love – all the manifestos of life that rhyme, everything that is slushy and cheesy, intellectually suspect, the opiate of the masses. I want spiritual riches, the power that raised Christ from the dead, life everlasting, joy, peace, ecstasy, power, riot, to this end I labour, struggling with all the energy of Christ, revelations, streams of living water, something so mesmerizing, so hypnotic, so compelling it sucks you in, consumes you, makes you lose control, fall on your face, tears streaming, let passion, love, life, God overwhelm me for once, and not this nothingness, not trapped, boxed in by this nothingness. Look at me, I'm dead. I'm dead. I look inside me and I'm dead. I'm never happy doing what I'm doing, when I'm doing something I'm always thinking of what I can do next. I don't want anything, not anything the world can offer. I can have anything I want, but I look at everything in the world and I don't want any of it. I had the only thing I ever wanted once, the only time I ever had it.'

You tell her about the white light by the river, how you saw God and were wounded by the light.

'I was reading a paper by Michael Persinger, he's a neuro-scientist at Laurentian University in Canada,' Clare said. 'He imitated the brain effects of stress by zapping the subject's brains with low-voltage, high-focus electricity. The people saw visions – angels, "God", demons. Brain events can induce the most deeply felt paranormal experiences. Have you read William James?'

'"The varieties of religious experience". 1902. Conversion is just another word for a nervous breakdown. What I experienced was all just due to chemicals in the brain, I must have had a fit, that's the only logical explanation, it couldn't be God, don't ever say it's God. God is just something people use to explain anything they can't understand because they're too stupid to explain it. So they take God away from me, and I go back, and stand in the black shade of the door. I look out at the world, I see everything on offer and I don't want any of it. I want God. Somewhere along the line they killed God, and I want him back. I want God resurrected, living in me. But I don't want the hippy, new age, pop culture, user-friendly, thought of the day, celestine prophecy, spiritual quest as narrated as an adventure novel – spouting Zen truths while machine-gunning from a jeep in the Tibetan mountains. I don't want the mass-produced, wrapped in plastic, sugar-coated, self-help shit. I want the real thing, a deep thing, a lifetime commitment, and not just a book, a weekend retreat, something to slot in between coffee mornings, Encounter groups and aerobics lessons. I want something that will fill all of me, every nook and cranny, touch every cell, course through the blood, fill the spaces of the mind, touch the unphysicality of the soul. I want God. I want the trees to shake, the window pane to shudder, the mountains to fall into the heart of the sea. I want that day when I glimpsed burning bushes, chariots of fire, angels with golden eyes with faces like the sun, blood and thunder, fiery arrows, pierced hearts, screams. I want church to be more than just a quaint social custom undertaken by elderly aunts and characters in Joanna Trollope novels. I want Faith, Hope, and Charity to be more than just a name for a new all-girl R & B rap group. I want the cross to mean something, to light the dark recesses of the soul. I want everything I used to believe in, I want everything I lost. I want it all, I want it all back.'

You don't know what got you started on this rant. You must

have kept it bottled up for ages, and it just came out. You couldn't control yourself. She is looking at you rather strangely. 'I'm sorry,' you say, 'I don't know what got into me.'

You open D—'s novel and begin to do some lucid textual analysis, and she begins to look more impressed. You are good at this, you can wax lyrical about literary texts in your sleep. You are dissecting D—'s text effortlessly, your studies have given you the ability to talk expertly about things you know absolutely nothing about, so you yabber on about D—, not even thinking about it very much, all you are thinking about is how to slip into the conversation the poem you wrote for Clare.

Even though it has nothing to do with whatever you were talking about, you suddenly say, 'I wrote something for you.' You shove her the poem:

'Burn'

Spiced baked hams squeezed against turkeys bewitched
to a dark gold; they crowded between the 12 varieties of
　　cheeses,
grapes lying on chicken breasts, devilled
eggs, green pork pâté. The white Italian cheese curled
round the black pudding. Waiters offered
chocolate truffles dusted with vanilla powder on silver trays.
　　The bar
served red wines, purple liquors and blue cordials. Caught
in the swirl of cigarettes and alcohol,
my stomach burned, and I missed you.

At church, I ate the body and blood of Christ. The wafer stuck
to the top of my mouth
it wouldn't melt
it still stuck
as I sipped the red wine
as I returned to the pew

it still stuck.

The wine was sour, my stomach burned, and I missed you.

I had two cups of coffee, Jamaican beans mixed
with chocolate and the essence of almonds. You know
how I get when I drink too much caffeine –
my heart pounds, my belly churns, and I can't sleep.
Saturday night, watching *Blind Date* on ITV,
I drank mugs of strawberry tea, hot chocolate, and even
three glasses of diet Coke.
Too much caffeine, my stomach burned, and I missed you.

You sit there and watch her go red. She does not say anything.
'What do you think?'
'I don't know.'

You sit there and finish your coffee. It is the longest coffee
that you've ever drunk. For the first time you realize that
'drinking a cup of coffee' is one of the dictionary definitions
for 'eternity'. The water fountain hums, and the waitresses
clang together the dirty forks and spoons.

You watch Clare get up, put your poem in her knapsack and
leave the cafeteria.

Finally, she says something. 'See you in class later.'

So this is it. Your English degree won't get you a job, you know
that, but now you know that it won't even get you sex. You
sit there, remembering Clare's silence and the black pit widens.

No wonder some people commit suicide. Why play this
game of chance called life? Why endure this emptiness known
as existence? You know why – somewhere, within the depths
of your soul, you hear a voice that says 'Live!', that regular,
insistent call that always tells you, 'You've got to carry on!' You
recognize those voices; it is the Endsleigh insurance company.
You still have three months of your life insurance to go, and
they want you to renew.

CHAPTER 22

Andy

I couldn't put it off any longer. The time had come: I was in my final year, and I had to find a job. These were the facts: I was a student in English from a so-so university, who would probably get a 2:2 degree, with no discernible gifts or talents. As for extra-curricular activities, I had spent the last three years in the pub (except for Thursday which is LCR night and Monday when it's student night at the Waterfront – only one pound with your NUS card). I had no work experience.

Now how could I convert all that into a seductive CV?

I started off pretty well, with

'CURRICULUM VITAE'

which was good, because it showed that I knew how to use Microsoft Word, and its basic features, like enlarging the font and centring the text. PC skills are essential in giving you an edge in the competitive job market, or so says the Careers Centre pamphlet.

So, encouraged by this happy start, I proceeded with the rest of my CV, typing out my name, address, telephone number and date of birth, thinking, 'Hey, this is easy, anyone can do it, maybe this whole job search thing isn't so bad.'

Under 'Languages' I put, 'Conversational French and German', which was a half-lie. My French consists of being able to go into a café and order a croissant and an Evian, and my German consists of phrases like 'Ich bin ein wiener schnitzel', which means I am a pork chop (I think). But hey, if the company is going to put me in some French or German situation, I can worry about learning the language after I get the job.

After I finished my finals, I went out and got plastered, celebrating the fact that it would be my last exam/test thingie. I was so wrong. When I started applying for jobs, I had to take these even weirder tests: matching squiggly shapes with boxes, word association quizzes, logic questions like 'A cat is to a book, as giraffes are to _____?' What's the point of all this? If I'm an executive at Unilever, you don't think some client will actually ring me up and say, 'So Andy, if a spanner is to a faucet, Persil is to what?' It's hard enough trying to get a job without having to be subjected to all sorts of inane questions.

Also, I hate filling out application forms. I must have written out my name and address over fifty times. And some companies have the weirdest fetishes. One insisted that I fill out the same application form three times, in black ink only (no typewritten and no other colours acceptable), warning loudly that 'PHOTOCOPIES ARE UNACCEPTABLE'.

I always do crap at interviews. It's not me that's the problem, it's the stupid questions they ask. Nowadays they don't ask you the usual, logical, sane questions that you expect, questions that are actually relevant to the job, such as 'Why do you want this job?' or 'What special qualities can you bring to our company?' Instead, they ask you stuff like, 'What do you think of European integration?' and 'What do you think is the future of transport?' and this was at a job interview for *Shell*. You think they'd ask about oil and lubricants or something, but they didn't.

I always do really badly on the trick questions. Once, an interviewer asked me, 'What is your greatest weakness?' so I gave the standard answer, 'I work too hard' and then he asked me, 'Why is that a weakness?' and I didn't know what to say. So basically, all my interviews were firmly in the region of Disaster-shire.

I went to a job interview with HMV, and they gave me this questionnaire with over a hundred questions, asking stuff like 'Who sang the backing vocals on Dusty Springfield's first album?', 'Who won the Oscar for best actress in 1984?', and 'What does *Wing Commander* have in common with the *Star Wars Trilogy*?' Of course I had no idea what the answers were.

'People come in and tell us all the time, "I'd love to work for HMV because I love music, I love the movies",' the interviewer said. 'So we make them fill out the questionnaire just to show them that they know absolutely nothing.' I had my doubts about working for a company who, right at the start, wanted to impress upon applicants their total incompetence, but that didn't matter in the end, because they turned me down.

I flirted with the idea of doing an MA in Studies in Fiction, because that would mean not having to think about getting a job for another year. But after talking to people who had completed the course, it seemed that all an MA enables you to do is to get a job as a sales assistant at Dillons or Waterstones. It seems that everyone on the shop floor of every book shop in England has at least an MA, and you wonder why you need to spend over four years in higher education just so you can key in £6.99 on the till, and say things like 'It's on the left shelf just behind Crime and New Age.'

'Some people think it's a waste, having an MA and being a cashier,' my friend said. 'But it has its pay-offs. Literature graduates love books, so it's ideal being able to work in a textual environment. Also, we get to meet many famous people. Just the other night, Nicholas Feraldon came to do a signing.'

'Nicholas who?'

'Feraldon. He's really famous.'

I wanted to say, 'No he isn't,' but I could see that look in my friend's eyes. She wanted so desperately for this Nicholas bloke to be famous, so that it would validate her sad little job, shine up her life with this claim to fame, as if her job at Waterstones enabled her to rub shoulders with the rich and famous. Why burst her bubble? Why be cruel? So I played along with her delusion. I might be a cynic, but I'm not a bastard, so I said, 'Oh yes, that Nicholas, I remember now. I loved his last novel, very entertaining.'

'It was about child abuse.'

'Yeah, um, it was entertaining in a kind of painful way. Cathartic.'

I couldn't get a job. Pushing aside doubts that the real problem may lie in the fact that I was poorly qualified, untalented and lazy, I decided that the *real* problem was that I hadn't found myself yet. 'I never took a year out. I don't have any life experience. It's not just books that count, you know. Not just head knowledge,' I said to Eugene and Loong. 'I went straight to university from A levels. Maybe that's what I need – a year "off". I need to explore, see new places, search my soul.'

'What you *really* need,' Loong said, 'is a job.' He suggested that I go work in Singapore. 'They're dying for teachers over there.'

'If I can't get a job in my own country,' I said, 'how am I going to get a job in Singapore?'

'Don't worry. I'll get my father to make a couple of phone calls,' Loong said. 'He'll sort out some relief work for you.'

'It doesn't pay very well does it?' I said. 'How am I going to afford a flat?'

'My parents have an extra flat in Singapore,' Loong said. 'Two-bedroom, easy access to the Clementi Interchange. I can get them to rent it out to you at a thirty per cent discount.'

'What's the catch?' Eugene said.

'Once a week, if you don't mind me and a couple of other friends using the flat – maybe Saturday night,' Loong said, 'just for getting together and placing a few bets.'

'Fine,' I said. It didn't seem any different from what we were doing in England.

'No it isn't,' Eugene said. 'It's illegal in Singapore. What if Andy gets raided?'

Loong shrugged. 'Nothing'll happen. All our deals are sealed by the tongue. The bookies will never testify against each other in court, so the police will never get enough evidence against us. I've been running this gambling thing for five years, and I've never been caught.'

'If it's so safe, why don't you run the betting house at your place?' Eugene said.

'My parents usually have guests over on Saturday nights. Diplomatic cocktail shit,' Loong said. 'That's why I usually use our spare flat in Clementi for betting.'

'I guess if I'm taking over Loong's flat, it's only fair that I let him use the flat on Saturdays,' I told Eugene. 'It's only once a week, and anyway, it should be fun.' I turned to Loong. 'You sure I won't get into trouble?'

'Without written records, without letters hammered in type,' Loong said, 'the police won't be able to convict us.'

'What happens if one of the punters loses a huge amount of money and he can't pay up and he does a runner?' I asked Loong. 'Do they send people to go and, um, "look" for them?'

Loong looked shocked. 'We don't do things like that. We're not secret society members. We're very gentleman.'

When I went to Singapore, that was a term I heard used by the punters a lot – 'We're very gentleman'. It was true of the system they set up, a business based upon a gentleman's code of honour, of keeping one's word. Because of the police, they couldn't write anything down. In the commercial world, where there are no gentlemen, you needed contracts, written agreements. But in the punters' world, all they had was each other's word. In the commercial world, if someone screwed you, you had your contract, and you could sue them. If someone cheated the punters, they just had to let it go, and wait for the man to make enough money to pay them back. It was a system based on trust, reputation, a good name and integrity. I found that so refreshing, so different from the business world, where all you could ever trust was a piece of paper, signed and witnessed.

I considered Loong's offer and weighed my options. I could either a) explore the Far East or b) Live with My Parents. Absolutely no competition.

Singapore loomed before me, a great escape route. You know, the exotic East and all that. Maybe I would find jungles and elephants, Buddhas in golden temples, Asian babes, especially babes like those girls in the Singapore Airline ads – 'Singapore Girl, you're a great way to fly'. Yes, I would fly a Singapore girl anytime. I wanted beaches, and palm trees, a place where my tanned limbs would be speckled with sand, and rinsed by the emerald waters. I wanted to breakfast with orang-utans in my bungalow, then go wind-surfing, and after that, feast on tropical fruits like guavas, papayas, mangoes, pineapples, and suck the juice straight from a fresh green coconut. In between all that, I might have a few James Bond type adventures – speedboat chases in mangrove swamps, near-death experiences while having sex with dragon ladies. I would travel the green waters in sampans, and the roads in rickshaws, pulled along by toothless old men.

But after Loong left, Eugene said, 'I . . . I don't think you should go to Singapore.'

'Why not?' I said.

'I don't trust Loong. It's too good to be true, him renting the flat to you at such a cheap rate.'

'You're paranoid,' I said. 'Loong's just being nice. I know you think he killed Charlie and everything, but Loong has never done a single bad thing to me.'

'He's just reeling you in. I know him,' Eugene said. 'He's just winning your trust so he can set you up.'

'Once I owed Loong about fifty quid,' I said, 'and I knew I had to get a part-time job to pay him off but it was tough because I was smack bang in the middle of finals. Loong knew, and he just cancelled my debt, just like that. He told me to forget about the fifty quid and just concentrate on my exams,' I said. 'Loong seems honest.'

'Devils often hide their blackest sins with heavenly shows.'

'You're impossible. If Loong so much as sneezes, you think that's part of his sinister conspiracy to infect the world with a deadly virus. If he does something nice, you think he's only doing that to lull you into a false confidence. If you look at him like that, he's never going to be able to do anything right in your eyes. You're just being paranoid. As usual.'

'You can't just go to Singapore by yourself. You shouldn't put yourself in Loong's hands completely. It's not safe.' Eugene fiddled with the remote control. 'Do you mind if I come to Singapore with you?'

'Yeah, great. Eugene – Andy's official babysitter. I'm not completely useless. I can take care of myself.'

'Since when? Who does all the washing up? Who melts off the ice from the fridge every month? Who checks the carbon monoxide detector every evening, before we go to bed? If it wasn't for me, you'd be dead.'

'All right, all right, you can come to Singapore with me. You can be my nanny.'

CHAPTER 23

DAY SIX: FRIDAY EVENING

Mei

An Indian security guard protected Loong's condo situated in the expensive Bukit Timah district. Slouched in the entry booth, playing with the dial on his transistor radio, the guard's main skill seemed to be his ability to listen to Tamil music without falling asleep.

'Who you want?' he said.

Just for the fun of it, I gave him a bogus name and a bogus block number. He grunted, rustled some sheets on his clipboard, yawned and waved me through.

Loong's condo was filled exclusively with upper middle-class Chinese, and Japanese expatriates. Why did they bother to employ Indian security guards? Certainly, it wasn't to deter burglars, since the guards had no police training whatsoever and displayed a level of incompetence that made them unemployable in any other profession. I always suspect that the guards weren't there for security purposes, but were there mainly to stop poor, non-Chinese people (like themselves) from wandering around the estate.

I pressed the intercom button. Loong answered, and buzzed me in. Potted plants lined the wall outside Loong's unit. There was the money plant of course, the standard of all condos, supposedly bringing wealth to its owner; there were also plants that could be used for preparing food – green limes, red chillies, and pandan leaves for wrapping glutinous rice; Loong's parents also collected white roses, periwinkles, chrysanthemums, and purple orchids. All the flowers were small, scentless, dry and stunted, struggling to grow in the dusty, fume-and-traffic-choked air. The perpetual cloud of smoke from the joss sticks stuck in the red altar above didn't help either. Only the hairy baby cactus seemed to thrive.

Loong looked exactly like I expected – a model Singaporean. He had short, neat hair, with an engineering degree-type face that was all glasses. He was good-looking, not in a sexy way, but in a solid, dependable, marriable sort of way. He was the SDU ideal, the type who would look good fathering 2.3 children. My mother would love him.

I introduced myself as Eugene's friend and Andy's lawyer.

Loong grinned and chatted away non-stop. 'Andy talks about you a lot. Um, I'm sorry my parents aren't here to greet you. They've gone to organize the Mid-autumn Festival games for the kiddies. Some mooncake treasure hunt.' Loong went to the stairs and shouted – 'Rose! Rose!' He slapped his forehead. 'Oh no. The maid's gone to help my parents. I'll have to do your tea myself. Sit, sit, don't need to be polite.' He ushered me to the sofa.

I looked around the living room.

'By the way, the decor in this room is completely my parents' idea,' Loong said. 'I absolutely dissociate myself from it. My parents just have too much money – look at all the rugs.'

Ten different rugs lay scattered across the living room.

'They're all expensive, but none of them match,' Loong said. 'My parents are *xiao*, they just go crazy sometimes. They have too much money, they go through these collection phases. Last year it was rugs. This year it's property. Right now they're buying every house in Malaysia and China. Especially China. Guess that's the in thing now – China. My father's going to be posted there. The government is so into China now. Frankly, I'm getting bored with it. Every day in the *Straits Times*, pages and pages, it's always buy this in China, invest that in China. I'm like – shut up, please.' He looked at me. 'Oh sorry. You haven't bought anything in China, have you?'

I shook my head.

'Oh, good. Whew.'

A stack of hideous Filofaxes lay on the coffee table. They looked exactly like the one the police had found in Andy's toilet.

'Do you want one?' Loong picked up one of the Filofaxes. 'My uncle – he runs a publishing company. He couldn't sell these. No surprise, look at them – eurgh! Anyway, he dumped over fifty of these on us. I know it looks pretty awful, but you can use it as rough paper. Or give it as a birthday present to someone you don't like. I've been trying to get rid of them for months. Take it. It's a gift. In fact, I insist.' He took a plastic bag, and put the Filofax in. 'See, I'll even throw in a free plastic bag with the deal. You *have* to take the Filofax.' He handed me the bag.

I took the bag, then said, 'Andy's been arrested.'

Loong sat down on the sofa. 'Is it?'

I waited for him to say something more, but he didn't. He seemed to have suddenly lost all his garrulity. So I said, 'The police raided his flat.'

'When did this happen?'

'Last Saturday.'

'But I thought Andy said there would be no betting that night. He called it off. Something about him finding Jesus, I didn't quite understand. Funny thing, religion. I remember going to a Billy Graham rally once. I spent the whole evening wondering how I could get up and go to the loo without the counsellors thinking that I wanted to make a commitment,'

Loong said. 'How did Andy get arrested if there was no one betting in the flat?'

'The police found a Filofax. It had all the bets in it. Someone planted the Filofax in his toilet.'

'Someone framed him? But who?'

'We don't know. Who do you think?'

'You know, sorry, I just realized I've been really rude. I didn't make you that drink. So *pei se*, very embarrassing, sorry. Don't move. I'll go to the kitchen, I'll be back soon.' Loong left the living room.

He returned with tea and biscuits. 'Orange tea and waffle biscuits. Got them from Holland.'

'Who would profit if Andy was arrested?' I asked.

Loong shrugged.

'What about Kwan?'

'Why do you suspect him?'

'Well, from what I've gathered, the police have been watching Andy's flat for a while, but they've never been able to get enough evidence to arrest him. They needed *written* evidence. So they get someone on the inside, one of the bookies, to write the bets in the Filofax, and plant it in Andy's flat.'

'But why Kwan?'

'He was arrested in a raid recently. He might have turned Judas in exchange for a lighter sentence.'

'That makes sense.' He frowned, hard in thought. Then he said, 'Your tea's getting cold. Don't you like it?'

'It's fine.'

'Drink it then.' He smiled. 'It's not poisonous, you know.'

'Kwan says that you were arrested in the same raid as him.'

'Rubbish. He's got no proof.'

'That's because your father put pressure on the right people. That's why your name's never mentioned in any of the official records.'

Loong grinned. 'I *like* you. You're really smart. I like the way you've tried to manipulate me into admitting that I could have done what Kwan might have done. You're suggesting that I worked with the police to betray Andy?'

'Yes.'

'Unfortunately, though you might be really smart, you are also really wrong. There are a few problems with your theory. For one thing, I don't think the Singapore police will ever stoop so low as to fabricate evidence against an innocent man like Andy.'

'They might.'

'Also, I have no reason to cut a deal with the police. I wasn't arrested during the raid. I wasn't running the gambling house when it was raided, I was just a participant, and you can't be charged with any crime just for participating. If you don't believe me, you can check the police records. I've never been charged with any crime.'

'That's because your father managed to keep your record clean.'

Loong laughed. 'Mei, my father is not the Prime Minister or God or Satan or whatever. He merely works for the Foreign Service. You're presuming that he has these amazing powers – he's just a diplomat. All he does is go to official ceremonies and sometimes he throws the occasional party for a visiting dignitary. Anyway, you know how strict anti-corruption laws are in Singapore. There's no way my father, or anybody, could doctor a criminal record.'

'What about the search warrant?' I said. 'It listed the owners of the flat as your parents, rather than Andy. The police couldn't have known that, unless someone told them. And you're the only person, apart from Andy and Eugene, who knows this.'

'I am? I don't know anything about the flat.' Loong frowned. 'Is that what this is all about? You think that I framed Andy?'

'Who else could have done it?' I told him what Eugene told me about the cat, and about Charlie.

He slapped his forehead. 'That's why you haven't drunk your tea. You really do think it's been poisoned. Me? A murderer? That's so ridiculous, it's hilarious.' He shook his head and laughed. 'I guess it's not a good time to ask if you'd like to go out for dinner with me some time.'

I pointed to the pile of Filofaxes. 'That looks *exactly* like the Filofax the police found.'

'So what? I've been trying to get rid of them for months. I probably gave a copy to all the bookies at the flat, even Andy. Anyway, you don't think I'm *that* stupid. If I really did plant the Filofax in Andy's flat, I wouldn't leave those Filofaxes out here, for everyone to see.' Loong grabbed my cup and gulped down the tea. 'See, no ill effects.' He wiped his mouth and burped. '*Now*, will you go out for dinner with me some time?'

'How do you live with yourself? Don't you ever feel guilty about what you've done?'

'What will you give me if I showed you my soul? Dinner next Friday, maybe?'

'Maybe.'

'Why don't you kill people?' Loong said.

'Be ... because it's wrong. How can you even ask that? Everyone knows it's wrong.'

'Yes, but why?'

'Because God says so.'

'I don't believe in God. Human life isn't sacred because it has no special source. Okay, so you've got secular humanism – the belief that you can do anything so long as it doesn't hurt another person. But that is based on the premise that people are basically good. That's bullshit. Take a look at your mother, your father, your friends. People are basically bad. We'd do anything as long as we could get away with it. We only help others because they can help us, or so that they won't hurt us. We're born to be selfish, it's the natural order of things. We're all profit-maximizers. You see, if you realize that there is no God, and that people are scum, it's incredibly liberating. You realize that you can do anything. You don't have to care about anything, anyone. See those ants?' Loong pointed to his glass of Fanta orange. The water vapour had condensed, running down the glass and leaving a rim of liquid on the table. A cluster of ants scurried across the black glass top and waded into the wet rim, searching for sugar. 'Do you remember the first time you killed an ant?' One ant scrambled up the glass, and Loong squashed it with his thumb. 'Of course you do. Maybe you felt a *little* guilt. But do it often enough –' Loong rapidly squashed the ants round his glass, '– and you don't feel any guilt at all. In fact, it can even become,' he pounded his fist on the last surviving ant, 'fun.'

I got up.

'Why, what's wrong? Many great men have said the same thing.'

'Like Hitler?'

'Like Shakespeare. "As flies to wanton boys are we to the gods, they kill us for their sport." God determines what is right and wrong. And so the trick is to be God. When you rule, you make the rules.' Loong picked up an ant from the floor and dropped it into his drink, drowning it. 'I'll see you next Friday? Seven-ish?'

'I'll see you in court,' I said.

CHAPTER 24

Andy

When I arrived at Changi Airport, the first thing I noticed were the toilets. When I think about what makes Singapore different from countries in the West, I think toilets. Due to their scatological nature, toilets are an under-discussed topic. That's tragic. Personally, the loo is very important to me. I would never go to a country which didn't have decent bogs. Toilets are the last refuge of civilization, 'cos when you're worn and weary, in need of comfort and succour, you need a seat where you can rest comfortably to relieve yourself.

The toilet at Changi Airport was one of those hole-in-the-ground things. It was an oval-shaped marble cistern in the ground, flanked by two rectangular marble tiles. You plant your feet on the tiles, squatting until you've completed your bowel movement. Now having to squat for ten minutes is pretty painful, and after five my thighs were sore (I don't think I ever had reason to squat for more than five minutes before this) and so I had to get up. Obviously, things started to drip from my posterior – and I shall now spare you the more graphic details of my first encounter with the sanitary facilities in Singapore.

Many of the public toilets in Singapore are pretty disgusting. The seats have black marks, and because the seats are dirty, people squat on them, which is how the black shoe marks get there in the first place. It wouldn't be a problem if they supplied toilet paper to wipe off the shoe prints, but they don't. I get *so* pissed off about this. There is nothing worse than not being able to wipe your bum after a crap. It's very stressful. At the National Stadium, they haven't even bothered installing toilet paper holders on the wall of the cubicle. Of course, the worst toilets in Singapore, but by far the most popular, are the public lifts. In the nineties, the government tried to combat this crime by installing urine-smell-sensitive detectors, that would activate a camera which videoed the perpetrator in action. Also, you could get arrested for not flushing the toilet.

Why am I telling you all this, you might ask? You see, when I came to Singapore, I thought, 'Great, I'm going to a new country, it'll be such a learning experience. I'll absorb a new culture, learn things (as Pocahontas sings) I didn't know I didn't know, explore my inner space, tap into the mystic East, paint with all the colours of the wind.' But that didn't quite happen.

I just learnt a lot about toilets.

Eugene had told me to stock up on chewing gum. You couldn't buy gum in Singapore – the government banned it because it was a litter hazard. I didn't know what to expect when I approached Customs. Would there be signs that read 'Welcome to Singapore. No drugs. No firearms. No chewing gum.'?

When I stepped into the tropical air for the first time – boom! – this giant hand slammed into me. The glass doors slid open, the flash of street lights blinded me, this orange glare – then the air – it rammed into me, rugby-tackle like. This must be how it feels when you break the sound barrier. Then I suddenly realized why Singaporeans could live without gum – the air was so thick and humid you could chew on it. It felt like the Michelin man had just sat down on me, and no matter how hard I tried, I couldn't shake him off, couldn't escape the heavy folds of flesh wrapped around my body.

'Great. There's Mei. She's come to pick us up.' Eugene waved his hand at this woman.

One look at Mei, and the weight lifted from my shoulders. On my way here, I read in *Silver Kris*, the in-flight magazine, that Singapore Airlines only chooses one out of eight hundred applicants to be a Singapore Girl. Mei looked like a Singapore Girl. Would she be a great way to fly? I couldn't wait to find out.

We zoomed on to the Benjamin Sheares Bridge, past the magical skyline. It's a sight of superlatives: the Westin Stamford, the tallest hotel in the world, the tallest building in South East Asia, a white shard among the silver skyscrapers. The banks and hotels tower above the dinghies that bob on the black sea. Spread in front of this financial district is Marina Square – blocks of gold, bathed in orange light, planted in reclaimed land. I could feel the money, the power radiating from the steel blocks, and I knew that if I could just wind down my window, reach out and touch the energy – the power that crackles at my fingertips – the dream-maker, wish-fulfiller – if I could only step into its arms, it would lift me to the top. I never believed that something so man-made, so calculated could make me feel like this. You know, I always thought these feelings of awe could only be created by mountains and snow-covered ponds, by those mighty, natural, works of God. I stared, all goldfish-gaping-like, at the silver towers.

'Uh-oh,' Eugene said.

'What?' I said.

'Um, I think you've got it,' Eugene said.

'Got what?' I said.

'The newbie disease. You always get it if you're a first time expat.' Eugene placed his hand on my forehead, checking my temperature. 'Uh-oh, you do have all the symptoms.'

'What symptoms?'

'First, you get a fever of excitement, like you've just gone boldly where no man has gone before. Everything is interesting because it's *new.*' Eugene described his first trip to England, how he was on a BR train, writing to Mei, describing everything, from the sight of the man reading the *Evening Standard* to the sound of crisps packets crackling open.

'You're just weird,' I told Eugene.

'No! No! Don't you get it? It was because England was new, so everything, even the most minute detail, was fascinating. But once you get used to it, once it becomes *home*, it gets boring. So you move to a new place, get excited about it for a month, then it turns into Boredomville, just like all the other countries you've been in. So you have to move, and start the whole cycle again. That's the expatriate syndrome. Familiarity breeds contempt. A cliché. Sad, but true.'

I didn't believe Eugene. The first week I was in Singapore, I believed I had found Shangri-La. It's amazing how much the weather influences our personalities, our lives, our culture. In Singapore, my whole life changed because the heat and the light enabled me to *go out*. In England, I hardly ever went out unless I absolutely had to. Everyone stayed indoors because of the cold and the rain, the grey. In Singapore, it's hot and bright, so there's street life, everyone and everything is open. I loved the shops at the bottom of my HDB block, they're door-less – they didn't need doors, because there was no cold to shut out. Outside the coffee shop, you would always find two old men, sitting in wicker chairs, with a bird cage on the table. They shouted at each other in Hokkein, while *wayang* blared from their transistor radio. In Fallensham, the streets are deserted after six, but here, after the sun sets, people still walk around chatting, eating or shopping (especially shopping). Boys play *sepak tawak* until midnight, kicking the soccer ball over a badminton net.

CHAPTER 25

Andy

You wake up in the morning. Unbelievable. It's traumatic enough having to wake up in the *morning*, but not only that, you actually wake up one hour before it's absolutely necessary. It's bloody five a.m., and you can't get back to sleep, because the mosque next door is wailing pre-dawn prayers – no words you understand, just a blare that goes 'waaaaaaaahhhhh' – like an alarm clock that you can't shut off. So you wake up in the morning, and stay awake in bed.

This particular morning, you will always remember. It is the week before you got arrested. The birds chirp outside your window, sunlight streams through the Venetian blinds, the school buses' horns honk for the children, a distant cock crows. All around, you feel the city rumbling awake, and you think, 'Yes, Andy, this would be a really good day for you to have a nervous breakdown.'

Things were going great before you got a job. But now Shangri-La has turned to Shit Hotel. You can see the daily grind before you: Start with morning registration. Scream for silence while the prefect reads the bulletin. Collect absence notes, photo money, Fort Canning trip money, orphanage appeal money. Promote the Walk-a-thon in aid of the new gym. After that, you will wrest ear and nose rings from the body of your students, and measure the length of the girls' skirts to ensure that they are of an appropriate length. Your principal believes that the sight of a skirt above knee level would send the boys into a sexual frenzy. Your blood pressure will get dangerously high, and it'll only be half-past seven.

When people ask you what you do, you tell them that you teach literature. It's quite good actually – by now, amazingly, you've reached that self-delusional state where you can say 'I *teach* literature' without laughing. I mean, if you consider forcing students to copy, verbatim, the text from *King Lear* into their brown exercise books, teaching, fine, because that's all you do. You've got no choice. It's the only way you can guarantee that those thickos have actually read the play.

You don't know why you even bother opening your mouth. It's not as if the kids ever *learn* anything. On your first day in class, you said, 'William Shakespeare was born in 1564. Though he was a man, he created complex female characters, like Goneril and Regan, who devour the stage. *King Lear* is a powerful study of order in the individual soul, in society, in the cosmos.' You carry on like that – *mua, mua, mua* (the noise that Charlie Brown's teacher makes) – feeling prouder and prouder of yourself, patting yourself on the back for remembering all that stuff from university. But then you look through their notes, and though you'd been lecturing about Lear for half an hour, all those thickos had written was 'Shakespeare. Born 1564. He was a man.' After that, you just gave up.

This morning, you walk to the sink, and for a half second, you feel (amazingly) fine. You were out getting pissed last night, and you don't have a hangover. You reach the sink, whistle merrily, look in the mirror – looking cool and funky today, then wham! Your head slams down towards the wash basin. Feels like you've been hit by a plank. Ugh. Stealth hangover attack.

You try to aspirin the headache, but it's no use. The pounding gets worse when you remember that you haven't finished marking your books for today's class, and you're already a week behind. You hate homework. You wouldn't give the kids any homework, but the fascist school inspector is coming next week, and unless you produce a pile of two hundred exercise books filled with (marked) assignments, you're going to get fired. Fuck that. You decide to play truant.

You take out a self-help book you bought the other day – *Happiness: Go For It!* It suggests that you make a list of positive statements, a list of things you're good at – talents, gifts, virtues – a self-affirmation list. You take out your pad and pencil, and think and think, but the only stuff you can come up with is:

'1) I have a great memory. I know all the lyrics to the songs in the 'Pretty Woman' (Original Motion Picture Soundtrack) CD. I can remember the team sheets for the Leeds versus Aston Villa Coca Cola Cup Final. I can also remember four out of five of the Metaphysical poets (just their names, not the poems). Not many people know what I know.
2) I have great powers of concentration. If I tune my mind into the right frequency, I can watch TV for ten hours straight. I can watch anything – from *Ultraman* to the Tamil news to Chinese variety shows, even Ma Ma Lemon Liquid ads – without moving my head once. Likewise, I can play Doom non-stop. I can stare at the VDU for five hours, without blinking, while tapping the keyboard at 50 wpm. Not many people can do that.
3) I look really cool when I'm playing the air guitar.
4) I'm taller than Mei. I'm taller than Eugene. I'm taller than most people in Singapore.
5) I am not very ugly. I might even be quite good-looking. In fact, if Rogue from the X-men was real, she would shag me. Maybe.'

You crumple the list.
You have a go at Doom. You pull up the Saved Games

screen. By the time the blood and fire fades away, you see that, for some reason, Mei's name is there. You load up the game to check which pathetic, beginner's level she is stuck at, and horror – she's at 'The Shores of Hell. Mission 25: Limbo'. Unbelievable. You have clocked in over three hundred and twenty-five hours, developed an incredible ability to run over toxic waste and dodge crushing platforms, you, the Doom Maestro, Bane of the Cacodemons, Terror of the Imps, *you* can't get past 'The Shores of Hell. Mission 12: Containment Area', but Mei is all the way up at Mission 25. Impossible. How did that happen? At this moment, all your sexist tendencies erupt. Girls cannot be better than guys at computer games. It's unnatural. You feel like you've just been told that you've been made redundant, because your replacement, a talking amoeba, is far more intelligent and qualified than you. Mei, better than you at Doom? Never. This is your last bastion, the one positive statement you know to be true, and which you are genuinely proud of – 'I am better than Mei at computer games'. It isn't fair. Mei is better than you at everything else. She has a better job, a better car, a better life, better *hair* – why couldn't she let you be better at computer games? Suddenly, a perfectly logical explanation hits you. You whoop for joy. Mei must have cheated. She can't have reached Mission 25 by her own skill and merit. She must have used the cheat code, IDCLEV, to warp to that level. She must have.

You ring her up, and the secretary says that Mei is in a meeting, but you say that this is an emergency.

'You used IDCLEV, didn't you?' you say.

'What?' Mei says.

'You cheated. I mean, I can't even get to "The Refinery". There's no way you could reach "Limbo" without cheating.'

'What are you talking about?'

'Doom. How did you –'

'You called me out of a meeting to talk about a *game?*'

'Did you cheat or not? You have to tell the truth. Did you type in IDCLEV?'

'What are you talking about? Andy, are you ill? Your voice sounds really strange.'

'How did you get to such a high level?'

'I don't know. I was just fiddling around.'

'Fiddling around? Just fiddled around and you got to Mission 25? Unbelievable. Exactly how did you fiddle around?'

'I just ran around and opened some doors – I can't remember exactly. Wait a minute. Why am I even having this conversation? This is insane. I have to go back to my meeting.' Mei puts down the phone.

You go back to playing Doom and after four hours, you are still stuck in the 'Containment Area'.

You return to bed and think of how your life could have been different. If you hadn't screwed up your Oxford interview, you would be working for a merchant bank right now, making ding-dong dillion dollars, sipping Singapore Slings at the pool of your condo, instead of being stuck with a Tiger beer hangover in a HDB flat.

You wake up. It's late afternoon. You start a letter to your parents. It's no use. Never before has anything looked so blank: your life, these words, the paper, this sun-soaked day. Today's like all the other days in Singapore, a day of white death, a day when the sun makes everything white. Outside your window, it's business as usual, but it looks like a funeral scene – white light bounces off the dark glasses of strangers, cars crawl slowly down the street, and the wind makes the palm trees bow down. This is the light of death – bright, blank, pale, empty as the paper before you. When you finally scrawl words on the page, they look like bones, a skeleton, a cage without flesh, without spirit; the black lines, curves, strokes, dots, gaps look like thin charred black bones choking on the dust in your room. A shaft of light filters through the Venetian blinds. Flecks of dust swirl in the white light. You wipe away a cobweb hanging between the two strips of the blind. The soles of your feet are powdered grey with dust. A tiny black thread clings to the ball of your right foot. You look at the blind, your finger, your feet, and do nothing.

You wake up, you go to work, you come home, you watch TV, you go to sleep. Rewind and repeat. Why the hell did you travel thousands of miles just to do exactly what you would be doing in England? Eugene is right. Wherever you go, it's going to be the same. You can't escape from the fact that human beings are consigned to the routine of wake-work-TV-sleep. Okay, maybe if you moved to another country, the customs would be different, small details like which side of the street you drive on, whether you have to take off your shoes when you enter someone's house, whether you use cutlery or chopsticks or your hands to eat, but after all that you still have to shower, do your laundry, post your mail. You still have to go to work to earn your bread (or rice or pasta). Even in the set-up of any place in any country, it's basically your residence with a row of shops – the chemist, the supermarket, and the bank. In Fallensham, it was Boots, the Co-op, and NatWest, while in Singapore it's the Guardian Pharmacy, NTUC and the POSB. Same things, different names. *Ennui* by any other name is still *ennui* – in France you do *ennui* in cafés, drinking that profound espresso, and in Singapore you do it watching crap Canadian productions like *Forever Knight* at one in the morning, alone in your HDB flat.

You don't want to stay in Singapore, but you don't want to return to England. You thought things would be better once you escaped from England. You believed if you went to a place that was as far away and as different as possible from England, that somehow things would be better, that you'd find something worth living for. But now you've done that, and you still haven't found, as U2 would say, what you're looking for. You are the living fulfilment of a bad rock anthem.

Maybe the city would cheer you up. You remember the buzz you got when you first saw the skyscrapered skyline. So you take the MRT down to Orchard Road.

It's no use. Eugene was right. You see the labyrinth of shopping malls and office towers, and you just want to nuke it. A city is a city is a city. Though the locals and the tour guides try to tell you differently, cities are basically the same around the world. Singapore, like all cities, has shops, banks, malls, skyscrapers, cinemas, trees, and a McDonalds or Pizza Hut every five hundred metres. Drifting past the black, white and grey blocks, nobody speaks to you and you speak to no one. You sink into the anonymity, blend into the sameness, become just another city dweller. In the heat of the day, you hide in the shade of the five foot ways. Any traces you leave behind will be swept away in the morning; the place where you left your prints will return to its original state, clean and green. Did anyone see you that day? Standing outside the bank/mall/cinema by the traffic lights, while the trucks, cars, and buses boiled cyclones behind them. Did anyone catch a glimpse of you? Did they notice that fleeting image at the blurred edge of their consciousness, a ghost fading in and out of the mirrored walls, a momentary reflection in the black shiny exterior of the city of glass? Perhaps someone saw you, but then the sun flared, the rays gleamed off the glass, dazzling them, and when they opened their eyes, the reflection had disappeared. They'd wonder if they really saw you, or if it was just a trick of the light?

You don't know what to do. Wherever you go, whatever you do, you are nothing.

*

It's night and it's raining. The water sweeps down in grey sheets, dark needles crashing in black blocks, rain so heavy it rolls off the rims of umbrellas like a waterfall, splattering the user still clinging pathetically on to the metal handle. The rain slams against windows, waking work-wearied couples from their sleep.

You go to the beach at East Coast Park. You watch the rain rust the deserted barbecue pits. The sea roars, wails, moans. Above the babel of the waves, you hear a voice floating above the chaotic tongues, a gentle spray, a siren song calling you into the water that pours from above, and swells from beneath. A wave rises like a wall of dark steel, stretches out, then crashes down, shattering the smooth surface. Maybe you should walk into the sea, let the water fill your mouth, nose, ears. Filled with the black water, no longer at ease with an alien world clutching their old idols, you should be glad of death.

CHAPTER 26

Andy

I'm embarrassed to admit it, but I'm really a lapsed atheist. You know people who claim to be Catholics, but don't practise? Well, I'm a non-practising atheist. I don't believe in God, but I can't help acting like I do. I know that God doesn't exist, but sometimes I'm walking down the street, the sky burns red, and I suddenly go – 'God, it's beautiful. You're amazing' – totally involuntarily. Then I have to quickly remind myself that God doesn't exist. The sunset is just nice weather. It doesn't have any divine transcendence.

I also try to completely avoid Christians, because most of them are so uncool. Their cringe factor is unbelievable. At university, you could easily spot the Christian: the girls looked as if they'd never experienced any vaginal penetration, the guys always carried guitar cases, and they all lived in rooms filled with posters of Bible verses, soft-focus rainbows, and fluffy kittens. But I have to admit I actually liked some of them. Sometimes, my more 'with-it' friends would spot me sitting in Americana with some Christian Union bird, and that's really dangerous, because if people think that you're a member of the celibate CU set, you'll never pull. So whenever any of my mates say that they saw me standing outside a church, I quickly do some lad stuff, 'I only went there to see if there were any girls I could "break in"'. Churches are great, they're like the original Virgin Megastore.' But worst of all, even though I don't believe in God, whenever I'm in trouble, I start praying. I don't know why. It just happens.

It happened again on the beach that night. I lay on the wet sand, crying for help. I prayed hard for God, but hoped just as hard that God wouldn't come, because if He really existed, what with the life I've lived – shit – I'd be in big trouble. If I converted, I'd have to stop gambling and drinking. I might even have to start flossing.

While I was praying, for some reason, I remembered a conversation I'd had with Mei a few weeks before. She had brought me to Haw Par Villa, a.k.a. the Tiger Balm Gardens. (Founded by a herbal doctor, Aw Chu Kin, the park was scattered with ads proclaiming the miraculous, cure-all qualities of Tiger Balm lotion.) Haw Par Villa is one weird place. It's like a Chinese religious theme park, a Confucian Madame Tussauds. We queued up for an hour to get on the Wrath of the Water Gods roller-coaster ride, took a tour of a dragon's mouth during our Tales of China Boat Ride. Every exhibit was didactic. All around you were examples of good being rewarded, and evil punished. 'Haw Par Villa is like a microcosm of Singapore,' Mei said. 'It's a simulated, totalitarian utopia. Like Disney World with a moral.'

We arrived at the Ten Courts of Hell. Concrete and wire sculptures depicted various gruesome tortures, all of it designed with loving attention to blood and internal organs. The artist also had a particular predilection for spilt intestines. To my left, a demon cleavered a food thief in half, soaking the wooden chopping board in blood. To my right, a green ghoul fried a man to death, a self-righteous smirk on his face, convinced that the victim was merely getting his just desserts.

Mei told me her grandfather first brought her here when she was six. Unbelievable. There are many things I don't understand about Singapore. The government won't let kids watch violent R(A) movies until they're twenty-one, but they'll happily allow parents to bring their toddlers to see a blue demon ripping out a man's kidneys. I don't know about you, but I find this rather strange, and more than just slightly disturbing.

'What are you supposed to do to avoid something like this?' I asked.

'That's the problem, people always want to know what to *do*,' Mei said. 'The most common question people ask when they first meet someone is – "What do you do?" as if our identity is defined by our activities. We think that as long as we *do* something, as long as we go some place, as long as we keep in motion, things will get better. Though we're unhappy, if only we could get a better job, get married, have children, wear nicer clothes, have a better haircut, take up a new hobby, meet new people – things will improve. If only we could afford to buy a dishwasher, and a car with power steering, air bags and auto gears – then our lives will be less hassle. If only we exercised more, reduced our body fat, toned our muscles, increased our flexibility – what we'd lose in weight, we'd gain in self-esteem. If only we didn't have Chairman Mao for a boss, if only we could get better grades, close that deal, win that account, break that world record, lift that trophy, appear on TV, then we'd have it made, we'd have done something with our lives.'

'You're talking about me, aren't you?' I said.

'No, not just you. Me and Eugene too. When we were kids, we all thought – whether it was Singapore or Holland or England – we were stuck in a dead-end place. We couldn't wait to get out, we all thought that if we travelled somewhere else, things would improve. There's excitement over the other side of the mountain, the horizon over the next hill blazes red and glorious. The grass is greener on the other side. That's why I was so angry with my parents for not letting me go to England. But then I talked to Eugene, and saw how unhappy he was. Even though he's lived in so many places, he's still miserable. I realized that being bored had nothing to do with Singapore, it had to do with *me*. If your life has no meaning, then no matter where you go, you won't find what you're looking for. You can change places, change environments, but you'll still feel shit, because *you* haven't changed. We're all looking for something on the outside. But the problem is with us, with the fact that inside, we're dead. We drift, like disembodied spirits, empty, wandering the famished road, desperate for someone to feed us, searching for something to give us life. We're all hungry ghosts.'

'But what can we do?'

'We're going to keep on wandering until we have God,' Mei said. 'That's what I always tell Eugene – God made us, and our hearts are restless until they rest in him. God is our ultimate reward. He doesn't give peace, he *is* our peace. He doesn't give power, he *is* our power. He loves us so much, he doesn't just want to *give* us everything, he wants to *be* our everything. He doesn't give joy or wealth or glory or power or freedom, he is all these things himself. He gives himself to us.'

'How did you find God?'

Mei told me about what happened to her while she was under the table at her grandfather's funeral. 'I know it's difficult to believe. How do you describe meeting God? Unless you've actually experienced it, it's difficult to believe that it can happen, because there's nothing else in the world like it.'

I told Mei about what had happened to me by the river back in Fallensham. 'If I really saw God, why don't I have the cup? Why don't I have any proof that it was really God I saw, proof that it wasn't just some accident? Why do I only have these scars on my thighs?'

'My Uncle Cheong told me a story once,' Mei said. Once

upon a time, there was a humble fisherman called Ahmad. He lived on the tiny island of Temasek, a long time ago, many, many years before Raffles turned this quiet fishing village into the busy port that we now call Singapore. One sunny morning, Ahmad went out to catch some fish, as he did every morning. He cast his net over the emerald waters, but he did not catch anything. Puzzled, he flung his net out again, but again his net came back empty. This worried him, for he knew how his wife, Puan Ahmad, would scold him if he did not bring home any fish. He loved her, but he knew that she had a bad temper, especially if she was hungry. So, with a sigh and a prayer, he threw his net one last time, and to his surprise, this time the net was so heavy he could barely lift it! He huffed, and puffed, until he finally heaved the net into the boat. Only after he saw what was in his boat, did he understand why his catch was so heavy. There, tangled in the middle of the net, was a mermaid!

'Please release me,' the mermaid begged. 'If you will let me go, I will bring you to my Master, the Ruler of the Sea, and He will surely reward you.'

'*Baik lah*,' Ahmad said, for he was a kind man, and not the type who enjoyed trapping mermaids.

The mermaid smiled and held Ahmad's hand. 'Hold your breath,' she said, and with those words she jumped into the sea and dragged Ahmad into the deep.

Ahmad was surprised yet again. He could breathe under water, just like he could in the air! He swam after the mermaid, past the swaying seaweed and the colourful corals. They swam and swam, until they finally arrived at the entrance of a black cave.

The mermaid knocked on the door, and when it opened, Ahmad could hardly keep his eyes open. The light from the cave dazzled him, for it was full of treasures – rubies, sapphires and other precious stones lay scattered, like stray rocks, on the pearl floor. The walls were made of gold, and the bright diamond ceiling shone like a lamp through the liquid air.

The mermaid took Ahmad gently by the hand, and led him to a feast. On the table were jugs of wine, loaves of bread and plates piled high with the fowl of the air and the fishes of the sea.

'Take and eat,' the mermaid said. 'Here is your reward. God is here prepared and dressed, God, in whom are all delights.'

Ahmad smiled, and ate to his heart's content.

After he finished, Ahmad bent down and picked up a pocketful of pearls.

When he returned home, he told his wife everything that happened.

'Why you never bring back any fish?' she said. 'You think you can trick me with that stupid story?'

Ahmad protested his innocence. To prove the truth of his tale, he put his hand into his pocket and pulled out – a pebble. 'But, darling, *sayang*, I really did take some pearls. These *really* were pearls.'

'Hah! I knew you were lying! I know what you've really been up to.' She sniffed his face. 'I can smell it. You've been out drinking and whoring.' She slapped the back of his head.

Ahmad returned to the sea the next day, and cried out again and again for the mermaid. When she finally appeared, Ahmad begged her to take him back to the cave.

She agreed, so Ahmad went to the cave and took three bars of gold to prove to his wife that he was telling the truth.

When he returned home, he said to his wife, 'Come, *sayang*, I show you I wasn't lying. See I got bring back these gold bars.'

He pulled out the gold bars, but they had turned into wooden logs!

'You've been out the whole morning again and again you

never bring home any fish.' She sniffed his face. 'Hah! I knew it. You've been out drinking and whoring.'

So yet once more, Ahmad returned to the ocean and begged the mermaid to bring him back to the cave. This time, when he entered the cave, he scooped many, many rubies into his basket. He swam back to the surface, but when he looked in his basket, he found that the rubies had turned into red rocks!

Ahmad moaned. 'What am I going to do?' he asked the mermaid. 'If I go home like this, my *sayang* will scold me again. How come all the treasure I take from the cave turns into rubbish?'

'You cannot take the things from Heaven to earth,' said the mermaid.

'Why?'

'If you want to enjoy the fruits of the cave, you have to go there yourself. My Master doesn't want people to believe in him because they've seen the gifts you bring. If you could bring the gifts from the cave to them, then they would rely on you and not go to the cave themselves. My Master wants people to believe in him, not because of the gifts you bring, but because they've been there and seen it for themselves. He wants them to come to Him and taste Him for themselves.'

For the first time in my life, I had actually met someone who could explain what had happened to me by the river all those years ago. But I still didn't know if I could commit. 'I don't know. I've been to church and it doesn't do anything for me,' I said. 'I'm just not into all that happy-clappy singing stuff.'

'Of course you're not going to meet God in *church*. Especially if you're just going there for the organ, the stained-glass windows, and the smells and bells. You're not going to find God just by sitting in a pew, and making the right noises at the right times. You need to have a real hunger for God. You need to have a sense of crisis. Jesus is like the rice, the manna, the white flakes that came down from heaven and gave life to the wandering tribes. He's the only thing that can feed us hungry ghosts. You don't eat rice by singing songs, do you? You have to go to Christ as if He is the rice of life. You have to hunger for Him, want to consume Him, meet Him in such a way that you actually eat His flesh, drink His blood. You have to get Him into your body, your blood, digest Him, let Him fill your all.'

In the end, it was embarrassingly simple. I guess that's my problem, I wished the answer was more complicated. I wished the solution lay in some scientific empirical experiment that you do with boiling test tubes and pipettes, some logarithms churned out by computers, or some complex maths formula like $\Sigma\alpha\text{-}\lambda\mu\subseteq(xy+z)^9\cong\Omega$. I wished the answer wasn't just 'Jesus Christ'. I wished it was something that could only be expressed in French or German or Latin, or maybe even a combination of all three, something like 'je ne lait achtung Spiritus Sanctus' – something that sounds really profound. I wanted the Meaning of Life illustrated in the form of a pie chart or a bar graph. The truth sounds so trite and catch-phrasy – 'Jesus Saves', 'God is all you need'. Life is complicated, why should the solution be so simple? If I were God, if I had my way, I'd make the answer so obscure, so incomprehensible that you could only grasp it after fasting under a tamarisk tree for a century or so. It's not fair, I went to university. I spent over a hundred hours in lectures, wrote over twenty essays and a ten-thousand word dissertation, searching for the Answer. Why should the solution be simply, 'Jesus'? All the effort I wasted, writing those papers, when I could be getting pissed instead.

So basically, it was simple. I prayed and it happened. Like a cold, black coal on the altar, I suddenly spurted to life. My soul caught fire, leapt like a spark, flew upwards towards the heavenly desire, towards the fountain flame. I changed. God created a new world in me. Bleeding like dawn on my soul, He touched and healed the cracks, and this deserted temple roared to life. I can't describe what happened exactly. It's like trying to describe the taste of black, the touch of white light. Just imagine what happens when the mouth is struck dumb, and the soul sings. It was exactly like what happened to Mei at her grandfather's funeral. If she hadn't told me what had happened to her, I probably would have just ignored my experience. Meeting God is like seeing a UFO. Your first reaction is to think that it must be a delusion, and you sure as hell don't want to tell anyone about it, in case they think you're barmy. But because I knew it had happened to Mei, it proved that I wasn't a freak. It showed that meeting God wasn't a strange, one-off experience that only happened to the mentally unbalanced.

I can only try to describe what happened to me. I don't know whether or not it proves that God exists, but I do know this: all the things I learnt at university – Nietzsche, New Historicism, post-post-structuralism, the Laffer curve, none of this could actually make someone enter me. That night, on the beach, an external presence possessed me, changed me, swooped into my soul the way the wind cuts through your body. His breath became my breath, His eyes became my eyes, and the world never looked the same. At that moment, the heavens dropped. When it first rained, it felt like hard black bullets, but then as the grains fell from the sky, the droplets looked clear and transparent. It looked like it was raining raw rice.

I don't know if this proves anything. Some people search hard for God, their knees pierce the earth, their eyes, the sky, but they receive no reply. Why? I don't know. For me, I've always been a doubting Thomas. I didn't *want* to believe. Faith is so un-hip. Atheism is much more glamorous. It's got that good old wrist-slitting vibe, that cool, hard, moody, let's throw-myself-off-Kingston-Bridge chic. I mean, if James Dean and Marilyn Monroe had become Christians, pop culture would be *over*. I didn't want to believe, but on the beach, God – damn Him – showed Himself to me so utterly, so completely, I couldn't deny what happened. That's how He dragged me to Himself. So finally, writhing and rolling, kicking and screaming, I fell into this irresistible, irreversible, inevitable faith.

CHAPTER 27

DAY SEVEN: SATURDAY

Mei

'What are you doing here?' I said.

Eugene was sitting in my office chair. 'I came to help Andy. You got anything against Loong so far?'

'No,' I said. 'Loong don't have a police record, and Kwan won't testify. We go to trial on Monday. We're going to lose.'

'Why you can't ask them to make the trial later?'

'Why?'

'So I can get more evidence against Loong.'

'But there's nothing.'

'There is. I've got extra evidence. Things I haven't told you yet.'

'Like what?'

'You promise not to tell anyone? Not Andy, not the police, nobody.'

'You know I can't promise that. I'm Andy's lawyer. I got to use everything I know to defend him.'

'If you don't promise me, I won't tell you anything.'

I didn't say anything for a long time.

'Well?' Eugene said.

'All right, I promise.'

'Go and get your Bible and swear on it.'

'Don't be stupid.'

'You don't get your Bible, I don't tell you.'

I did as he said.

'You got it?'

'Yes, yes, and I have my hand on the Bible and I swear I won't tell anyone what you're going to tell me.'

'Or you'll burn in Hell.'

'Stop being childish. Now what is it?'

'Loong didn't put the book in Andy's flat.'

'How do you know?'

'I know,' Eugene said, 'because I did it.'

My second silence was a lot longer than my first.

'You all right?' Eugene asked.

'I think I am. I don't feel anything. I can't feel my hands, my feet. I'm completely numb. If I wasn't actually hearing myself speaking right now, I'd think I was dead.' After I recovered, I asked, 'How could you frame your best friend?'

'I didn't plant the book to frame Andy. I put it there to frame Loong.'

'I'm sorry, but I fail to see the logic behind planting a book in your best friend's house in order to frame your worst enemy.'

'It seemed like a good idea at that time.'

'Like how?' I should have expected that from Eugene. When we were kids, he was always coming up with elaborate, harebrained schemes, like wearing wigs and false moustaches to trail suspected shoplifters. 'Why you want to frame Loong in the first place?' I said.

'I wanted to see justice done. I just can't get over Charlie's death. Every day I think about it; it's stuck with me. Charlie's death really bothers me.'

'But you didn't even *like* Charlie.'

'I guess he reminded me too much of myself. We both always wanted to be great secret agents. He was exactly like us when we were growing up, playing detectives.'

I guess Eugene was right. Our adventure with the 'murdered'

maid was exactly like Charlie's excursion in the park. Everyone wants to be a hero, everyone wants to catch the crook. Wasn't that why I became a lawyer?

'I keep thinking – if I didn't learn how to be streetwise, how to be bad, Loong could have tricked me. Loong could have killed *me*. You know, that's what gets me – Loong killed Charlie, and no one cares. Someone got to get justice for Charlie. I didn't want the same to happen to me – if someone murdered me, I'd like to think that, somewhere out there, someone would fight, someone would do everything he could to bring the murderer to justice.'

'But why you want to frame Loong? Surely there are other ways of getting justice. Why didn't you – I don't know – hire some people to beat him up? Or maybe think of some way to poison him? Or make some "accident" happen to him? I'm not saying that you should have done any of that. Only that something like that would have been a lot easier to pull off.'

'No. I want Loong in prison. I want him to be publicly humiliated. I want everyone to see him as he really is, a criminal. I want to wake up in the morning and read the headlines – "Oxbridge Graduate Given Life Imprisonment". That would teach everyone. Sending Loong to jail is the only way I can destroy the myth: everyone thinks that as long as you get good grades, you must be a good person. If Loong went to jail, that would wake the nation. That would destroy their ground once and for all.'

'So how did you plan to frame Loong?' I said.

'Loong placed bets regularly at the flat, but he never wrote anything down. Everything was word of mouth. I could only get Loong if there was written evidence against him, written proof.'

'So you typed all the things in the book?'

'Yes. I listed all the bets that took place in the flat. Now all

I had to do was connect Loong with this incriminating book.'

'How did you try to do that?'

'You know Loong has these really ugly notebooks? He's been trying desperately for months to give them away. He popped one of those things in a bag and gave it to me. When I got home, I realized that I hadn't touched the notebook. Loong put the notebook straight into the plastic bag and gave it to me. The books had Loong's prints! So I got a pair of gloves, took the notebook from the bag, and started typing the bets into the book. It was perfect – I had this book full of bets, a book that's absolutely covered with Loong's fingerprints.'

'But why did you plant it in Andy's flat?'

'There was no other place I could plant 't. Loong knows that I think he killed Charlie. He doesn't trust me. My parents bring me to visit Loong and his parents quite often, but whenever I'm at his house, he always keeps a close eye on me. There's no way I could have planted the book in his house without him noticing.'

'But got no other place, besides Andy's flat, where Loong and the bookies meet?'

'No.'

'So Andy's flat was the only place.'

'Now Andy runs the betting every Saturday night, right? Loong always attends – he's addicted, just like the other bookies. On that Saturday night, I called the police. I told them about the betting house, how it's run by this Chinese guy called Loong, and I even described how Loong looked like. I told the police they would find a book with bets that belonged to Loong, hidden in the toilet.'

'You were the one who told the police that the flat belonged to Loong's parents.'

'That's the beauty of it. You've got all the bookies in the flat, and if the police tried to pin it on Andy, Andy could simply say that the flat really belonged to Loong, and not him, because it was registered in Loong's parents' name. I told the police about the real owners to protect Andy. The police don't know that Andy is renting the flat from Loong's parents. So when I phoned the police, I told them that the flat really belonged to Loong.'

'Only problem – when the police raided the flat, Loong wasn't there.'

'I mean, I planned it all so carefully. I even checked the fixture for that Saturday night – Newcastle versus Man United – the championship match decider. I knew, for sure, that Andy was going to have the bookies round to bet, and Loong would be there.'

'But Andy called off the betting house.'

'How was I to know that he was suddenly going to find Jesus? Who plans for something like that? I had everyone figured out – Loong, Andy, the punters. I thought through every angle, then Jesus decides to *kaypoh* and mess everything up. It's not my fault.'

I saw how things got worse from there. 'The police raid the flat, Andy's the only one there, so he's the only one who gets arrested. And since he is the only one in the flat, the police presume that the book must be his.'

'The police don't even bother to dust the book for prints,' Eugene said.

'When Andy is questioned at the police station, the police give him the book to look at the bets, so now Andy's prints are all over the book as well.'

'You got to help me. I got to plant some evidence against Loong. He doesn't trust me, so I can't do anything. But he's not wary of you like he's wary of me.' Eugene gave me a Filofax. It looked exactly like the one that got Andy arrested. 'Now if you go to Loong's house, put this in his toilet . . .'

'Forget it.'

'Why? You got a better plan?'

I didn't say anything for a while. I couldn't think of a better plan. But then, at that moment, I was so shocked that I couldn't think of *anything*, period. Finally, I said, 'You can't just make up evidence. You can't fight evil with evil. You'll only end up becoming what you set out to destroy.'

'Look, I know you believe in God. I know you think vengeance is God's prerogative. But I don't. I believe that we only have one shot in life, one shot at justice, and if we want to do something, we have to do it *now*. You can't do anything once you're dead.'

'But you can't go around framing people. It's illegal.'

'So what? In the end, if the bad guy gets caught, everyone's happy.'

'It's just wrong.'

'The police do it all the time, what. They call it sting operations. Don't you ever watch TV? Why can't I do what they do?'

'Ding-dong, alarm call for Eugene. Time to wake up to reality. You think it's so easy to frame Loong? This kind of thing only works on TV. In real life, you try and frame someone, it'll just blow up in your face.'

'You're wrong. This works in real life.'

'Since when? Since when have any of your dreamland, airy-fairy, cuckoo ideas ever worked?'

'Since Marissa.'

'Who?'

'Mrs Lam's maid. You remember her murderer, Tom?'

'Yes.'

'Remember what happened when the police raided his flat?'

'They found Marissa's stuff in his cupboard. Her wallet and jewellery.'

'I put it there.'

'What? How?'

'I pulled the Scouts scam. Got in my uniform, went to his flat, asked if he wanted his windows washed. Then I dropped Marissa's stuff in his cupboard.'

'You framed him? The guy got the death penalty!'

'He confessed.'

'They hanged him. What if he was innocent?'

'But he wasn't. If I didn't put the stuff in his cupboard, you think he would have confessed? No. Without me, he'd still be free. He might have killed more maids.'

'I always thought you were stupid, but I was wrong,' I said. 'You're just insane.'

'You're the stupid one. Can't you see? Loong is just like Tom. All you got to do is plant the book in his toilet, call the police and bam! Loong will confess to everything. Just like Tom. Why won't you help me?'

'Because it's wrong. Illegal. Evil. Don't you get the concept?'

'Ugh. "Framing" – that's such an ugly word. I . . . I think of it as – oiling the wheels of justice.'

'Eugene, go to a police station, or a mental hospital. Tell them what you've done. They know what to do with people like you.'

'You know what your problem is? You don't care about victims. To you, Marissa was just a maid, just a domestic appliance.'

'That's not true.'

'What about your maid at home? Why do you make her eat in the kitchen? Why can't she join you at the dining table? Whenever she watches TV, she always peeks from behind the corner of the door, hoping that you won't notice her. She's human, she's not a machine, she's just like us.'

'I know.'

'No you don't. Remember that Eskinol bottle?'

'What about it?'

'I asked myself – why would Marissa want to make her skin whiter? Then I realized for the first time that Marissa was just like us, she wanted to make her skin white, to be blonde and beautiful. It got me thinking. The song she wrote – did Marissa dream of becoming a singer superstar, getting out, going all the way to the Star-Search Olympics? We were all the same, all stuck in a dead-end, sick of our boring roles in real life, wanting to be somebody else, somebody rich, famous, powerful, white. The guy who killed her – he didn't just kill a maid, he killed someone like us.'

'Your problem is that you identify too much with victims. You treat every crime like it was an attack on you.'

'Is it my fault that I've got empathy and you don't? That I can walk in the moccasins of another man, and you can't?'

'Spare me that pop psychology shit. You're the product of too much therapy.'

'I knew I shouldn't have told you this. I knew you would have problems with it. Why do you think I left it until so late to tell you? But what else could I do? If you don't plant the book in Loong's house, Andy's going to stay in jail. It's the only thing that can save him.'

I shook my head.

'I don't understand you. You're a lawyer but you don't care about justice.'

'What do you mean?'

'You've never cared about justice. When Marissa died, you didn't want to investigate her death. You didn't care who the murderer was. *I* was the only one who cared. Now I'm telling you how you can save Andy, and you don't want to do it. Why?'

'Don't you lecture me about justice. You know how we can get justice? Very easy.'

'How?'

'Why don't you turn yourself in?'

'What?'

'Go to the police. Tell them you planted the book.'

'I can't.'

'Why not?'

Eugene didn't say anything.

'Why? You afraid of jail? You – Big Mr Justice guy? Don't preach to me about justice. When I asked you to help bail Andy, why you didn't do it?'

Eugene didn't say anything.

'You were scared, right? Scared Andy would jump bail – lose you a lot of money. You say you want justice, but not if it means having to go to jail. You only want justice if it's free. You only want justice if it costs you nothing.'

I picked up the phone and called the Gambling Suppression Branch. 'Why don't you talk to Inspector Koh?' I said to Eugene.

'You going to turn me in?' he asked.

'I have to.'

'You can't.'

'Why not?'

'You promised not to tell anyone. You swore. On the Bible.'

He was right. I put down the phone. I'd made a promise, and I had to keep it, no matter what it cost. Even if it meant that Andy went to jail, and Loong walked free, I had made a vow of silence, and I had to keep it.

Eugene got up and left.

I let Eugene go, because I couldn't condemn him. Can anyone? Everyone agrees that justice is a good thing. But what price, justice? You see apartheid, prisoners of conscience, political hostages, and it's easy enough to pay your subscription to

Amnesty and sign the occasional petition, but would you go to jail for any of those things? What would I have done if I were Eugene? Would I go to jail for Andy? I don't know. If I'm ever faced with such a dilemma, I hope, by God's grace, that I will keep my promises, do my duty and make the right choice. But nowadays, you can hardly expect anyone to sacrifice everything for a mere principle. And why should we? We're just ordinary people. Like Eugene, we're just normal.

CHAPTER 28

DAY SEVEN: SATURDAY

Andy

'So how are we going to win this?' I asked Mei.

'I don't know,' she said.

'What are you going to ask Loong?' I was relying on Mei to come up with some brilliant cross-examination tactics.

'I don't think we should call Loong as a witness.'

'Why not? Isn't that going to be our key argument? That Loong framed me?'

'I don't think we should pursue that line of argument.'

'Why not?'

'It won't work.'

I threw up my hands. 'Why are you doing this to me? Why won't you fight for me? You're supposed to be my lawyer. You're supposed to *defend* me. But all you've done is try to get me to give up.'

'I've done everything I could. I've talked to Kwan, to Loong, looked up clippings, chased down warrants. What else do you want me to do?'

'Fight. I want you to fight. You never believed we could win this case. Ever since I got arrested, you just kept telling me to give up. When I wanted to get bail, you said I couldn't. When I wanted to claim trial, you told me to plead guilty.'

'I never told you to plead guilty. I just told you what your options were.'

'Yeah, but you were being such a big doom merchant, of course you scared me into pleading guilty. You always advised me to give up. Well I won't. Now I want you to put Loong on the stand and do whatever it takes to get him to say that he framed me.'

'I can't. I won't succeed.'

'Why not?'

'I'm just a lawyer. I don't do miracles.'

'Look. You believe I'm innocent?'

'Yes.'

'And that Loong is guilty?'

'Yes.'

'So why don't you believe that we can win? Why won't you even *try*? Why do you think we're doomed to failure?'

'Because I've seen it happen many times before.'

'What?'

She was silent for such a long time, I thought she wasn't going to answer me. But then she said, 'Bad people do bad things to good people. No one knows about this, not the police, nobody. And even if they did know about it, they can do nothing. The good suffer, while the bad go on to live happy lives. End of story.'

'What are you talking about?'

Mei told me about what happened to her at Red Hill.

CHAPTER 29

Mei

From the balcony of our flat, I could see 'Bukit Merah', which is Malay for 'Red Hill'. On any other night, the hill's silhouette rested like a black hump against the grey sky. But on that Mid-autumn night, over twenty years ago, the full moon lit up the hill. That night, as the white moonlight powdered the red soil, I understood for the first time why Singaporeans called it the Hill of Blood.

The Mid-autumn Festival was the time to remember Chang-E. The gentle wisp of black that floats against the moon's smooth canvas – that is Chang-E, the maiden of the moon. 'Once upon a time, got a bad Emperor called Hou Yi. He go and steal magic drink from the Queen of Heaven. Chang-E, his wife, was afraid that if Hou Yi drink the potion and live for ever, the people suffer a lot. So she go and steal the potion. She drank the potion, and *ta-dah* . . . she floated to the moon. Look, look she's there!' My father waved his finger at the moon.

My father had a bald head that was different from any I had ever seen on TV – it wasn't polished, clean or shiny (cf Kojak and Yul Brynner). Instead, it looked rather flabby. He looked like a walking buttock. He was dark, his dry skin permanently browned by the tropical sun. He wore the standard outfit for salesmen in Singapore – dark blue trousers and a light, plain, white long-sleeved shirt. My father always wore a singlet because he was afraid that people might see the nipples beneath his translucent shirt.

I never liked my father. My first memories of him were of the way he waddled towards me, his hands waving suggestively. He would taunt me, taking two steps forwards, two steps back, then flicking his fingertips at my cheek. I disliked those bulging eyes, but most of all, his moustache. It wasn't even really a moustache, just six thin hairs that strayed from his upper lip. As he puckered his lips, making kissing noises, the six strands of hair quivered.

Every Mid-autumn Festival, my parents would throw a 'moon appreciation' party, where they would eat mooncakes and pomelos, and light lanterns. That particular Mid-autumn Festival, when I was five, my father showered me with more gifts than usual. There was a deluge of food – four red boxes of mooncakes, and ten pomelos. The gifts came in even numbers, because the Chinese believed that it was good luck for gifts to come in pairs. The mooncakes were round pastries with a soft golden biscuit shell. Each mooncake that my father bought had a different filling – some had plain red-bean paste, but most had interesting variations, for example, red-bean paste with salted duck egg-yolks, dark bean paste with lotus seeds, custard paste with sunflower seeds.

'*Wah*, this mooncake inside even got durian. So expensive. See I so good to you, always buy you presents,' my father said. He winked at me.

I lowered my head. 'Thank you,' I whispered.

This gave my father an excuse to stroke my face and say, 'You so polite. Eat mooncake, don't shy. You so pretty. That's why we called you Mei, you so pretty.

'Why you cry for?' my father asked me. He peeled two pomelos. 'I want you to *have* everything.' The Cantonese name for pomelo was *yow*, which had the same meaning as 'have'. 'I also got a special present for you.'

It was a huge red lantern.

'This is the best in the shop,' he told me. 'The most expensive one. Only the best for my prettiest girl.' He stroked my face. 'Come, take picture, stand behind the lantern.' He shot some photos. I started to move away, but he said, 'Take more pictures, film is cheap, film is cheap. You look so beautiful tonight.' He snapped five more shots.

'Come, we go outside,' he said. 'I take you for a walk with your lantern.'

My mother wanted to come along too, but my father said, 'Ah, this type of thing, play lantern, only children do. You want to come along for what? I accompany her good enough already.'

Downstairs, the children ran with their lanterns but my father took me firmly by the hand and led me away from the others. 'Here so dangerous,' he said. 'Maybe they try and burn your lantern.'

If you were carrying a candle lantern, you were susceptible to attacks from children who would try to extinguish your flame by shooting pellets from their home-made blowpipes. The pellets would smash the lantern to the ground, and the children would cry '*kwei tu-tu*' as the lantern burnt, and the victim cried.

'I bring you to Red Hill,' my father said. 'There no children. Much safer.'

There was no other hill like Bukit Merah. It was red deep down, red soaked every grain, steeped every pore. Scrape the earth's crust, and you will find no grey rocks, green grass or brown weeds. You will find nothing, but red dust.

The car rumbled up the hill, boiling a fog behind it. Every moving thing created a crimson cloud of dirt; the dust took its

246

time settling down. My father walked out of the car, up the path, and lifted the cloud as high as his waist; I ran up the hill, my flip-flops snapping against the ground, and the cloud rose above my head.

The moonlight fell like chalk dust, and it mingled with the rusty cloud. The air was red and white powder.

'See here so quiet,' he said. 'Got so much space to run around.'

'I want to go home,' I said.

'Go home *lov*. But if you not careful, you walk off by yourself, after that you sink in the blood.'

My father told me the story of Red Hill:

Many years ago, the sea was infested with swordfish. They killed the fishermen, so the people on the island had no food. Whenever the Sultan sent his soldiers to attack the swordfish, they would pierce his men to death. One day, a little boy called Abdul said that he had a plan to destroy the swordfish. Abdul told the Sultan to line the seashore with banana stems. That night, when the swordfish rose to attack, their 'swords' were stuck in the banana stems. The soldiers easily killed the swordfish.

Abdul became the national hero, and this made the Sultan jealous. He sent four soldiers to this Hill, where Abdul lived. The soldiers sneaked into the attap house, and stabbed Abdul in his sleep. Blood gushed from the boy's throat, chest, stomach – it flowed like a river, and the soldiers tried to run away but the flood of blood was so great it drowned them. The hill flowed with blood for days, until all the soil was soaked red.

'That is why they call this place Red Hill,' my father said. 'At night, if you not careful, you try to run away by yourself, suddenly the soil become blood, and you will sink in the blood and drown.'

He pressed his body against mine, nailing me to the tree.

I tried to push my hands out but they were cold, frozen in mid-air. Then my mouth was filled with something wet, and it dribbled down my chest. I rubbed my hands against my chest to dry it, but it was no use, now my hands were wet too. My mouth, chest, hands, all dripping.

I used all the prayers I knew, prayers my Uncle Cheong taught me, flashes of what he sang to me when he closed my eyes to sleep, I didn't understand all he said but I used all the words that I found in my memory — *Father in Heaven hallowed be Thy name Jesus loves me this I know 'cos the Bible tells me so Your will be done forgive our transgressions as we forgive those who transgress against us maranatha for Thine is the kingdom and power and I am weak but He is strong yes Jesus loves me yes Jesus loves me as I lay me down to sleep I pray the Lord my soul to keep little ones to Him belong I am weak but He is strong maranatha lay me down to sleep Lord my soul to keep amen for Thine is the power and the glory now and forever in Jesus' name amen amen maranatha.*

After the prayer, I didn't feel what was happening to me. *The peace of God, which passeth all understanding.* Instead, I remembered. The two pomelos I ate earlier. Two was a lucky number. When I bit into the pomelo, the juice squirted in my mouth. Then I lit the lantern, the lantern that was still lit, now lying on the grass. The flame danced behind its red paper wall. The wind blew the flame, swerved it from side to side, bent it more and more each time. The flame vanished.

The previous time I was at Red Hill, we had played 'zero-point' — my friends held a rope made of looped rubber bands high above my head. I sprang, twisted my legs to hook the rope down but my feet got tangled in the bands and I slopped on to the mud. I rubbed at the stains on my frock, but the red spots wouldn't go away. When I returned home, my mother saw the soiled dress and raised her hand to smack me, but I lied, 'This boy, he anyhow push me I fell, cut myself,' transforming the mud into blood. Instantly, the lioness turned to jelly, quivering with concern, for the dried brown mud stains did look like spots of blood. My feet dangled in the air as my mother lifted me and shoved my head between those mountainous maternal breasts. 'I'll brew some ginseng tea,' my mother said. 'I'll make some black chicken, red date soup ... everything will be okay.' For this was Singapore, where there was no problem that a good medicinal meal couldn't solve.

Tonight, all would have been dark but for the moon. On previous nights, the moon hung above me, dirty yellow, like old cheese; tonight it bloomed to life, blazed like burning magnesium. It lit what was hidden on other nights, like the pale blue flowers emerging out of the damp wood in the roofs below.

The moon was like the one in *ET*. When I watched the movie, I didn't marvel at the boy cycling in the sky, rather, I gaped at the moon. Never had I seen anything so big, so bright. But my mother told me it was fake – they did some tricks with cameras and cardboard and blue screens, that the moon could never look like that in real life. But on this night, it did.

After the movie, my mother bought me a balloon, but on the way out, pushing through the crowd, a man bumped into her and jarred the balloon out of her grasp. The balloon floated to –? I always wondered where the balloons went after I lost them.

So I prayed, and God lifted me to the moon, to build a haven for lost balloons.

At the moon palace, I held Chang-E's hand, and watched what was happening to me below. My frock was dirty. I didn't know where the soil began, and the blood ended.

CHAPTER 30

DAY SEVEN: SATURDAY

Andy

After Mei told me about what happened to her at Red Hill, she said, 'Sometimes you can fight and win. Sometimes there's nothing you can do. You just have to leave it in God's hands.'

I shook my head. 'Okay, maybe I'll lose. Maybe I'll go to jail. But I won't give up. I'll get Loong in the end.'

I wanted to do a Schwarzenegger, storm through the streets with my Uzi with an endless supply of macho one-liners, find Loong, and make him dance with bullets. 'I don't know how, but when I get out, I'll find the man who put me in jail.' (Like Robert de Niro on *Cape Fear.*) 'Once I dig up enough evidence against him, I'll go after him. He'll have to spend the rest of his life on the run.' (Like Harrison Ford in *The Fugitive.*) I don't know why this happened. I was having this conversation and all these movie references kept popping into my brain. I couldn't control it and I don't know why. It was bloody strange and disconcerting. 'I'll chase him day after day, week after week, month after month, year after year . . . semester after semester. No matter how far he goes, no matter how high the mountain, how deep the valley, I will find him, you just wait, I will find him.' At this stage I shut up because I realized that I'd started quoting Daniel Day Lewis in *The Last of the Mohicans* and George Michael and Aretha Franklin's 'I knew you were waiting for me'.

My brain was definitely out of synch with my tongue, and

well plugged into my rectum. I had no words of my own, everything was derivative. I had never been in this state of affairs before – stuck in a Far Eastern jail for a crime I didn't commit. This scenario only happened in the movies, and before I knew it, I was spewing out all these cinematic clichés. What do you say if you're a normal person trapped in a movie-esque scenario? Under stress, you're in no position to think up any original lines, so you just start repeating things you've heard people say on TV.

I was inarticulate with rage. I just started spitting out the stuff I'd like to do to the guy who set me up, nothing made sense. Words clumped into my head, sent bolts to my brain, I couldn't think, couldn't form a coherent sentence, I could just spit the words out as the red mist descended and the words flashed before my eyes.

Mei just stared at me until I stopped foaming at the mouth. 'Have you finished?'

I nodded.

'If you want to express your indignation, fine. It's just that I expected something more original and cutting, maybe a Dorothy Parkerish rapier-sharp retort, from someone with a BA (Hons) in English. I hope your Local Education Authority doesn't find out about this, or they'll be ringing up your university, asking for a refund.'

'Why don't you stop making fun of me and help me for once? I'm stuck in here. You're the only one who can help me.'

'How?'

'Find more evidence against Loong.'

'But what if there's no evidence?'

'If you look hard enough, look long enough, you'll find something. I know you will.'

'I don't know.'

'You can't just give up.'

'It's not that. Why do you want to get Loong? Maybe he didn't do it.'

'If not him, then who?'

'Just don't get fixated on Loong. You don't want to go after the wrong man.'

'But it's him isn't it? Everything points to him. Who else could have done it?'

Mei pursed her lips.

'You think somebody else did it? Who?'

Mei didn't say anything.

'You know, don't you?' It hit me and I dropped back in my chair. 'You know and you won't tell me.'

'I *can't* tell you.'

'Why not? I'm going to jail and you can't tell me?'

'Forget it. Forget I said anything.'

'Why won't you tell me? Who are you trying to protect?'

Her silence was killing me. I stared at her, waiting for an answer, but she just sat there. Then I got it.

'You're in it with Loong, aren't you?' I said.

She jerked her head.

How could I be so stupid? Why didn't I see it before? 'You didn't get bail for me,' I said. 'You got me to plead guilty. You messed up my mitigation. All this time you've been trying to get me in jail.'

'I'll pretend I didn't hear that. I'll pretend that you've been under a lot of stress lately. Something –' She snapped her fingers. 'You can't be held responsible for this sudden insanity.'

'Then tell me I'm wrong. Tell me what really happened. Who framed me?'

She shook her head.

'What will happen if you tell me? You'll lose your job?'

'No.'

'Your life will be in danger? He'll kill you?'

'No.'

'So why can't you tell me?'

'I promised not to.'

'What? You mean, some kind of client-attorney privilege crap?'

'No.'

'You mean, it's just a promise?'

'Just my word.'

'I don't believe this.'

'You don't understand. I have to keep my word, no matter what it costs. It's a matter of principle. It's a Christian thing.'

'You expect me to believe you? You think I'm stupid?' I tapped the side of my head. 'How much did he pay you? Was it worth it?'

Her silence was killing me.

'I don't know how much you're getting, but you're worth every cent,' I said. 'You were great. Every time I talked to you, you just sucked all the life out of me. You never actually told me to give up, you just told me to – leave it to God. Very cunning.' I clapped my hands. 'And that rape story. It was a nice touch, very moving. Tell me this – did you rehearse it, or did you just make it up as you went along?'

Mei looked at me all business-like. 'Do you still want me to represent you?' she said in a neutral, telephone-operator voice.

'No.'

She snapped her briefcase shut. It sounded ten times louder than her voice. 'Your trial is on Monday. How are you going to find another lawyer in less than two days?'

'I can defend myself.'

'You sure?' She looked like a statue.

'At least I won't stab me in the back,' I said.

When she left, she didn't even slam the door.

CHAPTER 31

DAY SEVEN: SATURDAY

Mei

The Courts are opposite Peoples' Park. Music spilled out of the shopping complex into the streets, heavy metal competing with Cantopop; the different record shops played their own tunes at full blast, trying to drown each other out, pitting the ballads of Leslie Cheung against the guitar riffs of Bon Jovi.

It was a familiar scene, a real touristy area. The only people that wear hats in Singapore are tourists, and there were a lot of hats around that night. A German, in his giant bermudas and oversized sandals, moved from one Indian money changer to the other, comparing rates. Japanese women milled around, fully equipped with their Nikon cameras, Sony camcorders, Chanel handbags, as well as umbrellas to protect their electronic equipment from the rain. Some other *ang mos* sat in the Sports Station, their hairy legs surrounded by blue shoe boxes, trying to decide between a pair of red-and-black Nike Air Jordans and a blue-and-white Reebok cross trainer. White tissue paper littered the carpet. A group of five monks stood outside Hwa Wah Watch Shop, pressing their forefingers against the glass window at the gold Rolexes and chattering in Thai. With grey shaven heads and saffron robes, they looked like traditional monks. However, instead of wearing the sandals that you see in Shaolin Temple kung-fu movies, they sported brand new leather Oxfords.

Food was everywhere, of course. There was the ubiquitous McDonalds and KFC, but thankfully, also a few local hawker stores. The hawkers sold all kinds of titbits – prawn dumplings, baked buns, glutinous rice dumplings, and *popiah*. My mother never understands how I can watch the news and eat at the same time. 'You see all those earthquakes,' she would say, 'soldiers shooting people, those children – so skinny – how can you eat?' But disasters never dampen my appetite, they only fuel it.

I got the most calorific dishes possible – roast pork rice, fried kway teow, and fried carrot cake. After I finished, I took out Andy's file. I wiped my oily fingers on his documents, and burped. It felt *so* good.

CHAPTER 32

DAY NINE: MONDAY

Andy

The fluorescent lights curved around the ceiling, filling the
room with white. Looking above me was like looking at the
underside of a UFO. The wall behind the judge's desk was
just as surreal. Brown, with a pair of black metal air-con ducts
that looked like rectangular eyes and a Singapore crest in the
middle that looked like a nose, it looked like some sort of
primitive tribal mask. Everything in the room – walls and tables
– was wooden. The blue fire extinguisher stuck out in this sea
of brown, a rare flash of bright colour. One look, and you
could suss out the seat of power. The judge's desk was four
times the size of everything else in the room. Why that was so
I don't know, considering that the desk had nothing but a
calendar, two files and a green stationery holder. It didn't even
have a hammer.

Everything in Singapore is supposed to be really efficient,
but my trial was supposed to start half an hour before, and no
one was ready yet. Waiting just kills me. I sat in the dock – a
hollow chocolate box – trying to calm my nerves by rereading
the warning to switch off my pager and hand phone. To my
left, two kiddy policemen chattered in Hokkein. Finally, the
secretary, dressed in shocking pink Muslim headgear and blouse,
said, 'Okay, can we start?'

I nodded and smoothed my hair.

'Bangon!' the policeman shouted.

The judge entered and we bowed. As the clerk read out the charges to me, the judge sat there with a look of impatient irritation that suggested he wanted to get this over with as quickly as possible. He carried that look throughout the trial, as if witnesses and evidence were tedious inconveniences that had to be endured before he could deliver his verdict.

'The charges have been read to the accused,' the clerk said.

The judge nodded. With that pained frown and sage face, he looked like Confucius with menstrual cramps.

The prosecution called their first witness, Inspector Koh. After he told the court about the raid, I got the chance to cross-examine him.

'You've been watching my flat for a month?' I said.

'We suspected you were running a common betting house.'

'You suspected, but you had no proof.'

'We saw who went in, and who went out. They were bookies.'

'You saw who went in, and out, but did you ever see what went on *inside* the flat?'

The inspector paused for a while, then said, 'No.'

'So you had no idea what happened in the flat.'

He started with that 'We suspected —' line again, but I cut him off.

'When you raided my flat, what was I doing?' I asked.

The inspector thought for a while. Then he said, 'You were listening to music. It was very loud.'

'It was loud, but was it illegal?'

'No.'

'When you raided my flat, did you find any bookies? Did you see any gambling?'

'No.'

'Was I doing anything illegal?'

'No.'

'You never saw any illegal activity in my flat,' I said.

'No.'

'No what?'

'I never saw anything illegal in your flat,' the inspector admitted.

I waited for the judge to finish writing down that statement.

'For all you know I could have been running weekly Bible studies,' I said.

'Maybe,' said the inspector. 'I don't know.'

'There's a lot you don't know, isn't there,' I said. I was going to keep on insulting him when the judge made some disapproving noises from the bench. So I switched to another point. 'So why did you arrest me?'

'We found the Filofax.'

'So you only arrested me because of the Filofax,' I said. 'But how do you know the Filofax belonged to me?'

'We found it in your flat.'

'How many men went into my flat on Saturday night?'

The inspector frowned. 'About eighteen, twenty.'

'Couldn't the Filofax belong to one of them?'

'Maybe.'

'Did you ever question any of them?'

'No.'

'Why not? There were twenty alleged bookies in my flat. Why was I the only one arrested?'

The inspector didn't say anything.

'Because I was the only one there? Because you were too damned lazy to question any of the other men?'

More disapproving noises descended from the bench, so I calmed down.

'Did you find my name in the Filofax?' I asked the inspector.

'No.'

'My handwriting?'

'No. The entries were typed.'

'Did you check whether the letters in my printer matched those in the Filofax?'

'No. But we found your fingerprints.'

'You gave me the Filofax at the police station. Did you dust it for prints *before* you gave it to me?'

'No.'

'Why not? Do you know who the last person was to touch the Filofax before you took it from the toilet?'

'No,' the inspector said. 'But we found the Filofax in your flat.'

'And you arrested me for that?' I slapped my forehead in disbelief. 'Couldn't the Filofax belong to someone else? Couldn't someone else have put it there? Didn't you ever think that I might have been framed?'

'No.'

'How did you know the Filofax was in my toilet?'

'We got a phone call.'

'And the guy told you *specifically* to look in my toilet.'

'Yes.'

'How convenient. Isn't that suspicious? Doesn't it sound like someone's trying to set me up? He put the Filofax in the toilet, then he rang you.' I paused to let that thought sink in. 'Another thing that's really strange. You know the search warrant?'

'Yes.'

'Who was listed as the owner of the flat?'

'Mr and Mrs Lawrence Tay.'

'Why didn't you put me down as the owner of the flat? You were raiding me, not Mr Tay. How did you know who the real owners were?'

'The phone call. The man told us that Mr and Mrs Tay owned the flat.'

'Doesn't it sound like someone's trying to frame me?'

'The man knew you were running the syndicate,' the inspector said. 'He gave us a tip.'

'How long have I been in the country?'

'I don't know.'

'I've been here less than a year,' I said. 'What about the punters? Are they a trusting lot? Do they just bet with anyone?'

'No.'

'What language do they usually speak in?'

'Hokkein.'

'Don't you find it incredible that I can get all these Chinese bookies to trust me, to make me their boss? Look at me. I'm white. I don't speak a word of Hokkein. I've only been in Singapore for a couple of months. I don't even know which bus to take to Kallang Stadium. How in the world could *I* become the mastermind of a gambling syndicate?'

The inspector didn't say anything.

'The problem is – you have no idea what went on in my flat,' I said. 'You think I'm this big mastermind. But the truth of the matter is, you don't even *know* if there is a mastermind. And if there was, it could have been any one of those men in my flat, and not just me. Is that right?'

'Yes.'

I told the judge that I had finished. The prosecution didn't have any additional questions, so the judge called for a lunch break. That was a good sign. After lunch, I'd get Loong.

The next witness identified himself as Loong Tay of 148 Bukit Timah Road, and swore solemnly and sincerely that the facts he was about to give would be the truth, the whole truth and nothing but the truth. He wore rimless CK spectacles and a white shirt under a black Armani jacket. If the judge had a son, he would look exactly like Loong.

'What is your relationship to the accused?' the prosecutor asked.

'I met him when I was studying in England,' Loong said.

'Which college were you at?' the judge asked.

'Balliol. PPE.'

The judge smiled for the first time.

'When Andy decided to come to Singapore, he needed a place to stay,' Loong said. 'My parents offered to rent him our flat.'

'Did you go to flat of the accused on Saturday nights?' the lawyer asked.

'Yes.'

'Can you tell us what happened in the flat on Saturday nights?'

'I went there to watch soccer with Andy. He had many friends over. I didn't know they were bookies.' Loong looked embarrassed. 'I'm English-educated, I went to RI. I don't understand Hokkein.'

'So you didn't know what those men were talking about?'

'No. I only realized that Andy was using the flat to gamble when I read about it in the papers last week. My father was really angry.'

The prosecutor mentioned that Loong's father was the new ambassador to China, and the judge smiled in acknowledgement. The lawyer continued by guiding Loong through his CV, describing how, with an IQ of one hundred and seventy-five, Loong had entered the Gifted Educational Programme at Raffles Institution. He traced Loong's career through Oxford, which included a PSC scholarship, a First in Engineering, the Presidency of the Union and also the occasional bronze medal for swimming at the SEA games. Loong announced that he would be off next month to America on a Fulbright to get Ph.D.ed by Harvard. 'Slow, slow,' the lawyer told Loong as he raced through his achievements, leaving the scribbling judge in his wake. 'His Honour has to write down what you say. Give him time.'

When the judge finished, the lawyer said, 'The accused claims that he does not understand Hokkein. How did he communicate with the other men in the flat?'

'He had a friend, Eugene, who was bilingual,' Loong said. 'Eugene translated for Andy.'

The lawyer turned Loong over to me.

'Aren't you lying?' I said to Loong. 'Don't you speak Hokkein?'

'No,' Loong said.

'Which dialect group are you from?'

'My father is Cantonese.'

'And your mother?'

Loong paused, then said, 'She's Hokkein. But she never spoke Hokkein to me, not after the government's "Speak Mandarin" campaign.'

'Hokkein is your mother tongue,' I said. 'I can't believe you don't understand it.'

'My father is Hokkein, but I don't understand a word of it,' the judge interrupted. 'In fact, I can hardly speak Mandarin. We're English-educated. It's not an unusual phenomenon.'

'I didn't know that, your Honour.' I had made a mistake, I shouldn't have brought that up. Weakness at Mandarin was a sore point for some of the English-educated Chinese.

'Don't pursue this point,' the judge said. 'It won't bear fruit.'

'I'm sorry, your Honour,' I said. I turned to Loong. 'Someone told the police that the flat belongs to your parents. Do you know who he might be?'

'Maybe one of the bookies?' Loong said.

'That doesn't make sense. Now, you just said you don't speak Hokkein. So you couldn't have told them.' I placed my hand on my chest. '*I* didn't tell them. You didn't even *talk* to them. How could they have known that the flat belonged to your parents?'

'I don't know.'

'None of the bookies in the flat knew I was renting from your parents. Only you knew. You rang the police. You told them to put the name of your parents on the search warrant. You set me up.'

'I don't know what you're talking about.'

I asked the court to show the Filofax to Loong. 'Do you recognize this Filofax?' I said.

Loong opened the Filofax and flipped through the pages. 'I've never seen it before in my life.'

'Don't you have hundreds of similar Filofaxes languishing in your house?'

'No.'

'Look at the back of the Filofax, near the bottom, in gold letters. What does it say?'

'Tay Star Publishing Company.'

'Doesn't your uncle own this company?'

Loong hesitated. 'Yes.'

'Didn't he give you a whole pile of Filofaxes like that?'

Loong placed the Filofax on the desk. 'I've never seen this before in my life.'

'Isn't this what really happened? You tried to frame me. So you took the Filofax your uncle gave you, and recorded your bets in it. You planted the Filofax in my toilet. Then you called the police, and told them where to find the Filofax. You even told them who really owned the flat, so that the police wouldn't invalidate the warrant by mistake.'

'I never did anything like that,' Loong said.

The prosecution didn't want to ask Loong any further questions, so I asked if Inspector Koh could be recalled to the witness stand. The judge agreed, but said, 'I think we've had enough for today. Court is adjourned until tomorrow.'

Three weeks ago, Loong came to my flat with a pile of those Filofaxes to give away to anyone who would take them. Maybe somebody saw him.

Mei used to tell me that a good lawyer never asks a question they don't know the answer to. But I had no choice. I couldn't get any answers beforehand, because nobody would tell me anything. I could only get the truth now, here in court. All I could do was shoot a question in the dark, and hope to God that the reply would save me.

'Remember three weeks ago? Did you see that man,' I pointed to Loong, 'carrying an armful of Filofaxes into my flat?'

Inspector Koh frowned. After a while, he said, 'I think so.'

'Those Filofaxes,' I said. 'Did they look like the one you found in the toilet?'

'They did.'

'Yes!' I clenched my fist and pumped my arm. 'The phone call. The guy who spoke to you. What language did he use?'

'English.'

'Isn't that strange? Don't the bookies usually use Hokkein?'

'Yes.'

'Do you remember the guy's English? Did he use Singlish?'

'No.'

'Was he articulate? Did he use good, fluent English?'

'Yes.'

'What about his accent? Did he have an English accent? Did he sound like someone who had lived abroad for a couple of years?'

'I think so.'

'You've heard Loong's testimony. Did the man on the phone sound like the man sitting there?' I pointed at Loong.

The prosecutor made protesting noises, and the judge

stopped the inspector from answering me. But I think I'd done enough of a kick-ass job. I smiled and said, 'No further questions.'

The prosecutor didn't have anything more to ask, so I launched into the summary of my defence. 'The police have never caught me doing anything illegal. The only reason why I'm here is because of some Filofax in my toilet. That Filofax could have belonged to anyone, including Loong. If anyone can run a gambling syndicate, it's Loong. He's smart, and he's connected. Me? I'm just a lowly relief teacher. I know nothing, and no one.' I wished they would give me some water. The air-conditioning was sucking all the moisture from my throat. 'Loong might be a scholar, but he's also a liar. He said he never saw the Filofax before in his life. But the inspector saw him going into my flat with a pile of Filofaxes just like the one found in my toilet. What's going on? Also, the man who phoned the police, the man who framed me, this man spoke perfect English. Only one bookie fits that description.' I pointed at Loong. 'In view of the evidence, I urge your Honour to convict the real mastermind, and find me not guilty.'

The judge looked at the prosecution. After they summed up their case, the judge announced, 'I'll deliver my verdict after lunch. Court is adjourned.'

I couldn't swallow anything. My stomach was going into Pentium Overdrive, forcing me to make repeated trips to the toilet. I sat to crap and passed the time rereading the poster that reminded me to flush the toilet after use. When I got up to flush, another sign near the handle directed me to lift up the seat cover. On all four blue walls, smiling cats pointed their fingers at me as they told me to use the toilet as if it was mine. I have never been in a place which provided so many tips on toilet etiquette.

I returned to court and waited for the judge to deliver his verdict.

The judge looked at me and said, 'The Court finds that the prosecution have proved their case beyond a reasonable doubt, and finds the accused convicted of the charge.'

I didn't understand what the judge said. But then the prosecution started going on about my previous convictions (two for spitting and one for jaywalking) – I got it for the first time. Guilty. I was going to jail.

'I request that the Court impose a deterrent sentence,' the prosecution said. 'In the past year, seventy per cent of the murders in Singapore were committed by foreigners. Foreigners caused the crime rate to increase in Singapore for the first time in seven years. There were 3119 foreigners arrested in the first half of this year compared with 2492 for the same period last year. These people often come to our country to commit crimes, hoping to take advantage of our safe environment. A stiff sentence would deter other outsiders from following suit.'

I didn't get it. A deterrent sentence. Like why? I glared at the prosecutor. Why does this guy have a thing against me? What did I ever do to *him*?

The judge asked me if I had anything to say in mitigation.

Standing before the judge, I finally saw that I was always going to lose the case, and now I knew why. In the end, it was me versus Loong. And what chance did I have against Mr Singapore Fantasy? With good grades, solid family ties, branded clothes and landed property, Loong had everything every Singaporean valued in life. I, on the other hand, was an *ang mo*. Expatriates are always seen as a hostile force. In recent years, all the crimes in Singapore that hit the international headlines had been committed by expatriates, like Fay and Leeson. When a crime occurred, it would be all too easy to blame it on someone like me, to see him as the foreign body, the element that infected a once healthy society.

'Your Honour, this case comes down to one thing – my word against Loong's,' I said. 'Why do you believe him, and not me? Is it because I'm some symbol of British colonial oppression, and he's every Singaporean's wet dream?'

'You've committed a terrible crime. But instead of showing remorse, you stand here and question the integrity of this court,' the judge said. 'Are you calling me a racist?'

I kept my eyes shut and mouth clamped. These past weeks, the more I spoke, the more I struggled, the worse things got. Did Mei lie about the rape? Maybe not. Maybe this is how she felt. You know that what's happening to you is wrong, but nothing will ever change that – you never can, and never will be able to get justice for yourself. All you can do is close your eyes and pray silently, before the shadow looms above you and blocks out the light.

'Fine fifty thousand dollars and three years' jail, backdated one week,' the judge said. 'Court is adjourned.'

CHAPTER 33

Eugene

I went to bed. I felt cold, but then it was winter. There's a small window above my bed. A barren twig shook against the steel sky. The sky was grey, but then it was always grey, it was winter.

The past couple of days, I'd slept a lot. When I did wake up, I ate, I watched CNN International ('Farmer in Idaho Finds New Method of Growing Potatoes'), and slept. I thought I felt okay actually, that nothing was wrong – but then as time passed and I continued wanting to sleep, I knew I wasn't okay. I did feel guilty. But not guilty enough to go back to Singapore and spend three years in jail. I liked Andy, but not that much. I didn't like anybody that much. But then, who does?

I decided to go for a walk, even though it was snowing. Snow is pretty to look at, but hell to walk through. My boots chomped along the street, melting the snow, dirtying the white ground with streaks of grey.

After walking half a mile, I leant against a lamp post. The stares of the passers-by bore into my back. My shoulders shook.

I returned home, and microwaved my meal – pot noodles, a mixture of ingredients designed to provide maximum taste (the manufacturer's opinion), and minimum nutrition (my opinion). It tasted terrible, so I drank a brandy to sit on its chest and hold it down. That's all I do nowadays. I sleep, wake up, then drink to hold it down.

CHAPTER 34

Mei

I came home late at night, and as usual, my mother tried to pick a fight. She always begins with an innocent question, but usually ends up launching some thermo-nukes.

'What did you do today?' my mother said.

'Nothing,' I said.

'Really? You just go to work and come back?' she said.

I grunted and continued watching *Seinfeld*.

'Mrs Kwek said she saw you at People's Park today. At Metro. At the Great Singapore Sale. You bought a white blouse.'

'Uh-huh.'

'So you didn't do nothing. So you didn't just go to work and come back. You went shopping. And you didn't even tell me.'

'Uh-huh.'

'You going to show me your new blouse or not?'

'It's in my room. You can have a look at it if you want.' I did not move from the couch.

'Why you never talk to me?' my mother said. 'All my friends' daughters tell their mothers *everything*.'

I could see my mother moving the cruise missiles in position, so I decided to take swift defensive measures. 'All right, all right. If it'll make you happy, we'll do something together,' I said.

My mother clapped her hands. 'We can look through your old photographs.'

'Anything but photographs. Let's get a video.'

'No, if we watch video, we never talk. We just look at the TV. We need to spend *quality* time together.'

My mother took out a stack of photo albums, two and a half feet high.

'You're going to break your back carrying them,' I said.

When I was a child, my father would take a picture of me every five seconds. I am not exaggerating. If you flip through my photo album quick enough, it's like an animation book – you can watch me jumping and crying and throwing my pillow at the camera. I guess my parents tried to make up for not being able to afford a video camera. I flipped through photographs that I had not seen for over ten years, like the photos from my Wonder Woman phase. I had a red bath towel draped around my six-year-old shoulders, with the corners of the towel tucked into the collar of my T-shirt. There were mini basketball hoops around my wrists – they were my Wonder Woman bracelet shields.

'Remember when you played Wonder Woman at the clinic?' my mother said. My mother had come down with a cold, and had brought me along to the clinic. I remembered the smell of antiseptic, the coughs and sniffles of the patients, the air that tasted thick with disease. I looked through the women's magazines on the waiting-room table, but I was at an age when neither cake recipes nor summer fashions interested me. I was bored, so I played 'Wonder Woman', spinning myself as I had seen Lynda Carter do on TV. Turning and turning, I got so dizzy that I lost control of my legs. My jelly limbs wobbled backwards until I fell, and hit the edge of the glass table with the back of my head.

I never tried to be Wonder Woman again.

I opened another photo album. There was a picture of me in a lacy white frock. 'Talk about lace explosion,' I said. My mother used to stitch dresses for me from torn curtains and old cushion covers. '*Ai-yoh*, those gingham dresses you used to make,' I said, 'I looked like a walking tablecloth.'

'You were so happy when we got the lace dress,' my mother said. 'First time we *buy* a dress from Chinatown.'

'I loved that gun,' I said. In the snapshot, I pointed a pistol at the camera, my left hand resting on the black gun belt round my waist. Covered in white lace and pink ribbons, I threw my best Clint Eastwood stare.

'Today you got eat fruit or not?' my mother said. 'You pass motion now still got bleed or not?'

'*Ma* – that stopped three months ago. I mentioned it to you *once*, and you have to keep bringing it up.'

'I just worry you got not enough fibre. I go peel an orange for you.' My mother went to the kitchen.

In the next photo, I crouched in a compartment in the wall – how I had loved sitting in my own little pigeon-hole, the rough grains of the brick prickling my hand. A vase sat there now. I couldn't believe that I was once small enough to fit into the wall. Turning the page, I saw it – the Mid-autumn photo. I stood behind the lantern my father had bought me. The lantern loomed in the shot, obscuring the tiny child. Only the top of my face was visible, two small black eyes peering above the glowing red mass.

I didn't tell my mother what happened that night. Surely she would have said, *Why you so useless, just stand there like that? He didn't tie your hands. Why you didn't push him, why you didn't scream, why you didn't run away?*

'Eat your orange.' My mother placed the plate on the coffee table.

I kept quiet. My mother must have known that something

was wrong when I came back that night; that night, like tonight, sitting on the sofa, staring at the magazines stacked neatly on the left side of the table, waiting for my mother to notice that something was wrong.

'*Oi*, you think so easy to peel an orange?' my mother said. 'I now got all these white bits from the orange stuck inside my fingernails. You better eat, don't let me waste all my effort.'

'Can't you see that I'm looking at the photos?' I said. 'Always yak yak yak yak yak. Just leave me alone.'

'I'm your mother. If I don't take care of you, who's going to take care of you? I can't leave you alone.'

I went to my bedroom. 'Stop following me around,' I told my mother. 'This flat is too small. I really have to get a place of my own soon.'

I walked back to the living room.

'Why do we always have to fight?' my mother said. 'Why you hate me so much?'

'I don't hate you. Stop imagining things. You're driving me crazy. You're going to make me *gila*.'

'You always get angry with me for no reason. You never talk to me, and when you talk to me that time, you always scold me. I'm your *mother*. How can you scold me? No respect.'

I stared at Jerry Seinfeld.

'Why you always angry with me?' my mother said.

'Oh help, here we go again,' I muttered under my breath.

'You say what? I couldn't hear you.'

'Nothing.'

'Why you even whispering now?' my mother said. 'Even at home, right in front of me, you won't talk to me, you start whispering.'

I flicked through the six channels.

'Why you always angry with me?' my mother said.

I flung the remote control. 'You want to know why? I'll tell you why, it's . . .'

'Tell me.'

'You don't want to know.'

'Tell me.'

'You always say you want to know but every time I tell you, you always get upset.'

'Tell me.'

'Why you always let Daddy touch me like that?'

'Touch you how?'

'You know how.'

'He loves you *mah*.' My mother sighed. 'I should have been more like him. Sometimes I think you don't like me because last time you young that time I never hug you enough.'

'Didn't you ever think – what happened to me at Red Hill that night?'

'What are you talking about?'

'I always thought it was my fault. But now, look at this photo – I was five, tiny – my lantern, so small – against the tree – black – my arms – so cold – heavy, like blocks of ice – my mouth filled – how could I scream how could I push how could I do anything? Look at this photo. How could he have done such a thing to someone so small? I was so small – barely taller than the lantern. I was only two feet tall.'

My mother took a tissue out of her sleeve, and held it out to me. 'Don't get your blouse wet.'

I pushed my mother's hand away.

'What did you want me to do?' she said. 'What could I have done?'

'You could have confronted Daddy. As you always say, you're my *mother*. You're supposed to protect me, expose him, bring him to justice . . . You could have killed him. You're my mother. You're not supposed to sit here and go, "Sorry, I can't do anything, why don't you just forget it, girl."'

'You didn't tell me till now. I didn't know. How am I supposed to do anything? And now he's dead. I always did everything I could for you. But now he's dead. There's nothing anybody can do now, not me, not you, not the police.'

I got up.

'Where are you going?' my mother asked.

'I'm going to visit Daddy.'

'You don't be crazy. You very upset now, why don't you wait until tomorrow. Calm down, then you go. You do bad things to his grave, like that – very bad luck for the rest of your life.' My mother grabbed my arm. 'The police come and catch you, people think you're crazy. Maybe he alive that time, can report to the police, but now he's dead, nobody can do anything. Why don't you just leave it alone? You anyhow do anything to his grave, you'll only harm yourself – very bad luck for the rest of your life!'

'Look at what I was, and what I've become. Look at what he did to my life. Do you think anything worse could happen?'

Outside the crematorium, three elderly Chinese women tossed ghost money into a flaming container. The rusty red cylinder, the size of ten oil drums, bellowed black smoke as the orange flames licked the red money heavenwards. One of the women lit a joss stick, shook it three times, her lips murmuring a prayer. She dropped the stick, and ground out the burning end with her slipper. The ground was littered with joss sticks – thin red ones, and thick, brown ones. Ash was everywhere, grey powdered the white cement. The breeze blew, swirled the ash around like nuclear snow.

I found my father's square. My mother had placed a flower

in the offering slot the day before and now the water droplets slid down the hibiscus stem into its red holder.

I wanted to reach out and claw him out of the grave to face what he had done to me. I pressed my palm against the cold white marble. My hand slid away. It was just a photo.

My mother was right. Here ends the story: my father was dead and there was nothing I could do. Once, there was a time to accuse, and to avenge; but the time for judgement and justice passed when they laid his ashes in the grave. He died, he was mourned, and unpunished, and that was that, and that was how it was always going to be. I never wanted to admit that I was powerless. All those photos of me as Wonder Woman – I always told myself that I could have fought back, unleashed a superhuman kick that would have sent my father flying through the air into the red pit, that I wasn't weak. I wasn't nailed against the tree, helpless.

Standing there, I felt like my mother, knowing that nothing could be done. And even if something could be done, would I have the strength to do it? Probably not. Even in the grave, only my father had the power. Staring out at me in the photo – the bulging eyes, those six hairs quivering above the cracked lips, gloating, untouchable, beyond the arm of justice . . .

I stood there before him in frozen silence.

When I returned home, my mother asked me what I did.

'Don't worry, I didn't do anything that would cause any . . . bad luck.'

'What do you want me to do?' she asked.

My mother looked out of the window for a long time, staring at Red Hill. Sometimes she shut her eyes, but all the time, she said nothing.

Usually, the moon glowed sullenly, dim and yellow like her teeth, but tonight it shone like the sun, lit up the streets so it looked like day. Perfectly round and bright, it shone like a searchlight, flooded the air with white, exposed all the rotting memories. I wondered – did my mother hear nothing, see nothing, know nothing? Or was my mother like me, closing her eyes only to fall into the dream of the five-year-old that repeats and repeats, woken only by the moon that cast light on old wounds, waking to the twilight chorus of crickets, waking to blank spaces in the throat.

The rape has always been a foreign body in my system, infecting all of my life, it's always with me. Whenever I look at the night sky, or kick a puff of dust walking along a sandy road, or squirt my mouth by biting hard on a pomelo, or even just sitting on the MRT train, looking at the route map and seeing the Red Hill stop on the West line – these common, everyday activities set off a slow motion replay in my head, and I see everything that happened at Red Hill that night. All I can do is go away and sit down somewhere in the dark, and try not to fade to black.

Every time I talk to my mother, when she asks me why I hate her, her words only enlarge the foreign body, making the bone pierce deeper into my heart. For years I blamed my mother for doing nothing to stop my father. I blamed her for not doing enough for my grandfather, despised her because she abandoned him in the old folks' home. Now I realized that my mother did nothing, not because she didn't want to, but because she *couldn't*. My mother did not have the power, just as I did not have the power. It wasn't fair for me to expect my mother to right wrongs. My mother wasn't evil, she was just weak. If my mother was evil, then I could hate her. But she was weak, she needed me. She depended on me to save her. Even when I was ten, in the car, she had relied on me to soothe my raging father. My mother always needed me. And I couldn't hate her for that.

'You don't have to do anything,' I said.

My mother handed me a letter. 'From Andy,' she said.
I opened the letter:

Dear Mei,

I don't know whether to kill you or to kill myself. I keep thinking of what you did over the past weeks, what you didn't do – what you showed me, and what you might have hidden – and I don't know. I just don't know anything any more. Sometimes I think you did a Judas, sometimes I don't. I don't know what to think. What shall we do? If you did betray me, then there is nothing you can say to me; if you didn't betray me, then no words of mine can ever heal the hurt I caused you. I don't know whether to strangle you or to fall at your feet. Who am I? Villain or victim? I don't know. I guess I'll never know, unless you tell me who framed me. But I guess you've already said that you won't, so I'll never know. And even if you do tell me, will I be able to believe you? I don't know. Will we see each other again? Probably? Not?

But whatever happens, there is something that I need to tell you, something I want to tell everyone. You told me that everyone needed God. You were *so* wrong. When I stood in the dock, I looked at Loong, stared down those deep, black eyes into his soul, but I could see no gap, no longing for God, no lack. All I saw was joy and peace. Loong might be a lot of things, but he is not a hungry ghost.

So I asked myself – what's in it for me? Why should I believe in God?

But why should I take my flesh in my teeth? Though He slay me, yet will I trust in Him. As he lay there on the ground, guiltless, scraping his sores – his servants sliced by the Sabean sword, his cattle charred by Heaven's fire, the bones of his sons and daughters crushed by boulders, buried under the house he built for them – when told to curse God, all Job said was, *Though*

He slay me, yet will I trust in Him. His words echoed through my soul, not the words of Job any longer, but my words, the syllables of my spirit – *Though He slay me, yet will I trust in Him.*

I guess I can never forget those times where I laid by the waters and saw Him face to face. His love fills me – not the soft, cuddly, sentimental, Santa Claus, let's-all-get-along, flower-power type, but God's love, a love beyond reason, blind and obsessive, dangerous; a love that devours and destroys, a love that is lethal. I could never desert him, because He put that love in my heart, the howl Solomon felt for his Bride – *Love as strong as death, as cruel as the grave.*

I look into my future and unlike Loong, I see no joy, no peace, not even a toothbrush that I can call my own, just a life forever striped by the shadows of these prison bars. But I don't care – I love God not for what He gives, but for who He is. I love him because He is God. I don't care how much He hurts me, I will still love him, because no matter what I do to Him, whether I drive nails hard into His hands or spear His side, He will still adore me. Even though I crucified Him, He still lives for me, so though He slay me, yet will I trust Him. I know it's illogical, probably heretical and for most people, utterly repulsive. But that's how our love works, me and Him.

Yours?
Andy

A long time ago, my Uncle Cheong told me about the Fisher King, the guardian of the grail, the maimed monarch who ruled over the dry and wasted land. When Andy told me about his vision and the wound in his thigh, I thought – no, it couldn't be. How could Andy be the Fisher King? Joseph of Arimathea collected the blood from Christ's wounds as it dripped from the cross into the cup. How could Andy possibly possess this sacred vessel? Andy was a lager lout who spent most of his life performing reverse communion, turning his own blood into alcohol. How could he possibly be the keeper of the grail? I guess I was wrong. Andy always had the cup, but he spent most of his life denying it. But now that he has clasped the chalice with both hands, now that he is willing to share the cup of love with all the world, who knows what will happen?

As for me, I could only do what I hated most – wait. Unlike Andy, I know what I want. I want justice. I want my father to be punished, Loong to be imprisoned, Andy to be free. I want to be free of all the secrets stuck inside me – the rape, Eugene's confession, everything – but I can't be freed, not now, but if I wait, one day I will be released.

I stared out of the window at Red Hill. The overhead fan whirred noisily, its blades beating out breezes in uneven gusts. There was nothing I could do, nothing but whisper, 'Maranatha, Oh Lord come,' and wait for that day. Now I see nothing, nothing but shadows, but then I shall see Him face to face. When the trumpet sounds, and the dead in Christ arise, when the old becomes new, and the corruptible, incorruptible, on that day, gazing into His golden face, I will be transformed into His likeness, from heart to heart, from blood to blood. And in that moment, I shall, finally, be set free from the flesh that hungers, released from – no longer trapped with – this foreign body. On that day, a time of wonders in the heavens and in the earth, of fire, of screams, and pillars of smoke, when the sun turns to darkness, the moon to blood, and all the princes and the powers flee to the refuge of the rocks, running from the wrath of the Lamb, in that hour, when the dust hangs in the morning like fog, Christ, the pale rider, will return to claw the guilty out of the black earth and lift them against the ruby sky, and the land will groan its vengeance like it did that day for Abdul, the murdered boy. In the day of the Lord, blood from the hill will flow again.

foreign bodies

Hwee Hwee Tan

A Readers Club Guide

ABOUT THIS GUIDE

The suggested questions are intended to help your reading group find new and interesting angles and topics for discussion for Hwee Hwee Tan's *Foreign Bodies*. We hope that these ideas will enrich your conversation and increase your enjoyment of the book.

Many fine books from Washington Square Press feature Readers Club Guides. For a complete listing, or to read the Guides on-line, visit

http://www.simonsays.com/reading/guides

A Conversation with Hwee Hwee Tan

Q: To what degree is *Foreign Bodies*—a novel about Singaporean culture, what it is to be an expatriate, and the intersection of Eastern and Western cultures—based upon your own life?

A: I grew up in Singapore. I left when I was 15, spent three years in Holland (Den Haag) and then went to college (University of Oxford) in England for 5 years. I now live in New York City. I've been an expatriate for half my life, so the idea of being a "Foreign Body" resonates greatly with myself.

Q: Do you ever go back to Singapore? Do you still have close family there?

A: I've been back to Singapore every year. I usually stay with my parents during that time, which can be difficult. I am very close to my sister but still struggle when dealing with my parents.

Q: Have your parents and family read this novel? How do they feel about it?

A: When the book first came out, my mother wouldn't speak to me for 2 weeks. She was convinced that I needed to see a psychologist. My father, oddly enough, had no response to the book. I don't think he even read it (but then, I don't think he's ever read a novel in his life).

Q: Why did you decide to tell your story through three different voices? What challenges arose once you made this choice?

A: I was inspired by Faulkner's *As I Lay Dying* to use different first person narrators. I think the book's strength lies in the voices and it was a method to vary the range of the book by allowing different characters to speak and also making the book more interesting via unreliable narrators.

Q: While Andy is a wonderfully recognizable "type"—the seemingly irredeemable, perpetually laddish slacker— he's also full of surprises and charming idiosyncracies. Did his voice come easily to you?

A: I spent 5 years in England surrounded by Andys. Andy really encapsulates the twentysomething lad, so the voice came easily.

Q: You've discussed in interviews your own experiences with sexual abuse. How much do Mei's traumas—and her way of coping with them—resemble your own?

A: I was never raped by my father. I did have about four friends who had been raped or abused as children, but who never confronted their abusers. Hopefully, the novel will be able to give a voice to the voiceless.

Q: If you had to put up with being assigned one media-friendly, all-purpose label for yourself, which of these descriptions would you find the least reductive?: A. transcultural writer; B. Christian writer; C. the mouthpiece for twentysomething stasis. Do you object to any of these labels in particular?

A: I've always seen myself more as a retractable can-opener.

Q: Maybe not since Graham Greene has a novelist so boldly employed Christianity as her story's moral framework—and as the engine for her characters' potential redemption. Why do you think Christianity and struggles with faith have become such unusual subjects in novels today?

A: Someone once wrote that the gospels recount a history while relating a mystery. If one sees Christianity as presenting a magic fusion between faith and fact, a presentation of truth in spirituality, rather than mere dogma, then, one can consider any piece of truthful fiction as "Christian" fiction even though it might be populated by ungodly characters.

Q: One of the things that is most striking about *Foreign Bodies* is your complex, highly ambivalent rendering of the mother-daughter relationship. Tell us how you set about writing Mei's relationship with her mom, what your intentions were, and how you feel about the result.

A: There was a time when I felt very close to my mother, but at some stage that feeling stopped. Writing *Foreign Bodies* was an attempt to explore the events that led to this shift in our relationship. Like Mei, as I was writing the book, I came to realize that my mother did not protect me from my father—not because she didn't want to but because she couldn't.

Q: How do you explain the significance of your novel's title?

A: The novel is structured like a metaphysical poem inspired by John Donne's *Batter My Heart* which is about God and spiritual rape. Just as a metaphysical poem is structured around puns and word play, *Foreign Bodies* is structured around the double meaning in the title.

Q: When Eugene mentions the infamous Michael Fay caning case, he says he "couldn't understand what the big deal was." Was this a common reaction among people you know?

A: It's a common reaction from expatriate kids (who tend to be over-spoilt and over-protected.) Most people in Singapore considered Fay's crime to be serious.

Q: You delightfully and invaluably skewer cultural and generational stereotypes in this novel, and many reviewers have commented upon how refreshing it is for a younger writer to abandon altogether the familiar conventions of cynical "Gen-X" writing and multicultural literature. How do you feel about these kinds of reactions to your work?

A: Characters, if truly drawn become fully fleshed people rather than cardboard cliches, so it was gratifying that the reviewers felt that the characters weren't flat.

Q: Growing up, what novels affected you the most?

A: Like Mei and Eugene, I read a lot of crime fiction, for example, the *Hardy Boys* and *Three Investigation*.

Q: And whom, among contemporary novelists, do you admire most today?

A: *Foreign Bodies* was probably most influenced by Amy Tan, Douglas Coupland, Michael Ondaatje (*Running in the Family*), and Robert Olen Butler (*A Good Scent from a Strange Mountain*) .

Reading Group Questions and Topics for Discussion

1. Describe the different "foreign bodies" with which each of the novel's principle characters must contend, and explore the individual journeys each character takes. Does Loong have a foreign body? Explain.

2. In the midst of her grandfather's marathon of a funeral, eleven-year-old Mei experiences a religious epiphany in the form of an "unutterable kiss" from God. "This phrase suddenly popped into my head—Christ took my sins and cleansed every stain. Of course I always knew this...but before today, it was nothing but a dry, empty slogan....Under the table that day, I suddenly realized what it really meant." What does the phrase mean to Mei? How do her understandings of faith and Christianity shape the choices she makes in the course of *Foreign Bodies*?

3. "The good suffer and the bad go on to live happy lives." How does the outcome of Tan's novel serve to support, challenge, or complicate this statement?

4. When Mei first meets Andy in the airport, she sees him as "a baby angel, empty of guile." She instantly senses that she will end up devoting her "life to protect that innocence, preserve that purity, shelter him from an evil and cunning world." What is the author already beginning to establish only a dozen or so paragraphs into the novel? How does Mei's first impression of Andy foreshadow the major themes and events in *Foreign Bodies*?

5. Compare Mei's faith with Andy's. What happens to Andy the day he runs off, leaving his parents standing in the ladies' changing room at Debenham's? Consider the parallels that exist between Andy's otherworldly experience with the bright, round light and the legend of Ahmad the fisherman, which Mei tells Andy late in the novel. How might the moral of Mei's story be applied to Andy's situation?

6. What is the story of the Fisher King? Are we meant to believe that Andy is literally the keeper of the Holy Grail? What is Tan suggesting here?

7. What happens in "the story of Red Hill," which Mei's father tells Mei as a deterrent to keep her from running away? What bearing does the story have on the rest of Mei's narrative?

8. What is the significance of the caved-in sidewalk? How might the sidewalk function as a metaphor for faith? In what do Loong's parents place their faith? Loong? Eugene?

9. Mei's father accuses her of being a "banana": "Yellow outside, white inside." What does he mean?

10. Discuss the various religious allusions Tan injects into her narrative. For example, you might discuss links between the Bible's stories about various prophets and their divine visions with the epiphanies of Andy and Mei. Or you might identify the ways in which Andy's plight echoes or is informed by the Biblical story of Job.

11. In Mei's account of her rape on Red Hill, she tells us that her father "nailed me to the tree." What makes this particular description of the event so evocative and effective?

12. What are the elements and ingredients that make up *Foreign Bodies*? Is it a mystery thriller? A contemporary comedy of manners? A parable of faith redemption? A cautionary tale? Discuss all of the genres and literary traditions Tan is riffing on, alluding to, or updating in her novel.

13. Explain Loong's personal philosophy: he fancies himself a Nietzschean superman; he doesn't believe in God; and he totally rejects the possibility that the concepts of "right" and "wrong" possess any universal, objective meaning. Loong is wholly corrupt, but he also embodies the highest ideals of Singaporean society. What do you suppose Tan is suggesting by investing the character of Loong with so much irony and contradiction?

14. Why do you think Tan tells the story through the eyes of three different characters? How would the novel be different if it were told only from the perspective of Mei? Andy? Eugene?

15. Which character would you say is the most "reliable" narrator? Why?

16. "Going abroad was the core motivating principle of my life," Mei tells us. What motivates Eugene and Andy? What sorts of escape did they dream about when they were children?

17. "The monk's robe fell open, revealing—Levi 501's." What is the effect of Tan's pointed, pitch-perfect descriptions of the dual nature of contemporary Singaporean society—where references to Robert Ludlum and REM stand beside references to the Chinese *tei yuk*?

18. Most Singaporeans, Mei tells us, speak "Singlish," a pidgin English that also features "Chinese, Malay and Indian words." How might Singlish act as a metaphor for Singapore as a whole?

19. By the end of *Foreign Bodies*, do you believe any of the characters have been/will be redeemed? Considering the fates of each of her characters, what does Tan seem to be saying about conventional notions of justice and conscience, good and evil, and morality and corruption?

About the Author

HWEE HWEE TAN was born in Singapore in 1974, and has also lived in the Netherlands and in England. Her stories have been broadcast by the BBC and published in *PEN International*, *Critical Quarterly*, *New Voices*, and *New Writing 6* (A. S. Byatt, editor). In 1997, she graduated from Oxford, and *Foreign Bodies* was published in England. Currently a *New York Times* Fellow in Fiction at New York University in Manhattan, Tan is at work on her second novel.

What book will you choose for your next reading group?

Visit

www.simonsays.com

to keep up on the latest new releases from Washington Square Press as well as author appearances, news chats, special offers and more.

Our WSP Readers Club Guides will help enrich your reading group discussions by offering more questions, better and more focused discussion topics, and exclusive author interviews.

To help choose your next reading group book and to browse through our vast library of available reading group guides, visit us online at **www.simonsays.com/reading/guides** today.